Death at the Digs

A Paige Harper Mystery

Christine Tipper

Copyright © Christine Tipper 2024

The right of Christine Tipper to be identified as the author of this work has been asserted in accordance with the Copyright, Designs and Patents Act 1988.

All rights reserved. No part of this publication may be reproduced, stored in or transmitted into any retrieval system, in any form, or by any means (electronic, mechanical, photocopying, recording or otherwise) without the prior permission of the author. Any person who does any unauthorised act in relation to this publication may be liable to criminal prosecution and civil claims for damages.

This is a work of fiction. Names, characters, businesses, places, events and incidents are either the products of the author's imagination or used in a fictitious manner. Any resemblance to actual persons, living or dead, or actual events is purely coincidental.

ISBN 978-1-7384307-2-7

To Lynn,
Can you unearth
the murderer?
Enjoy!

**With thanks to Alan, my family
and friends.
Let the adventures continue...**

love
Christine

Christmas '24

Chapter 1

Tuesday 12th February

On a cold February afternoon Paige Harper peered out of the upper floor window of River Books at the lights along the River Exe quay. It was half past four. The light was fading. She didn't like the dark afternoons of winter, but the bright window displays of Riverside's shops raised her spirits. The reflection in the pane of glass showed a slim, tall woman with blue-grey eyes and long blonde hair surrounded by higgledy-piggledy shelves piled high with books. Who'd have thought that she would be running a bookshop in the South-West of England in her thirties? She certainly wouldn't have when she'd been happily working as a semi-professional skier in the French Alps before her life there had taken such a nightmarish turn. She sighed. It was no use dwelling on the past.

"Paige? Are you up there?"

Paige poked her head over the banister to answer her sister. "Here, Mary. What's up?"

"It's really quiet. If you want to shoot off early, I'll lock up. I know you've got that talk at the University this evening."

"If you're sure? It doesn't start until 7."

"I'm sure. You can return the favour by opening up tomorrow morning. Harriet's asked me to take her and some of her friends to the station. They're planning on taking the train to Plymouth for a day's shopping."

"Not a problem. I'd forgotten it's half-term at the college."

Mary's daughter, Harriet, was studying at Exeter College. The girl was passionate about fashion and design. Unlike her mother who favoured the classic look, Harriet's fashion sense was what could be best termed as experimental. She liked to dye her hair vibrant colours and wear outrageous outfits. Paige grinned to herself. She was convinced that her niece's clothing was chosen more for its ability to shock her mother than her actual fashion likes.

"I wonder what she'll buy? Some stunning outfit or make-up," Paige goaded and was rewarded by a groan from her big sister.

"Don't. I really do not want to think about it."

"Oh, come on, Mary. She'll grow out of it eventually. The more upset you get, the more she'll do it."

"When did you become so wise?"

"How do you think? I'm a straight A student when it comes to winding you up. Harriet's following in my footsteps."

Mary shuddered. "I sincerely hope not."

Paige laughed as she retreated to her office to collect her things. She galloped down the stairs and called out, "Bye," before setting off towards home along the footpath beside the river. Her breath hung in white clouds as she walked in the chill air.

At 6.30pm Paige called for her friend and mentor, Professor Dominic Giraud.

"Evening, Dom. Ready to learn about Roman remains?"

"*Bonsoir, ma chérie.* I am indeed," said the elderly

gentleman as he folded himself into Paige's Mini.

"I'm not that interested in history but I wanted to support Zac. Let's hope the whole thing isn't too boring."

Dom tutted. "How can you not be interested in history. It's beyond me."

Paige laughed. "Lots of things are beyond you, *mon cher grandpère.*"

"That's enough of your cheek, young lady. Remember I'm doing you a favour by accompanying you," he replied lightheartedly.

She reached out and gave his bony knee a quick squeeze. "Thank you."

The buzz of conversation in the small lecture theatre died down as Professor Marcus Watkins entered the stage. Paige stretched out her long legs, hooked her blonde hair behind her ears and sat up straighter in the less than comfortable seat. To her right, the aquiline nose and sharp profile of Dom stared straight ahead. Suddenly, as if intuiting her gaze on him, he winked.

"Now, let's concentrate and see why young Zac was so insistent that we should attend this lecture," he whispered.

The young Zac in question was a student employee at Paige's book shop. An archaeology student at the University, he was involved in the recent digs at the Cathedral, where Roman ruins had been discovered. The lights dimmed and the large screen behind Professor Watkins lit up.

"Ladies and gentlemen, thank you so much for coming out on this cold winter evening to hear about our latest discoveries from the Roman period in the Cathedral's Cloister Garden. Some of you may have noticed the plaque on the path outside commemorating the findings of a Roman bath house and buildings dated between AD 50 and 60 under the Cathedral Green. What we've unearthed now, beneath the foundations of the medieval cloisters, are the remains of an early Roman street and timber buildings, along with the wall of a Roman town house. We are hoping these will provide us with new clues to Exeter's past. The street and timber buildings date from AD 50-75 and were part of the Roman legionary fortress. They were most probably part of a barrack building where soldiers were housed. We are extremely excited by some of the artefacts we've found. The University is grateful to the Cathedral for allowing us to be included in the groundbreaking work."

Watkins paused and waited for the ripple of laughter at his awful pun to fade before continuing. Paige zoned out whilst he continued to thank the long list of sponsors who were contributing to the costs of the excavations. Her ears perked up when she heard Zac's name mentioned. "Now, if I could ask Zachary Jones, one of our most promising students, to join me on stage."

A stocky, ginger-haired young man, wearing chinos and a pink shirt that did nothing for his pale, freckled complexion, climbed the four steps quickly and stood next to the professor. His brow was damp from sweat and his complexion was flushed. His eyes darted nervously around the room.

"Zac has been cataloguing some of the finds from the dig. What you need to know is that we believe this site covers a turbulent time in Roman history. Emperor Claudius arrived in Britannia in AD 43 and then came a quick succession of Roman Emperors. The infamous Nero, who you will all have heard of, was in power for twelve years between 54 - 68 AD. In quick succession followed Galba, Otho and Aulus Vitellius until some stability returned with Vespasian who ruled from 69-79

AD. You can see why we are excited about the possibilities of what discoveries this dig could provide." The professor paused and turned to the student, "Zac, over to you."

"Thank you, Professor." He launched straight in, "Roman Emperors were keen to stamp their authority on their territories and one of the most efficient ways to do this was to issue coins with their heads on them. Legionaries serving in distant lands would find out who was in power by whichever Emperor's head was on the coins they were paid with. Now as Professor Watkins mentioned, there were a total of seven Emperors who ruled during the time period of our excavations. So far we have uncovered coins from the Emperors Claudius, Nero and Vespasian. If we were to find coins from the lesser known Emperors, then these finds would be of international significance." He finished speaking and looked towards Professor Watkins.

Paige felt her dream catcher warm at her throat. *Oh, no. Not now.* When it heated up it was not a good sign. Her vision clouded and she saw in her mind's eye Zac drowning in a sea of coins. She blinked and focused on the young man. He looked as if he was struggling to stay where he was. Professor Watkins, oblivious to the heightened nervous state of his protégé, continued to drone on. The young man rocked slightly from side to side waiting to be dismissed.

Finally Professor Watkins seemed to notice that Zac was still standing there and said, "Oh sorry, Zac. Off you go."

A scowl of mingled embarrassment and annoyance flashed across Zac's face before he stepped down to quickly take his seat in the front row.

Paige pondered over what was going on between Zac and his head of department. It could just be nerves, of course. Giving a presentation to the public was daunting. And yet, she felt there was something else in play. Zac had been working for them since she'd joined the rugby club six months ago. Originally, he'd just covered her shifts on match days, but lately he'd been doing a few more hours. He seemed a pleasant lad, but there was something sneaky about him that she couldn't quite put her finger on. At times she felt as if he was playing the role of 'model bookshop employee'. A nudge in the ribs brought her back to reality.

"*Chérie*, time to go and congratulate our young Zac. He's waiting for us," Dom said.

"Of course. We can't disappoint him."

Shaking away the disturbing image she'd had of Zac, Paige linked arms with the tall, aristocratic gentleman next to her and made her way towards the stage. Today Dom, always a stylish dresser, was wearing a cobalt blue tweed suit, paired with a pale sky blue shirt, matching tie and pocket handkerchief. His silver-topped walking cane tapped on the polished wooden floor as they approached the group of history buffs swarming around the exhibits that Zac was guarding.

"Zac, my boy. Wonderful work." Dom's voice, which had been used in many a lecture theatre during his years as professor of French, carried easily above the background hum.

The young man flushed crimson at the praise. "Thank you, Professor Giraud. I'm thrilled you could make it. As you heard, these discoveries are exciting and could reveal so much. So far, there have never been any findings of coins with the heads of the Emperors Galba, Otho or Aulus Vitellius in the British Isles. Imagine how famous the person who discovered them would become in international archaeological circles. It could make a person's career. I'm honoured to be a part of it."

"Indeed. You are one of the guardians of Exeter's history," Dom said.

Paige felt rather than saw Zac's unease.

"Well, when you put it like that," he stuttered.

Dom tapped him lightly on the shoulder. "I'm sure that you take your responsibilities seriously. We expect great things from you, don't we, Paige?"

"Yes, Zac will become an internationally renowned archaeologist and we'll be able to say we knew him before he rose to dizzying heights." Paige gave Zac a reassuring smile, but again a vision of him drowning in a sea of coins flashed across her retinas.

Chapter 2

In the week that had passed since the talk at the university about the dig at the Cathedral, Zac had done two shifts at River Books. To Paige he'd seemed agitated and nervous around her. A couple of times his 'model bookshop employee' mask had slipped and he'd snapped at mild-mannered Olivia, the longest serving student employee. Olivia, with her owl-like face and thick-lens glasses, was a treasure that Paige hoped she could hold on to as long as possible. Olivia was serious, hard-working and, as a student of Modern Languages at the university, a real asset to their foreign languages section. Paige, herself a French graduate from Exeter, felt a kinship with her. It was at Exeter University that she'd first met Professor Dominic Giraud, who over the years had become a dear friend to her, replacing the grandfather she'd never known.

"Olivia, good morning, how are you?" Paige asked, flashing the shy girl a wide smile.

"Fine, thanks, Paige. We've received an order of French and German fiction that I was about to go and bring up from downstairs." The young girl blinked and made as if to go down to the stock room.

"Whoa. There's no rush. I'll go and fetch them. Lugging them upstairs will count as part of my exercise regime today."

Olivia relaxed. "Well, put like that, how can I resist? I wouldn't want to come between you and your exercise," she answered, showing a rare sense of humour.

"I've got my reputation to keep up and lots of work still to do if I want to become the best player in the Riverside Ladies team," Paige said, referring to the local rugby team she played for. "Olivia, can I ask you a sensitive question?"

Olivia shrank. "Er, okay."

"Don't worry. It's just that I'm a little concerned about Zac. He doesn't seem himself. I wondered if he'd said anything to you."

The girl's shoulders dropped in relief. "Actually, he told me that he had a few problems at his digs."

"At the archaeology dig?"

"Actually I'm not sure. I assumed his rented flat but he might have meant the dig at the Cloisters. He said that there was something he needed to sort out, but he didn't elaborate on what that was. When I asked him, he waved my question away and said he was perfectly capable of sorting it out himself. Not that I'd offered to do anything. He does seem a bit touchy of late."

Paige was amazed. That was probably the longest speech Olivia had ever made. She was definitely worried now. Paige knew Zac less well than the others. Because he was employed mainly to replace her when she had a rugby match or training that clashed with the bookshop's opening hours she rarely worked the same shift as he did. Nevertheless, something was off.

Down in the stockroom, Paige set about collecting the books to take upstairs. The basement was still her least favourite place in the store. It brought back memories of the death of Logan, a young employee, not long after she'd taken over River Books. A shiver ran down her spine as she remembered the vision she'd had of Zac being swallowed up by a pile of coins. Surely, lightning didn't strike twice? Shaking her head vigorously to dispel the dark thoughts that threatened to overwhelm her, she took a deep breath and picked up the first pile of books. Paige jogged up the two flights of stairs with them and deposited them on a table next to where Olivia was standing.

"First delivery," she gasped, before turning on her heels and sprinting down the stairs again.

"Paige, where's the fire?" Mary's voice stopped her in her tracks.

"Just getting some exercise in, big sis," she said.

"Why on earth would you want to do that?" Mary asked her younger sister.

"Each to their own. You're the classy IT whizz," she replied, her eyes taking in her sister's smart Boden blazer, stylish trousers and suede ankle boots, "and me, well, I'm not. I'm the gung ho sports lover."

Not for the first time, Paige wondered how they were both from the same gene pool. Mary took after her mother - petite with an innate dress sense. Paige was like her grandmother. Or, at least, like what she'd gleaned from the few photos that she'd seen of her. Tall, leggy, blonde and a lover of comfortable clothing, her grandmother had died when she'd been a young child and she only had a fuzzy memory of her. Paige's parents had been killed in a road accident on the other side of the world when she was eighteen. The sisters' parents had been the 'hands off' types and, as soon as Paige had turned eighteen and was officially an adult, they'd sold the family home, packed up their belongings and emigrated to Australia without a backward glance. So even though Mary and Paige were miles apart in looks and temperament, there was a strong bond between them, forged by being left to bring themselves up.

Paige's fingers strayed to the dream catcher that her grandmother had left her. Had her grandmother also experienced visions and had a heightened sense of intuition? Paige liked to think that her grandmother had recognised a similar sensitivity in her, her youngest granddaughter, which was why she'd bequeathed the dream catcher to her and not Mary. The necklace had strange powers. It heated up as a sign of impending danger. At the moment it was cool to the touch.

The bell to River Books jangled and Violet, the local gossip, sailed in. Today she was dressed in a turquoise floaty suit that made her look like a walking seascape.

"Cooeee! Hello my dears. How are you today?" she called across the shop as she headed like an exocet missile for the last free table at the café.

Sunny, the Nepalese manager of the café, walked over to where Violet had plonked her considerable bulk. "Violet, how nice to see you. What can I get for you today?"

Violet beamed at Sunny whose calm and gentle manner worked wonders on the customers.

"Sunita, my dear. Do you have any of those delicious violet cupcakes?"

"Sorry, Violet. Not today. I do have a tasty carrot cake. Would you like to try that?"

The older woman's red-lipped mouth turned from pout to smile. "Why not? And one of your cappuccinos, please."

The chair creaked ominously as Violet leaned back. "I bring news," she clarioned.

A hush fell on the shop. Everyone was eager to hear the latest gossip.

Satisfied that she had the customers' attention, Violet said, "There has been a development at the archaeological dig. Apparently, the TV cameras are swarming around Cathedral Green."

"Do you know what's been found?" Paige asked.

Violet's smug expression faltered momentarily before she replied, "Not exactly. But I've been told it's something that could change how we view the history of Exeter."

"I'm surprised..." Paige began before Mary cut her off.

"That's exciting, Violet. I imagine Zac should be able to fill us in when he arrives for his shift," Mary said quickly stepping in before Paige could bait Violet. It was, after all, one of her favourite games.

"I'm sure he will. As you all know, I do like the Riverside community to be well-informed of any local developments," Violet replied.

Violet took her role as President of the Riverside Association very seriously. She used it as an excuse to feed her insatiable thirst for gossip. Her main rival in the gathering of gossip was Dom, who after years of being Professor Dominic Giraud, Head of French and master of the dark arts of departmental politics, had retired as Professor Emeritus. With less influence at the university, he'd turned his attentions to the Riverside community, much to Violet's annoyance. River Books had belonged to his family for years before a scandal implicating a former manager had temporarily closed the shop. Fed up with unreliable and criminally-inclined managers he'd decided to sell it to Paige for a nominal price when she'd needed a fresh start after abandoning her life as a professional skier in France.

As if her thoughts had conjured him up, Dom strode through the doorway, his silver-tipped walking stick tapping out a brisk rhythm. He came to a halt as he saw Violet smiling like the cat who had got the cream. "Ah, I see that I am too tardy. I presume that you have all heard about the dig?"

Violet chuckled. "My dear professor, I'm afraid that

is old news now." Her sumptuous chest expanded until Paige was afraid it would smother the table.

"Well played, old girl," Dom said.

"Less of the 'old girl', you ancient skeleton," she said haughtily.

Dom, who was indeed rather thin and skeletal, laughed. "Sorry, Madame President. Please accept my profuse apologies," he said, sweeping an imaginary hat in a flourish before him.

Violet deflated and grinned. "Thank you, kind sir. Please, join me."

Dom folded himself onto the seat. Sunny bustled over to take his order.

"Sunita, my dear. What delicacies do you have today?"

She beamed at the elderly gentleman. "Just for you, I have a slice of sticky ginger loaf. Would you like that? I think a pot of Earl Grey tea would complement the flavours of the cake."

"Sunita, I trust your excellent choices. You have never failed me," he said, his eyes shining with kindness.

Sunny blushed and went to prepare his order. She quickly returned with his food. Dom tucked into the ginger cake while Violet was making serious inroads into her carrot cake. Paige left them and went to have a quick word with Mary.

"Shouldn't Zac be here by now?"

Her sister frowned and consulted her watch. "He's forty-five minutes late. It's not like him. I've tried ringing him, but it goes straight to voice mail."

Paige's spine prickled. "Something's up, Mary."

"Are you having one of your feelings?"

Paige nodded. "Look, I've got to run a book over to Miss Fletcher, who broke her ankle last week. I rang her earlier and promised I'd drop it off. Tell me Zac's address and I'll pop in on him after I've seen Miss Fletcher. I'll take Sprite. Miss Fletcher always makes a fuss of her and she'll be disappointed if her favourite dog isn't part of the delivery service."

"Good idea. Here's Zac's address. It's in Heavitree too so it won't be out of your way."

As Paige entered the address in her phone, her vision clouded and coins spun in front of her eyes.

Chapter 3

Paige found a parking space a few yards from Miss Fletcher's home and turned off the Mini's ignition. Paige had brought her Norfolk Terrier, Sprite, along with her, who one day had turned up on Paige's doorstep thin and undernourished. Paige had taken her to the vet who'd given her a check-up. The combined efforts of Paige and the vet had failed to track down an owner so Paige had adopted her, although she was convinced that Sprite had in fact chosen her. They'd clicked immediately as if they'd known each other all their lives. Now Paige couldn't imagine life without her pet.

She undid Sprite's harness and the little terrier jumped out of the car onto the icy pavement. Slinging her bag over her shoulder, Paige walked towards the neat, compact garden that fronted the small terraced house. Azalea bushes lined the paved path to the navy front door. Sprite inspected them with interest, her terrier instincts searching for a scent. Her attention was interrupted when she heard the sound of someone on the other side of the front door. It opened to reveal a narrow hallway where Miss Fletcher, balanced precariously on crutches, greeted them with a smile.

"Come on in. Hello little Miss," she said, beaming at Sprite.

The dog raised her cute furry face and gave a friendly bark.

"And I'm pleased to see you too," Miss Fletcher replied. She always spoke to Sprite as if she could understand her.

Paige and her pet entered quickly to stop the heat from the house escaping. Following the elderly lady as she manoeuvred her way into the kitchen, Paige saw that a Victoria Sponge and a teapot were set out in readiness. She didn't have the heart to tell her that they were an employee short in the shop and that she needed to get back. Instead she took off her coat, sat down and chatted to Miss Fletcher while eating a delicious slice of the moist sponge. Eating cake was no hardship for Paige. When the plates were empty and Sprite had been given a doggy treat, Paige cleared the table and washed up the dishes.

"There's no need for that, Paige, dear."

"I insist. Is there anything else I can do while I'm here?"

"No, I'm fine. I've organised meals to be delivered. I've got a key safe so they can access the house without me having to get up. Once I'm settled in my armchair by the window in the front room, I can watch the world go by. And read the latest Eve Mallow mystery," she said, tapping the cover of the Clare Chase book Paige had delivered.

"I'll wait until you're settled and then be off. I've got to check on Zac. He's not answering his phone. It's unlike him."

"The ginger-haired boy?"

"Yes."

"I sometimes see him walk past. He must live near here."

"He does."

"I hope he's alright," Miss Fletcher said, a frown crinkling her lined forehead.

"I'm sure it's just a misunderstanding. He's probably got his shifts mixed up and is sleeping in," Paige said reassuringly.

"Nevertheless, I'll call you if I see him. I can pretend to be in that Hitchcock film. You know, that one with James Stewart when he's at home with a broken ankle and spies on his neighbours. What was its title?"

"Rear Window," Paige said with a smile. "Now don't you be getting into any mischief." She wagged her finger at the old lady and was rewarded by a wide grin.

"Ah, those were the days," Miss Fletcher said with a twinkle in her eye.

Once she was installed in her armchair with her foot up on a stool, Paige checked everything was within her reach.

"I think that's everything. We'll be off now."

Miss Fletcher ruffled Sprite's neck. "Bye, bye, sweet thing."

Paige replied for both of them, "Goodbye. Thank you for the tea and cake. Do give me a ring if you need anything, won't you?"

"Don't fuss. I'm fine. Thank you for bringing the book and your delightful little dog."

Paige carefully closed the door behind her and shut the gate before turning to wave at Miss Fletcher, who was watching them through the window.

"Right, Sprite, as Zac only lives a street away and parking isn't always easy around here, we'll walk round, okay?"

Sprite perked up her ears and followed Paige along the pavement and down the next road on the right. Paige checked the address she'd entered in her phone. "It's that one there," she said to Sprite pointing to a small terraced house. This house was in stark contrast to Miss Fletcher's. The paint on the window sills was peeling away and a gutter was dripping on the cracked paving to the left of the discoloured front door.

Sprite growled and Paige's dream catcher started to burn. A vision of Zac drowning in coins sent a chill down her spine.

"Come on girl, something is definitely wrong. No one leaves a front door ajar in the middle of February."

Carefully, Paige pushed the door open with her gloved hand and poked her head inside the tiny entrance. A small table that had held the students' post was tipped over on its side. Envelopes and pizza delivery leaflets were scattered on the grubby grey carpet.

"Hello. Anyone there?" Paige called. Silence.

All of the doors leading off the hallway were open. Surely, the individual students would keep their rooms locked? She peeked her head around the first door. The only thing out of place was the smoke alarm. It was hanging open from the ceiling. With a rising sense of doom she looked into each ground floor room in turn. In every one the smoke alarm dangled open. Sprite had sprinted upstairs and was barking outside the first room on the left. Paige hurried up the stairs. She skidded to a halt beside her dog. A middle-aged man was crumpled on the floor next to an overturned stool underneath the smoke alarm which also hung open. A coppery puddle of blood surrounded his head. The corner of a nearby desk was smeared red. It looked like he'd hit his head on the desk when he'd fallen off the stool. Paige sniffed the air. It smelt of smoke. She noticed what looked like a cigarette burn on the bedside table where the pale wood was charred black. Was that why this man had been checking the smoke alarms? Had there been a fire?

But, that didn't explain why the room had been ransacked. Books had been swept off bookshelves, the mattress had been upended and slit open, drawers had been wrenched out of the dresser and their contents emptied on the beige carpet.

Paige stepped carefully around the objects strewn all over the floor, took off her gloves and bent over the man to feel his neck. He wasn't breathing and she couldn't find a pulse. She pulled out her phone and dialled 999.

During the time she waited for the emergency services to arrive, Paige had a quick look round the room. She was careful not to touch anything as she took photos with her phone of the smoke alarm, the items scattered on the floor, the torn mattress and the books that had been rifled through. They were all on archaeology. This was definitely Zac's room. She recognised the pink shirt he'd been wearing when he'd given his presentation about the Cathedral's Cloister Garden digs amongst an untidy pile of clothing that had been chucked out of the wardrobe.

Once she'd gathered as much information as she could without contaminating the crime scene, Paige left the room and went downstairs to await the ambulance and police. She poked her head out of the doorway and saw the blue flashing lights appear at the end of the road. She waved to the crew, informed the 999 operator, who'd been on the other end of the line, of their arrival and hung up. Paige directed the paramedics to the upper floor.

Paige stood just inside the front door in an attempt to keep out of the bitter cold. She clicked on the 'big sis' icon in her mobile's contacts list.

Her sister answered immediately. *"Paige, where the hell are you?"* she snapped.

"Mary, I'm at Zac's. Listen, don't panic. There's a dead body."

"Not again! I don't believe it! Is it Zac? Please tell me we haven't got another dead employee."

"No, it's not Zac. But the body is in Zac's room

and Zac is nowhere to be found."

Paige heard Mary sigh. *"That doesn't sound good."*

"No," Paige admitted. *"It doesn't. Look, I've got to go. The police have arrived."*

She heard a car draw up and stepped outside to see a patrol car double park next to a saloon car. Her heart sank as DS Brown got out from behind the wheel of the dark blue BMW. DS Brown was a female detective whose sharp tongue and attitude matched her severe clothing style. Paige and the woman had crossed swords in the past. Paige had made the mistake of speaking about her special abilities in front of the policewoman after she'd discovered Logan's body. Since then, DS Brown never missed an opportunity to mock Paige's intuition.

"Well, well. If it isn't Miss Harper," DS Brown sneered. "You turn up at my crime scenes like the proverbial bad penny."

Paige gritted her teeth and forced a smile on to her face. "DS Brown, a pleasure as always," she said sweetly.

"Don't tell me. You had a message from the spirits that someone had died."

"No, sorry to disappoint you. I came to check on a member of staff."

"Another of your employees is dead?" The malicious curl of the woman's mouth competed with the steely glint of her eyes.

"Not this time. Shall I show you the way?"

"No, I don't want you interfering in my case. Just tell me where it is."

"He," Paige paused to emphasise the pronoun, "the dead man is on the first floor, first room on the left. The ambulance crew are already up there with him."

"Stay here. The constable will take your statement." DS Brown garbled something into her phone, then putting paper bootees over her shoes and pulling on blue nitrile gloves, she went inside the house.

PC Patel had been waiting patiently as the detective had spoken to - or should that be - at Paige.

"Hello, Miss Harper. Shall we sit in the patrol car? It's very cold out here." He gave a sympathetic smile as his hand rested on the door handle.

"Thank you, PC Patel, that's a marvellous idea. Is Sprite allowed in too?"

His eyes softened as he said, "Of course she is." He crouched down and gave the ginger fur ball a stroke.

Once seated in the relative warmth of the car whose heater was working overtime, Paige explained to the police officer how she'd come to be at this address and what she'd found. She cuddled Sprite as she spoke.

"And have you managed to contact Mr Zac, er, what's his surname?"

"Jones. Zachary Jones. No, I haven't. I'm worried. There were signs of a struggle in the room."

"He could be the killer, Miss," Patel ventured. "Maybe he's done a runner."

"I honestly don't know what I can tell you, constable. I'd hope that I was a good enough judge of character not to employ a killer." Her fingers reached instinctively for her dream catcher.

"Anyone can kill, Miss. You just have to read the newspaper headlines. Neighbours and friends always say that they couldn't imagine the person accused of murder as a murderer."

Paige nodded. Was Zac a killer? If so, what had he been involved in? She felt her chest tighten. If she was honest with herself, she suspected that Zac was guilty of something. But what?

Chapter 4

Paige opened the door of River Books and quickly slipped inside with Sprite close on her heels. As soon as the bell tinkled, Mary appeared at the door of her office and rushed to her sister's side.

"Are you okay?" she asked, giving Paige a penetrating look.

Paige shrugged. "Sort of. I'm not sure. I must be cursed. I keep tripping over dead bodies."

"Don't be stupid. You're not cursed. So who was it?" Mary asked leading Paige by the elbow to a café table.

"I don't know. A middle-aged man who looked like he'd fallen off a stool and cracked his head open." Paige slumped in her chair.

"But, it wasn't Zac? So that's good, isn't it?" Mary asked.

"It wasn't Zac but his body was in Zac's room and that had been ransacked Mary. His stuff had been tossed all over the place. Even his mattress had been ripped open. And there was a really weird thing," Paige paused and lowered her voice, "all the smoke alarms were hanging open."

"What?"

"The doors of all the students' rooms were wide open and in each one the smoke alarm was hanging open. How weird is that?"

"Maybe the man you found was a maintenance man

and he was replacing the batteries?"

"Even if he was, why had Zac's room been turned over like that? It doesn't make sense. And," again Paige hesitated before continuing, "Olivia said Zac was worried about something at his digs."

Mary scrunched up her forehead. "She didn't say anything to me."

"Don't worry. She didn't volunteer the information. She told me because I asked her if she'd noticed Zac was acting twitchy of late. Surely, you've noticed he's been a bit off recently?"

"I can't say I have. As long as he gets on with his work, I leave him be. He's efficient and hard-working"

"Yes, he is, but I sometimes feel as though he's playing a role and that these last few days he's forgotten his lines. Apparently, he snapped at Olivia."

"That's not like him," Mary admitted.

"No, it isn't. Anyway, he told her he had problems at his digs. She didn't know whether he meant his rented accommodation or the archaeological digs. He told her in no uncertain terms that she shouldn't get involved, that he could fix it."

"Paige, do you think he could have killed the man you found?" Mary whispered uneasily.

"I honestly don't know. Maybe by accident. I know that he's in trouble." She stopped when her sister raised a questioning eyebrow. Paige held up her hands as if in surrender. "Yes, I've had visions. But what they mean I haven't worked out yet."

"Let's hope he's found soon and the mess can be sorted out," Mary said.

Paige caught a movement and looked up to see Sunny making her way towards them holding a tray loaded with a tea, a cappuccino and two slices of lemon and blueberry cake. "Ah, Sunny, thank you. Just what we need," Paige said. She felt full from the earlier slice of Miss Fletcher's sponge but Paige didn't want to disappoint Sunny, who was always so thoughtful.

"How are you feeling, Paige," the young woman asked, her chocolate drop eyes soft with compassion.

"I've been better, but cake and tea always help." She picked up her tea, took a long sip and smacked her lips. "Perfect. Nothing beats a strong cup of Assam to perk me up. Sunny, had you noticed anything different about Zac lately?"

In a jangle of bangles Sunny sat down at the table with them and leant forward before saying quietly, "He's a boy with lots of turmoil in his past. Recently, I've sensed he's been fighting shadows."

Mary looked nonplussed. "You're talking in riddles. What do you mean?"

"I'm not certain. I think he was struggling with a dilemma. Sorry, I can't be more helpful. It was just an impression."

Paige laid a comforting hand over Sunny's. "I understand. I felt it too."

Mary harrumphed. "Oh, to be surrounded by rational people," she exclaimed. She pushed her glasses up her nose and wrapped her hands round the mug of cappuccino.

It was almost closing time. Sprite had been lying under a café table in the hope that a crumb or two might fall her way. Now she jumped up and bounced towards the shop door. It flew open as a Chocolate Labrador bounded into the shop with his owner desperately trying to slow him down. Alejandro Ramos, a tall, slim man with dark curly hair that flopped over his almond gold-flecked eyes, gave up the battle and let go of the dog's lead. Sprite and the young dog greeted each other by enthusiastically rolling on the floor.

Paige's stomach fluttered as it inevitably did when

the handsome Spaniard was anywhere near her. She and Alex, as most people called him, had a strange relationship, if you could call it that. Paige had been badly hurt in the past and found it difficult to trust, especially dashingly good-looking men. They were her kryptonite. She regathered her thoughts and brought the dogs to heel.

"Hello Rafa," she said, stroking his silky brown fur and being rewarded with a slobbery lick. "Hi Alex, how are you?"

"*Bien, gracias.* But I think it should be me asking you that question, no?"

He strode towards her. Paige's heart galloped at the close proximity. She took a calming breath and said, "How did you find out?"

"Inspector Denton contacted me. He's asked for my assistance on the case. There are some worrying details he wants me to investigate."

"But surely he hasn't had time to find anything yet? I only discovered the body a few hours ago."

"I don't know. He's asked me to attend the case briefing this evening." He gave her that particular smile that melted her insides and said, "Could Rafa come to stay at your house tonight? I'm not sure how long I'll be out and," he dipped his head before muttering, "he's been misbehaving when I leave him for too long."

Paige bit the insides of her cheeks and swallowed a giggle. It was a continuous source of frustration to Alex that Rafa didn't listen to him but was well-behaved for Paige. She bent down and stroked Rafa's side. "Rafa, have you been a naughty boy?" The dog gazed at her with innocent eyes and gave a short bark. "He refutes your claims, Alex."

"Well, he can deny all he likes. The evidence doesn't lie."

"What evidence?"

"The now empty bag of doggy treats I found on the kitchen floor which was full when I left to give my lecture this morning. He'd eaten the whole lot."

Rafa looked at Paige as if to say "Who me?"

"Don't worry, he can come to stay. Do you have his bed and bowls in the car?" Paige asked. When Alex nodded she handed over her car keys. "Here. Go and put them in my Mini. It's parked…" She didn't get to finish her sentence.

"I saw where it was. Thank you," he said doing that strange heel click he did with his cowboy boots before hurrying out of the shop.

Mary grinned at her little sister. "So how is it going between you and the handsome Spaniard?"

Paige ran her fingers through her hair. "Honestly, I don't know."

Paige and Alejandro had been attracted to each other for months, but the relationship had been fraught with misunderstandings and arguments. Paige wasn't even sure that they had a relationship, although their dogs, Sprite and Rafa, were great friends. Alejandro was a criminal psychology lecturer at the local university. He was often seconded to help the police when a case presented complex psychological elements. That was how they'd first met. He'd been called in to help investigate the murder of, Logan, one of River Books' employees. Yet, for all his training in psychology, he was first and foremost a scientist. He liked facts. Whereas Paige was an intuitive who saw visions and had premonitions. They were like oil and water.

"Maybe it's time you found out. Have you any idea why he's here in Exeter? Why he left Spain? What relationships he's had in the past?" Mary asked concerned.

"Not really," Paige mumbled.

Mary wasn't taken in. "Paige Harper, you pride yourself on your intuition, your empathy and your curiosity. What's stopping you? What are you afraid of? And don't say you're too fragile after what Xavier put you through. That was almost a year ago now. You're not normally a coward." Mary touched a nerve as she knew she would.

Paige spluttered, "I'm not a coward."

"I'm just saying, little sis. Think of it as a dose of tough love from your big sister who always knows best." Mary winked.

Paige laughed but inside she was questioning herself. Why hadn't she shown more interest in Alejandro's past? What was she afraid of finding?

Chapter 5

That evening Paige, Sprite and Rafa knocked on Dom's door. When he answered, she said, "Hi Dom. Do you want to come for a walk with the gang?" She motioned to the two dogs who were sitting on their haunches eagerly waiting for his decision.

"How can I resist such an invitation. Give me a few minutes to wrap up warm and I'll be right with you." He disappeared inside and pushed the door to behind him.

Paige waited outside. She was wearing a fuchsia pink down jacket, a matching scarf, a blue Exeter Chiefs bobble hat and warm gloves. Dom emerged from the house in a beige woollen overcoat, a tartan patterned scarf and matching tartan fedora. Thick tan leather gloves completed the 'English gentleman' look.

"So, *ma chérie*, where is the dashing Spaniard?" he asked as they walked down the path.

"He's at a police briefing. He asked me to look after Rafa tonight as he didn't know how long it would go on and," she stopped and pointed at the Lab, who was walking to heel, "that young lad has been misbehaving and can't be trusted on his own."

Dom grinned. He was well aware of the battle Alex had with controlling Rafa. The boisterous young dog constantly disobeyed his master. He also knew how Paige delighted in teasing Alex about it.

"Ah, what was it this time?"

"A whole bag of doggy treats stolen from the side

and demolished in one sitting."

"Won't he ever learn that Labradors are programmed to steal food and that food needs to be locked away?"

"Apparently not. Anyway, Sprite's happy to have her boyfriend staying for a sleepover." Paige chuckled as Sprite gave her a smug look.

"I noticed that you avoided saying what the police briefing is about," Dom said, giving her a sideways glance.

"Let's get to the park and then, once the dogs are off their leads, I'll explain."

Dom raised a questioning eyebrow but held his peace until they reached the park. While the dogs ran off to explore he and Paige walked slowly along the lit path. "Right, what's up?"

Paige stopped and turned to face him. "*Grandpère*, I sort of discovered a body earlier today."

Dom blanched. "Oh *ma chérie*, that's awful." He gathered her into his long arms. "*Comment vas-tu?*"

Paige let herself be held before replying, "A bit shaken. The man was lying with his head cracked open. She gave an involuntary shiver, "There was blood everywhere."

"And where did you find this body?"

"At Zac's lodgings. He was late for work and not answering his phone. I'd promised to deliver a book to Miss Fletcher - you know she broke her ankle recently?" Dom nodded. "Zac's place is just round the corner from her house in Heavitree so I told Mary I'd pop in to check on him."

"It wasn't Zac?"

"No, a middle-aged man. Thin and scrawny with a weasel face. He had calloused hands like he did a manual job. He'd fallen off a stool and split his head open on Zac's desk."

"What was he doing on a stool?" Dom asked baffled.

"The smoke alarm was hanging open. All the smoke alarms had been opened in every one of the students' rooms." She looked up and saw the questioning look. "All the doors were ajar. I didn't open them, honest," she said holding up her hands.

"Behaving yourself for once? Good." He rubbed his chin. "Maybe he was replacing the batteries?"

"That would have made sense except Zac's room had been trashed. Someone was searching for something."

"And what does Zac say?"

"He's missing, Dom. I'm really worried for him. Since that talk we attended at the university about the Roman digs, he's been edgy and snappy. Now he's disappeared."

Dom lifted Paige's chin and levelled his brown eyes at her blue-grey ones. "And what have you seen?" The elderly gentleman had accepted long ago that she had special abilities.

She sighed. "Coins. Zac drowning in coins."

"Ah. You think his disappearance has something to do with the Roman digs at the Cathedral rather than the break in at this flat?"

"Dom, didn't you notice the tension between him and Professor Watkins that evening of the talk?"

"What I noticed was when I said that he was a guardian of Exeter's history he looked uncomfortable."

"I saw that too!"

"Tomorrow I'll have a word with Alex and ask him what he knows. For some reason, he's more inclined to confide in me than you," he chuckled.

"Ha, ha. So I once betrayed his confidence. I didn't

do it on purpose." Paige pouted.

"No, you didn't. You did what you normally do - you rushed in to help without thinking it through." Dom focused on her. "It's not a criticism, Paige. But don't forget the saying, *Fools rush in where angels fear to tread*. Be careful. I worry about you. Now let's go home and have a hot chocolate."

"Do you have marshmallows?"

"Is the Pope a Catholic?"

Paige whistled and Sprite and Rafa came running over. "Time to go," she said attaching their leads.

After a warming mug of hot chocolate complete with marshmallows savoured in Dom's kitchen, Paige and the dogs returned to her house across the grounds. Her lodge house was part of the original estate owned for generations by Dom's maternal family. Even though his father had been French, Professor Dominic Giraud could trace his maternal family's historical links with Exeter back to the seventeenth century. The first of his ancestors on record was Christopher Lethbridge, who'd been Mayor of Exeter in 1660 and one of the *Worthies of Devon*. There was a monument to this ancestor in St Mary Arches Church and a monumental brass in Exeter Cathedral in memory of the Lethbridge family. Hence Dom's remark to Zac about the responsibility of guarding the city's history. He took his heritage seriously. Dom claimed his family was descended from the Norse king, Ragnar Lodbrok, who wreaked havoc in England during the ninth century. Paige couldn't quite picture the tall, almost skeletal man as a descendent of the warring Viking, although he was an expert in the art of verbal warfare.

Sprite and Rafa settled down for the night in their beds in the kitchen. Paige made sure that all food was shut away in cupboards. She didn't want to put temptation in Rafa's way. Also, she needed to show Alex that when Rafa was her guest, he behaved. She shook her head.

"How pathetic, Paige," she muttered to herself. "Can't you give your competitive spirit a night off? What are you hoping to prove?"

In bed she tossed and turned, plagued by nightmares of Zac drowning in a pool of coins and of the unknown man laying on the floor. At 5am she gave up on any attempt to get more sleep and turned on the light. She would have loved a cup of tea but she didn't want to go downstairs and wake the dogs so she made do with a glass of water from the bathroom. Paige picked up a notebook and pencil and wrote out what she knew about Zac. It wasn't much.

1. Paige had noticed that he'd been on edge at work. According to Olivia, Zac had been worried about something at the digs. He hadn't elaborated and had warned Olivia off when she'd questioned him.

2. He could have meant the student digs he lived in or the archaeology dig. There was obviously a problem at his student accommodation because a man had been found dead in Zac's room and the room had been turned over. What had the person who'd done that been looking for? Had they found it?

3. Why had all the smoke alarms been hanging open? What was the story there? Was it simply that the dead man had been replacing the batteries?

4. Why had Zac's room smelt of smoke? Had he noticed that the smoke alarm wasn't working and contacted the letting agent? Or had he opened up the smoke alarm himself?

5. Paige had picked up on tensions between Zac and Professor Watkins at the lecture. Did that have any relevance? Part of Zac's duties was to document the finds. Had he noticed discrepancies between what had

been unearthed and what was presented to him to catalogue?

6. Why had Paige had a vision of Zac drowning in coins? What was the significance of those coins?

Paige read through her list hoping for a spark of inspiration. None came.

Chapter 6

Wednesday

At 7am Paige stumbled downstairs feeling tired after her restless night. The moment she walked into the kitchen she felt better when she was mobbed by two very affectionate dogs.

"Good morning, my angels." She knelt down and hugged a dog under each arm as pink tongues enthusiastically licked her cheeks. "And I love you too," she said, struggling to her feet. "Now it's time you patrolled the garden."

Sprite hurried to the back door with Rafa right behind. Paige opened it and stood in the doorway. The garden looked like it had been dusted with icing sugar. Frosty rime ran along the top of the fence as if it were piped icing on a gingerbread house. The grass crackled under the dogs' paws as they explored every inch of the garden. Rafa barked and jumped excitedly at a cat that had foolishly clambered on the fence. It disappeared with lightning speed back from where it had come. Sprite gave Rafa an approving yap. The young Lab strutted with pride. Paige wrapped her arms around herself to keep warm. Here in the south west of England, frosty mornings were rare and she wanted to cherish this moment of crispness. When she'd lived in the French Alps, she'd loved those magical days of fresh snowfalls sparkling under cobalt blue skies. In January she'd gone back to France for a week's skiing.

Not to the town where she'd lived previously, but to one of the resorts where she'd competed in her former life as a professional skier. It had been great to feel the buzz of negotiating a black run with ease. These days she got her thrills as best she could on the rugby pitch.

A mad barking brought Paige back to the present as both dogs charged towards the gate. She recognised the head of dark curls that could be seen over the top of the fence.

"Paige, I tried ringing at the front door."

"Alex, you're early." Paige said, as she walked over to let him into the garden.

He bravely rode the tide of the dogs' adoration and made it upright to the kitchen. The dogs tumbled in after him.

"I was just about to feed the dogs and make breakfast. Would you like some?" Paige asked, tightening the belt on her dressing gown self-consciously.

Alex sat down and sprawled his long, jean-clad legs out in front of him. "*Gracias, cariño. Tengo mucho hambre.* I'm very hungry."

"I can cook you an omelette or would you like some porridge?"

"I will be English and eat porridge. It is good for cold mornings, no?"

"It is. Do you want to be even more English and drink tea?"

The handsome Spaniard's face fell. He rubbed the dark stubble on his chin. "*Cariño, por favor.* Please - not tea. I have been up most of the night. I need strong coffee."

"Don't worry, Alex. Just teasing. One espresso coming up." She put a capsule in the coffee machine and pressed the button. A rich, dark aroma filled the kitchen.

Paige fed the dogs. Then she prepared her pot of Assam tea and cooked the porridge in the microwave. She set out dried fruits, bananas and honey on the table. Alex fetched his cup of coffee and drank it quickly.

"It is my fuel. I am going to have another one, okay?"

"Sure. Help yourself."

He removed the used capsule and placed a fresh one in the machine. Once the coffee was made he sat down next to Paige to eat his bowl of steaming porridge. Paige added a banana and a drizzle of honey to hers. Alex did the same. Rafa had gobbled down his food and was sitting drooling next to Alex.

"Rafa, you've eaten. Go to your basket," Paige said, pointing to his bed.

The dog gave his master a forlorn look. Alex ignored him. Reluctantly, Rafa returned to his bed. He put his chin on its padded side and focused sad puppy eyes on the mean adults. Paige laughed. "That trick won't work." The dog's dark gaze never wavered. She scraped out her bowl, placed the spoon inside and took it over to the sink. She returned to her seat.

"So, now that I've eaten and fed you and your dog, are you going to tell me about the case?" Paige drummed her fingers on the table top.

"*Cariño*. I'm impressed. Your patience is improving." His gold-flecked eyes danced with amusement as he pointedly checked his wristwatch. Paige threw a serviette at his grinning face.

"Very funny. Actually, I'll have you know I don't do anything before I've eaten breakfast. Now that I've finished, spill."

Paige burst through the door of River Books a few moments after Mary had opened up.

"So sorry, Mary," she gasped. "I know I'm late.

Alex came to pick up Rafa and time slipped away from me."

"How is Alejandro?" Mary asked, then realised she'd fallen into her sister's trap of moving the focus away from her tardiness.

"Fine. He told me some things about the investigation." Paige's eyes were clouded with concern.

"Such as?"

"The most important piece of information for us is that Zac is being sought by the police. You haven't heard from him, have you?"

Mary shook her head. "No. Nothing. I'm worried. Do the police think he killed that man?"

"Honestly? I don't know. Obviously, finding a dead body in his room makes him a prime suspect."

"Why did he run away if he's innocent?"

"That, big sis, is the million dollar question." Paige frowned. "We need to hold a staff meeting and ask everyone if they have anything they can tell us."

"Already organised. We are closing early at 4 today."

"Why am I not surprised that my super efficient store manager has that arranged already?"

Mary smiled and brushed an imaginary fleck of lint off her jacket. "Just doing my job."

The staff meeting was held in Paige's office. Mary opened by thanking them all for being there and said, "What we need to know is anything connected to Zac that might be pertinent to the case."

"How will we know what's pertinent?" Beth asked, whose body piercings portrayed an image of a tough nut that was in sharp contrast to her gentle nature.

"We don't," Paige said. "I'll tell you what I know so far and am allowed to divulge and then we'll go round the table. Each of you can tell us about your recent interactions with Zac. I'm probably the person who knows him the least, as he's employed to cover for me. I'm counting on you all to fill me in. I'll start and we'll go from there." Heads nodded in agreement.

"I can tell you that a man was found dead in Zac's room." A collective gasp escaped from Malik, Beth and Olivia. "I can also tell you that that person's name is Andrew Hammond who worked for a letting agency that managed several student rental properties around Exeter. He was known as Handy Andy." A whisper of a smile played on their lips. "I know, not terribly original, but there you go." She paused. "Zac's room had been ransacked." Another gasp went round the table. "Obviously someone was searching for something. What it was, the police don't know. Zac is missing and the police are actively looking for him. That's all I can say at this point." Paige watched as the student employees digested what she'd said.

What she wasn't able to share was what Alex had told her about the smoke alarms and the reason for which he'd been brought into the investigation. The police had discovered that the smoke alarms were fake and were actually spy cams. Unfortunately for them, all the SD cards from the alarms had been removed and there were no clues as to who'd been involved in installing them.

"So who'd like to start? Olivia?"

Olivia's eyes blinked owl-like behind her tortoiseshell frames. She took a deep breath and said, "It's like I told you, Paige. I noticed that Zac was distracted these last few weeks. He was even rude to me, which wasn't like him at all. When I asked him what was wrong, he said he had problems with his digs but could sort it himself without anyone's help. At the time, I didn't know whether he was talking about the archaeological digs or his student digs. I assume now that he meant his student digs."

"Thank you, Olivia. Beth, Malik did he say anything about this to you?"

The pair exchanged a look and shook their heads. "No, but there is something we need to tell you," Beth said, watching Malik who nodded to her to continue. "Okay, here goes. It was just after we'd closed one day and I was downstairs getting ready to go home. I was hanging my jacket on the hook next to my locker when the clasp on my bracelet broke. I stuffed the bracelet in my jacket pocket and went to the loo. When I came out of the toilet, Zac was holding my jacket. He said that it had fallen off the hook and he was picking it up for me. I didn't think anymore about it until I was walking home and put my hand in my pocket. The bracelet wasn't there. I know that I definitely put it there. They're deep pockets. The bracelet couldn't have fallen out. I believe that Zac took it. I told Malik and we decided not to challenge him. We didn't want an awkward situation with a co-worker but we've been much more vigilant around him since then."

"Beth, why didn't you say anything?" Mary asked.

"It wasn't worth much and I had no proof," Beth replied.

"Thank you for sharing that with us, Beth. Malik do you have anything to add?"

"I've noticed that Zac has been on edge recently. Because of what happened with Beth, I've been wary around him. I admit that I may have been less friendly. I got the feeling that Zac craved acceptance. That he's insecure." He stopped and said self-consciously, "Listen to me and my psycho-babble."

Paige jumped in to reassure him. "Don't put yourself down, Malik. Your opinion is valid."

Mary smiled warmly at the young man. "Thank you,

Malik. Can I ask all of you to let us know if Zac contacts you, please? Right, I'll let you get off home now."

The youngsters gathered their belongings and made their way downstairs where Paige let them out.

"Bye, and thank you all again. I'm sure that there's a simple explanation for Zac's disappearance. See you all in the morning," she said locking the door behind them.

Paige returned to her office where Mary hadn't moved. Her brow was furrowed.

"A penny for them?"

Mary shook her head. "I'm just thinking about what Beth said. It reminded me of an incident on a Saturday when you were off playing a rugby game."

"What happened?"

"A customer had taken off her coat and left it on a chair while she browsed the shelves. When she put her coat back on, a brooch that had been on her lapel was missing. Zac was on duty in that area that day. We searched down the side of the chair and on the floor, but couldn't find it. In the end, the woman convinced herself that it must have fallen off in the street. But, and it is a big but, what if Zac had taken it?"

"Mary, do you think he's a jewellery thief?"

"That sounds a bit extreme, doesn't it?"

"It does, but the evidence is pointing that way," Paige said, her shoulders slumping. "I've also got something to tell you. I couldn't say anything in front of the others as Alex told me in confidence. It's information that the police aren't releasing. You remember I told you that all the smoke alarms were hanging open?"

Mary nodded. "Yes. We thought the handy man was replacing the batteries."

"We did. He wasn't. Apparently, the smoke alarms weren't real."

"Not real?"

"No, they were spy cams!"

"So the police will be able to see what happened."

"They would if all the SD cards hadn't been removed."

Mary's eyebrows shot up. "No!"

"Yes. And there's more," Paige said, her eyes glittering with excitement. "When I was in Zac's room I smelt smoke and saw a burn on his bedside cabinet."

"And?"

"What if Zac accidentally set fire to something and when the smoke alarm didn't go off, investigated why?"

"You mean he found the spy cams? That would explain his comments about problems at his digs."

"It would. And maybe he saw it as an opportunity to blackmail the person who'd installed them."

Mary narrowed her eyes. "But, if the man he was trying to blackmail was the dead handy man, he must be the police's prime suspect. This isn't looking good, is it?"

"No, but I think that we need to keep an open mind. I'm assuming that the reason Zac's room was turned upside down was because someone was searching for those SD cards. We don't know whether they found them. Maybe Zac had already removed them. He could have hidden them here. We ought to check his locker, Mary. I imagine the police will be rolling up to do that any time soon, but we can have a peek first. What do you think?"

"It's an intrusion of privacy, Paige. I don't think the circumstances warrant us opening it," Mary said, standing up and moving towards the door.

"But, Mary. There might be valuable clues in there."

Mary turned a steely gaze on her sister. "No, we are not crossing that boundary."

Paige shrugged off her irritation. Her big sister was such a stickler for things like this. "Okay. On to plan B. I'll carry out a thorough search of the shop to see whether anything seems out of place."

"That's a bit of a long shot, isn't it, even with your photographic memory? He could just as easily have hidden them in his locker at the university. As for me, I'll see if I can find any videos on the web that might have come from the spy cams. It's despicable behaviour by whoever put them there. Not only were they spying on students in the privacy of their own rooms, but they were leaving those same students at risk if a fire occurred."

"It's reprehensible behaviour. However, we have a plan. Let's go home and tomorrow we'll get cracking." Paige high-fived her sister.

Chapter 7

Thursday morning, Paige and Sprite set off early for River Books with the purpose of carrying out a search. They walked briskly along the river bank. A sludge grey sky hung low over the horizon.

"Come on, Sprite, we're almost there. You'll soon be in the warm and we'll be safe from the sky falling on us."

Sprite gave her mistress a quizzical look. Paige laughed, "I was thinking of the Asterix books where the Gauls' only fear was that the sky would fall on their heads."

The dog seemed to shrug her shoulders as if to say, "Whatever." As the shop door came into view Sprite put on a spurt. Paige hurried after her. She unlocked the door, disarmed the alarm and locked the door behind her. It was only 8am. That gave her almost an hour to search for anything that seemed out of place. She knew her chances of finding what Zac might or might not have hidden were slim. And yet, not so long ago she'd found vital evidence in the shop that had helped solve Logan's murder.

Sprite gave herself a shake and began patrolling the ground floor.

"We're looking for anything out of the usual," Paige said, walking behind her terrier and scanning the shelves. "He may have put the SD cards inside a book or between books to retrieve later."

Paige worked her way along racks of shelves looking for anything unusual. The first area she searched was the archaeology section, but she found nothing to indicate Zac had left anything amongst the books there. Crawling on all fours she searched under and behind bookcases. All she found was rather a lot of dust and made a mental note to be more thorough with the duster and hoover in the future. Sprite had been watching her mistress' antics with mounting curiosity. She held her nose in the air, took a deep breath and scampered over to the cookery section. Her little body turned rigid. Paige's pulse accelerated.

"What is it girl?" Sprite barked and placed her front paws on the lowest shelf. Paige crouched down. There was a slip of paper sticking out of the top of a book. What on earth was *Studies in the Roman and Medieval Archaeology of Exeter* doing here? It was in completely the wrong place. Was that the point? Hiding it on a shelf where other readers interested in archaeology wouldn't find it did have a certain logic to it. Surely, it must have been Zac? Paige turned to the page where the piece of paper was inserted. The chapter contained a recent research paper about Roman coins from Exeter and Devon. Paige rocked on her heels as the vision of Zac drowning in coins flashed across her retinas and landed with a thump on her bottom. Her heart rate began to stabilise as the vision faded. Checking the editor's details, she saw he was a professor at the University of Exeter. Was that the reason Zac had marked the page? Because it was a person he knew? Or was it because of the dig he was involved in? An untidy scrawl in black ink said *"check coins from the dig??!!"*

"Well done, Sprite. Judging by the string of question marks and exclamation marks, it seems that Zac had questions about the coins that they've uncovered in the

Cathedral Cloister Garden. Good girl." She gave her pet a hug. "Let's continue. If he marked this book, maybe he's done the same in others."

Although Paige scanned more shelves for wrongly placed archaeology books, she found no more of them.

"What now?" Paige asked Sprite. In response Sprite bounded towards the stairs leading to the basement and staff lockers. She gave a sharp yap.

"Okay, so you think we'll find something down here. Let's see."

Paige followed Sprite down the stairs and walked over to the lockers. A shiver went through her as she remembered Logan's body that she'd discovered down here not so very long ago. He'd been such a lovely lad. She shook the thought away. "Concentrate on the problem in hand," she told herself.

Sprite was sitting in front of Zac's locker and looking at Paige expectantly.

"I'm not sure I should open Zac's locker. Mary was very firm about it yesterday. However, it is an emergency. We don't know where he is and there may be some clue in there to help us find him."

Sprite continued to stare at her mistress as if to say, "Enough with the procrastination. Just get on with it."

"Right. I'll go and fetch the skeleton keys that Mary keeps in her office."

Paige returned a few moments later with a key ring and some gloves. She didn't want to leave prints inside the locker which she was sure that the police would search before too long. She put the gloves on and then carefully opened Zac's locker. Stuck on the inside of the door was a photo of Zac with his arm wrapped around an elderly lady's shoulders. It was signed, *"Good luck Zac, love Grandma."*

"Ah, that's nice," Paige said to Sprite. "Now let's see what else is in here."

A spare shirt and pair of trousers were hanging on a hook. Paige's fingers carefully felt in the pockets. Zac's staff ID tag was stuffed inside a trouser pocket. Paige took it out, examined it and replaced it.

"Well, his ID is here. A spare change of clothes too. Nothing out of the ordinary. Hang on. There's a small, white plastic bag," she said, crouching down and pulling it towards her. Inside shiny objects glistened. She gasped and her heart sank. "I think we might have found Beth's bracelet and other stolen pieces of jewellery, Sprite."

Paige laid the contents of the bag out on the locker floor. A collection of cheap trinkets covered the surface. "It doesn't look like he was a master jewellery thief like Raffles. These are mainly costume pieces. They're pretty but not of any real value. I wonder what this means. Why steal them? Perhaps that's a question that Alex can answer." Paige's lips curled into a smile at the thought of the dark, handsome Spaniard. "There aren't any SD cards hidden here, Sprite. Where could they be? Did Zac take them or was it the person who ransacked his room? I think we're going to have to get Mary to use her super IT skills to do a deep dive on the web to see if she can find any footage taken by those hidden cameras."

Sprite yapped her acknowledgement and left Paige to replace the items in the plastic bag while she headed upstairs at the sound of the shop door being opened.

Mary's voice called out, "Paige. Where are you?"

"Down here. Won't be a minute."

On the ground floor, Mary was taking off her woollen coat and standing by her office's open door. "What have you been up to?" she demanded hands on hips.

"We searched the shelves and found an interesting

note in an archaeology book. But no SD cards. So we extended our search." Paige paused and Sprite, sensing that things were going to get heated, slunk away. "So much for solidarity," Paige muttered watching the terrier's retreating rear.

"I'm waiting," Mary said, tapping her toe.

Paige pulled out the key ring from her pocket and handed it to her sister.

"The staff locker spare keys! Paige I thought we agreed yesterday that we wouldn't invade Zac's privacy."

"I know, but we thought that as the police were no doubt going to search Zac's locker, it'd be a good idea to have a peek."

"We? Are you saying that your dog convinced you to take a look? That's a bit of a cheap shot, isn't it, blaming Sprite?"

"You're right. I take full responsibility." Paige held up her hands in surrender. "Anyway, do you want to know what I found?"

"The SD cards?"

"No, unfortunately not. But I did find a stash of stolen jewellery."

"So Beth was right."

"Yes. What I assume is her bracelet is there and also a brooch like the one you described to me. Other trinkets as well. But the thing is Mary, they're cheap stuff. The pieces are all very sparkly but don't look expensive to me. I mean we are not talking about a professional jewel thief here. Not that I'm an expert in jewellery. You'd know more than me. The glittering items reminded me more of the things you'd find in a magpie's nest."

"Well, what you found makes things look bleak for Zac. And for us. We employed a thief." Mary's head dropped.

Paige moved towards her sister and put an arm around her. "Hey, sis. It'll be alright. We'll get to the bottom of this. In the meantime, I was thinking that your magic fingers could work on finding videos of what those SD cards recorded."

Mary harrumphed. "You're losing it, little sis, we already agreed I'd do that yesterday."

Paige slapped her forehead. "Silly me."

The distraction worked. Mary was back to her efficient self as she said, "If the operation has been up and running for a while, there must be videos on the web. I'll find them." She flexed her fingers.

A sharp rapping on the shop door brought the conversation to an end. Standing outside were PC Patel and another officer.

"I do believe that Zac's locker is about to be officially searched," Paige said as she fixed a welcoming smile on her face and went to open the door.

Chapter 8

"PC Patel, hello. Any news on Zac?" Paige asked as she let the police officers inside the shop.

"Sorry, Miss. He's still missing. You haven't heard from him, have you?"

"No. We're really worried about him. He's normally so reliable. Something horrible must have happened to him."

"Or he did something awful and is now in hiding," PC Patel said.

"I won't believe that until there's firm proof of his guilt," Paige said with more conviction than she felt.

"I understand. Anyway, we're here to search his locker. If you give your agreement, that is. Otherwise we can get a warrant."

Mary arrived by Paige's side. "PC Patel," she said, "How can we be of assistance?"

"We'd like to take a look inside Zachary Jones' locker, Mrs Richardson. Do we have your permission?"

"Certainly. Let me fetch the spare key." She turned on her heels and strode towards her office.

Paige smothered a grin. The keys were in Mary's jacket pocket where she'd shoved them when the police knocked on the door. Mary opened her desk drawer and, by a sleight of hand that impressed her younger sister, pulled out the keys.

"I'll show you the way," Mary said, leading the police towards the stairs. "If you'd like to follow me."

While Mary escorted the officers downstairs, Paige got ready to open the shop. Today she and Mary were on their own until mid-morning when Malik was on shift. The door bell jangled and Sunny entered with her arms piled high with fresh produce. Paige rushed to relieve her of the baguettes balanced precariously on top of the heap and closed the door behind her.

"Morning, Sunny. How are you?" Paige asked as she followed the diminutive woman to the café kitchen.

"Fine. Did I see the police outside?"

"Two officers are searching Zac's locker as we speak. Mary's with them."

"Oh, dear. Still no news on Zac?"

"No. However, I suspect we'll have DS Brown and a SOCO team turning up very shortly." Paige winked at Sunny.

Sunny gasped. "Paige what have you been up to?"

Paige put on her most innocent face. "Me? Not much. Well, I may have had a little look-see in Zac's locker earlier," she whispered.

Sunny shook her head. "And you found something of interest?"

Page nodded. "Yes. Can't say more. Time to open up," she said with a grin as she walked to River Books' door and turned the *Closed* sign to *Open*.

A quarter of an hour later, DS Brown strode into the shop, closely followed by a team of SOCO officers carrying cases.

"Miss Harper. I believe that PC Patel is here," she said abruptly.

"Good morning to you too," Paige said.

DS Brown didn't even blink. "Where is he?" she demanded deadpan.

Paige gave up baiting the sergeant. "He's

downstairs checking Zachary's locker. Do you want me to accompany you?"

"No. I know the way," she said marching towards the stairs. The forensic team waddled behind her like ducklings in their clumsy suits.

Minutes later Mary reappeared from downstairs. "I've been dismissed by Madame Sharp Edges. Although, she's more civil with me than with you, she still needs to work on her people skills."

"So, what did they find?" Paige asked.

Mary raised her eyebrows in surprise. "But…"

Paige pointed to her ear and then towards the stairs. Mary understood the silent message.

"Oh, Paige, it's horrible. They found a bag of jewellery in Zac's locker."

"No, really?" Paige exclaimed.

"Yes, and it looks like they are stolen pieces. Beth's bracelet was there. The police have already said that they'll need to speak to her when I explained how it went missing. I believe the customer who lost the brooch was a tourist so I don't know how the police will trace her." Mary let out a deep sigh. "Let's hope those other items weren't stolen from our customers. It's bad enough he stole from a member of staff," Mary added.

Paige felt her stomach drop. Would Beth make an official complaint? Just when Paige needed a busy morning to keep her mind off what the police were processing in Zac's locker, time dragged. Finally they were packing up and leaving. Malik walked past them as he arrived for his shift.

"What's happening?" the young man asked.

"The police were examining Zac's locker," Paige replied. "It seems that you and Beth were right. They found her broken bracelet there."

Malik clenched his fists. "I knew it. The little weasel. Why would he steal from a workmate? It's not like it was an expensive bracelet. Beth liked it because it sparkled."

"We don't know the answer to that question yet. I'm sure the police will get to the bottom of it. In the meantime, Zac is still missing and no one knows what's happened to him."

Malik's tensed shoulders and a darkening of his eyes told Paige that as far as he was concerned Zac could go to hell.

The rest of the day passed uneventfully. Malik and Paige dealt with customers while Mary hid away in her office searching for evidence of spy camera feeds from student accommodation. At 4pm Malik left. A few minutes later Mary emerged from her office bleary eyed.

"That was like wading through a sewer. There's obviously a big black market in hidden camera feeds. I feel like I need to have one of those disinfecting showers to get rid of the grime sticking to my skin." She gave an involuntary shiver.

"Did you find anything that might be connected with Zac?" Paige asked, picking up on her sister's leaden movements. She took her hand and led her to a table.

Sunny hurried over. "What can I get you, Mary? You look like you need a pick-me-up."

"Thanks, Sunny. A strong americano should do the trick."

"Anything else?"

Mary rubbed her stomach. "No, thanks. After what I've just seen I couldn't eat a thing right now."

"I don't have that problem, Sunny. I'll have a tea and *pain au raisin*, please."

Mary groaned. "I can't understand how you manage to always have room for cake. You should be the size of a house."

"I've told you before. My fitness regime and high metabolism are the answer."

Sunny laughed as she returned to the counter to make the drinks.

Once the beverages were on the table Mary leant forward and in hushed tones began to tell Paige about what she'd found.

"It made me sick seeing images of young girls and boys being secretly filmed. Some of the videos seem quite innocuous in themselves until you remember that the people in them have no idea they're being recorded and that their personal lives are being broadcast to all and sundry. There were sites with live feeds and others that were montages of clips. Those were sexual in nature."

"How did you access them?"

"I managed to side step firewalls on the tamer sites. Many sites that are subscription based are more explicit. And more difficult to access but I got into enough to get a general picture of the sort of content they're peddling. It's not pretty, Paige." Mary wrapped her hands round her mug and took a gulp of her coffee. "I did find some video feeds that have been recorded here in Exeter. I recognised the university logo on sports gear. The rooms looked like private rentals, not university accommodation. That would fit with the dead man in Zac's room working for a private letting agency."

"Any sign of Zac in any of the videos?"

"No, but that doesn't mean he wasn't recorded. Most of the clips show students wandering around naked in their rooms after a shower or having sex. I imagine the less interesting parts are edited out."

"What if Zac had been doing something illegal in his

room and wanted to stop the images being transmitted? That would give him a motive for killing Handy Andy and laying low."

"Whoa, Paige. We don't know anything yet. The police will have their own IT specialists searching the web for evidence of what the SD cards were recording. And they'll have photos of the students in Zac's digs that they'll be able to match to online images." Mary drank the last of her coffee and stood up. "Do you mind closing up tonight. I've got a pounding head and need to get home to have a long hot shower to make me feel human again."

Paige watched with a pang of guilt as her sister dragged herself across the room and entered her office. She was the one who'd asked Mary to do the search. She hadn't realised how much it would affect her sister. Mary reemerged wrapped up warmly against the winter chill.

"Bye, Paige. See you tomorrow."
"Bye. Take care."

Chapter 9

Friday morning Paige was surprised to receive a phone call from Miss Fletcher at 8am.

"Miss Fletcher, is everything okay?" Paige asked, her chest squeezing with anxiety.

The elderly lady ignored the question and plunged straight in, *"Paige. I promised I'd let you know if I saw Zac."*

"You've seen him?"

"I caught a glimpse of his red hair as he scurried back along the path after posting an envelope through my door. It's addressed to you, dear."

"To me? Okay. I'm coming over to fetch it now," Paige said, feeling a rush of adrenaline fizz through her.

Paige grabbed her coat and bundled herself and Sprite into the Mini. Peak rush hour traffic meant that the journey to Heavitree took almost half an hour. A space miraculously appeared as Paige turned into Miss Fletcher's street and Paige gave silent thanks to the parking angels. With the Mini parked, she jumped out of the car followed by Sprite, who'd picked up on her mistress' excitement and didn't even dawdle to sniff the tempting plants along the path.

The door opened for them before they'd had time to ring the bell. Miss Fletcher was propped up on a walker, which was a vast improvement on the crutches she'd been using the last time the pair had called on her.

"Come in, come in," she said, her eyes sparkling

with excitement. "I told you that I'd make an excellent spy, didn't I? Watch out Jimmy Stewart."

Paige laughed. "You did indeed. Now tell me exactly what happened this morning." She trailed the elderly lady into the kitchen. On the table was a brown envelope with *Private and confidential. For the attention of Miss Paige Harper* written in black marker pen. Paige resisted the urge to tear the envelope open. She'd take it to the shop with her and then call Alex. She wanted to know what was in it before going to the police with the envelope - if she had to.

Miss Fletcher perched on the seat of her walker while Paige pulled out a chair opposite her. Sprite settled on the floor between the two of them.

"I was sitting in the front room. Although it was still quite dark outside, I'd pulled back the curtains and was watching the street. I'd glanced down at the Radio Times to see what was on the radio this morning when I heard something drop through the letterbox. I raised my head and saw Zac rushing out of the gate and down the street."

"You're sure it was Zac? You know he's been missing for three days now. We've been so worried about him."

"Definitely Zac. His red hair's a giveaway and he was wearing his University of Exeter anorak. There's no doubt in my mind it was him. Of course, I heard on the local radio about the body being found. Was that you who found the man? It must have been terrible." Miss Fletcher gave a shudder but her voice vibrated with excitement.

"It was." Paige stated flatly. She changed tack. "Well, thank you, Miss Fletcher for ringing me. I'll take the envelope and get off to work."

"You're not going to open it now?" Disappointment was written all over her face.

"No, sorry. I'm going to have to handle it with care. It may well be evidence in a suspicious death investigation."

Miss Fletcher's disappointment turned to elation as she asked, "Oh, will I have to have my finger prints taken for elimination? Or be called to the witness stand?"

Paige grinned. "I can't say one way or the other, but I promise to let you know if I find out anything I can share with you."

"Perfect."

"We'll let ourselves out and, once again, thank you."

Sprite sauntered over for her customary stroke and gratefully accepted a doggy treat that Miss Fletcher magicked out of her pocket. "Here you are, sweetheart."

"You spoil her," Paige said, earning herself a glare from Sprite who was carrying the treat in her mouth like a precious gift.

"Not at all."

Paige realised she was outnumbered. "Goodbye and thank you."

The door's bell jangled as Paige and Sprite burst into River Books. Mary, standing by the till, pushed her glasses up her nose and watched her sister bounce like a rubber ball across the shop towards her.

"What's got in to you?"

"You know I sent you a text to tell you I had to call in on Miss Fletcher on my way here?"

Mary nodded. "And what's got you so excited about visiting an old lady?"

"Mary, let's go into your office," Paige said wrapping her arm around her sister's shoulders and ushering her into the small room.

Mary let herself be led away, but not before she signalled to Olivia to watch the till.

"Okay, what's so mysterious?" Mary demanded.

Paige pulled out the envelope and placed it on the desk. "This."

Mary stared at Paige's name on the envelope. "And? It's addressed to you. What's special about that?"

"It was posted through Miss Fletcher's letterbox by Zac. I need to see what's inside."

"But, isn't it evidence?" Mary's forehead crinkled with worry.

"We won't know that until I open it."

"Paige," Mary's voice ratcheted up a notch. "Please, don't go playing amateur detective again."

"Look, Zac trusted me enough to get this envelope to me. I need to honour that."

"Honour amongst thieves, eh?"

"Mary, that was a cheap shot. The boy's in trouble. If it'll make you feel better we could ask Alex to come." Paige prayed her sister would say no because Alex would definitely tell her to hand it over to the police. "Or I could call Dom to come here," Paige offered brightly.

Mary spluttered. "What? Very funny. The dear Professor who is as irresponsible as you? Oh, let's just get this over with," she said, resigned to the fact that Paige was determined to open the package no matter what. She pulled out her drawer and gave Paige a pair of cotton gloves normally used for handling rare books, "at least wear these so as not to contaminate the evidence."

Paige donned the gloves and carefully peeled back the seal of the envelope. Her dream catcher burned at her throat and her sight blurred as a vision of Zac drowning in coins flashed across her retinas. A tremor shook her hands and she took a moment to steady herself before emptying the contents onto the desk. A small plastic pouch containing SD cards and a letter fell out. She unfolded the letter and read it out loud.

Paige, I've felt that someone's been following me for a while and now that I've found spy cams in the house I'm convinced of it. There's a dead man in my room. Was it me they meant to kill? Why? Is it to do with the dig? I don't know who these people are but I'm scared. I'm afraid they'll convince the police I killed that man. I'm going into hiding. Can you check on my grandmother? Please. Zac. I'm giving you these SD cards for safekeeping.

"Mary, I think I will call Alex. This is serious. Zac doesn't want us to pass on the SD cards to the police but I do think we should. However, can you make a copy of them before we hand them over? At least that way we'll have evidence of what was on them should, heaven forbid, someone try to tamper with them."

Her big sister silently put on another pair of gloves and removed the cards from the pouch. Glumly she inserted each one in turn into her laptop and copied the content. "There, satisfied?" she grumbled. "Making me into an accomplice."

"Thank you. Look I'm calling Alex now. You've no need to tell him about copying the SD cards. We need to know what's on those cards for Zac's sake. Actually, I'm having second thoughts, do you think we should hand them over at all?" Paige asked.

"Why don't we give ourselves until later on today to decide. Don't call Alex for the moment. Once I've had a look at what's on them, we can make a decision then." Mary shook her head. "I can't believe I'm saying this. What have you done to the real Mary Richardson?

I'm meant to be the sensible and law-abiding sister."

"Are you starting to understand the thrill of sleuthing, big sis?" Paige chortled. "Seriously, let's put everything back in the package and lock it in the safe. We'll take the rest of the day to investigate information we glean from the cards. Then we can make an informed decision as to what to do."

"In that case, you're in charge of the shop while I get to work digging around in the murky depths of hidden spy cam footage. But I'm warning you that you owe me big time."

Paige's heart gave a nervous jolt. "Mary, are you sure? Yesterday's search left you drained. I don't want to put you in a situation where you're uncomfortable."

Mary waved off her concerns. "I was searching the dregs of the internet sites. These will only contain things recorded in the student house and shouldn't be so disturbing as the filth I trawled through yesterday."

"If you're certain?"

Her big sister nodded and shooed Paige out of her office. By the time she closed the door behind Mary was engrossed in her screen.

Paige walked up to Olivia and said, "Mary's tied up with some admin work so I'll be working downstairs today. Can you cover upstairs?"

Olivia blinked her owl-like eyes and nodded. "Okay, Paige."

Sunny caught Paige's eye and beckoned her over. "Okay, what's going on?"

"It's new information about Zac," Paige whispered. "Mary's magic fingers are on a trail. Zac's in trouble Sunny and I'm trying to help him."

Sunny's solemn chocolate eyes softened. "I understand. You do what you do best, Paige. Solve the mystery of what Zac's involved in."

Paige clasped Sunny's tiny hands in hers, "Thanks for your faith in me. Let's hope I don't let you or Zac down."

The rest of Friday was a torment for Paige. She was on edge and twitchy. Whenever she entered Mary's office for updates, her sister waved her away and muttered "Later." It was torture. She so wanted to know what was going on. She was anxious for Zac's safety. Would he contact her again? Where was he hiding? Who was shielding him?

When Violet blew in to the shop at 4.30pm with her usual offering of gossip and half-truths, Paige actually welcomed the distraction.

"Cooeee, Paige. Have you heard?" Violet trumpeted across the shop.

"What?"

A hush fell over the shop as customers tuned in to what Violet was about to say. Violet preened and manoeuvred herself on her short, dumpy legs to a café table with the unbelievable grace of a ballerina . She sat down, unwrapped her thick turquoise shawl and removed her matching toque. "The police are searching for your employee, Zachary. Apparently, he's a murderer," she bellowed, making sure everyone within a five mile radius could hear.

Paige felt her blood boil. She was already on edge after reading Zac's letter and this stupid woman's unsubstantiated claims released all the pent-up anxiety and apprehension she'd been battling to contain since. She exploded.

"Violet Tucker, you should be ashamed of yourself. Spreading lies and gossip about one of Riverside's own," Paige yelled.

Violet's pale jowls wobbled in shock as Paige's body developed a will of its own and careened at speed towards the Riverside President. A diminutive gold and green clothed figure appeared through the red mist that had descended over Paige and barred her way. As the mist cleared Sunny stood there shaking her head.

Paige screeched to a halt, turned on her heels and galloped upstairs to her office, slamming the door behind her. Inside she slid down on to her haunches. How could she have lost control like that? Her thoughts were interrupted by a scratching at the door and a small yap. Rising to her feet on candyfloss legs, she cracked open the door enough to let the little terrier in. Firmly shutting it behind her she gathered Sprite into her arms and hugged her. Gradually the blood pounding through her veins calmed to a gentle pulse.

"Oh Sprite. Why did I let Violet get to me? It's not as if I don't know what she's like. Somehow she presses all the wrong buttons in me. Having been on the receiving end of malicious gossip, it's so hard not to overreact. I suppose I'm going to have to apologise for my behaviour. She's a pain in the butt, an inveterate gossip and busybody but she's also the powerful President of the Riverside Association and River Books can't afford to be blackballed by her." Sprite responded with a gentle lick of Paige's cheek. "Let's get it over and done with." Paige rose to her feet, straightened her spine and took a deep breath before exiting the room.

Peering over the banister, Paige saw that Mary was seated at Violet's table. It was overflowing with cakes and coffee into which Violet was making serious inroads. Paige crept down the stairs and dragged her feet over to stand next to them both. As she opened her mouth, Mary gave an almost imperceptible shake of her head before saying, "Paige, I was just explaining to Violet that you received some bad news today which upset you. I'm sure you'd like to apologise unreservedly to Violet for your uncharacteristic outburst."

Violet placed a chubby hand on her copious bosom and said, "I'm so sorry to hear of the death of your French friend, my dear. Suicide in a young person is so awful. And to think they took their own life because they'd been wrongly accused of a crime. I forgive your earlier rudeness," she said, with a flourish of her right hand as if granting a royal pardon.

"Yes, she was such a good friend to me. I can't believe she's gone." Paige wiped a sleeve over her face. Did the woman not realise that what she was proclaiming about Zac was the same thing? She took a deep breath. "However, I do owe you an apology, Violet. I'm very sorry I reacted like I did."

Humble pie eaten, Paige slunk away mouthing 'thank you' to Mary behind Violet's back. She busied herself rearranging a shelf display. Paige had absolutely no idea what tale Mary had invented to save her from Violet's wrath. She definitely owed her sis big time now.

Violet, having efficiently demolished the bribe of cakes and coffee provided by Mary and Sunny, waltzed out of the shop giving Paige a simpering look of pity as she passed by. "I hope you feel better soon, dear," she said in a loud stage whisper.

Paige gave her a weak smile.

Chapter 10

Friday evening

Paige admitted to herself that she was being a coward using Dom as a shield against what she imagined Alex's reaction to her discovery would be as she sat in Dom's living room awaiting his arrival. Their early warning system, Sprite, jumped up and ran to the door wagging her tail. He'd arrived. Paige went to open the door and let him in. Rafa crashed into the room and gave her a big slobbery kiss as she crouched down to scratch his neck. He accepted the attention and then followed Sprite into the room to where Dom was lounging in his armchair.

"Alejandro, *que tal?*" Paige asked, giving him what she hoped was a winning smile.

"Bien cariño y tú?"

"I'm okay," she replied, leading the way into the room where the two dogs were fighting for Dom's attention. Dom gave both dogs a stroke and then pointed to the blanket. As they reluctantly settled down the professor turned his attention to the Spaniard.

"Alex, wonderful to see you, young man. Take a seat. Can we get you anything to drink?" Dom asked.

"No, thanks." Alex settled himself in the other armchair and stretched out his long legs. His black jeans showed his well-defined muscles. Paige had to tear her eyes away.

"Concentrate," she muttered to herself.

Dom looked at her askance. She nodded.

"Alex, Paige and Mary discovered several things today pertinent to the investigation into Zac's disappearance and the death of the man found at his lodgings. She wanted to let you know what they found out and to ask for your guidance."

Paige silently applauded Dom's strategy of appealing to Alex's ego. It didn't stop the Spaniard's almond eyes flashing with irritation.

"Paige, how many times have you been asked not to interfere with ongoing investigations?" he huffed.

"Alex, it's not my fault. Zac sent me a package."

"Zac sent you something and you didn't contact the police immediately?" he growled through clenched teeth. "You know he's a person of interest in a suspicious death investigation."

Paige turned to Dom. "I told you he'd react like this," she whined.

Dom gave her a stern look. "Carry on with what you need to tell Alex," he said firmly. "And Alex, let her explain before biting the poor girl's head off."

Both looked suitably chastened. Paige regathered herself and stood up. She placed the envelope on the table in front of Alex. "This was posted through one of our customer's door this morning. The customer, Miss Fletcher, called me to come and fetch it. As you can see," she said, pointing to the writing on the envelope, "it's clearly addressed to me. Miss Fletcher thought that it could have been Zac who pushed it through her letterbox, although she wasn't sure." Paige allowed herself this little white lie. The elderly woman had been pretty certain it had been Zac. "I took the envelope back to the shop and Mary and I opened it together. This is what we found." She opened the envelope and tipped the contents onto the table top. "It's a pouch filled with SD cards. I'm assuming they are the ones that were in the fake smoke alarm spy cams. There was also this letter."

Paige waited while Alex read the letter. He lifted his head. A frown knitted his brow. "I understand why you've hesitated to contact the police, Paige. Zac doesn't know who to trust. Do we? What can we do? We need to come up with a plan. Do you know what's on the SD cards?" He slapped his forehead. "Stupid question, of course you do. Your super hacker sister will have been crawling all over these. So what did she find?"

Paige handed Alex a sheet of paper that Mary had prepared for him. It listed the people who were on the SD cards - they were the students living in the digs - and what activities they'd been filmed doing.

"Why has Mary given me a list? It's much easier if I see the images, no?" Alex asked.

"Mary has it all encrypted on her laptop. She didn't want to take the risk of sharing the images. And she wasn't certain that you would want to see them. Both you and my sister have strong ethics about what is right and wrong in an investigation."

Alex gave a curt nod. "We do. But so far this doesn't seem very interesting," he said running his finger down the list.

"That list isn't, but this one is," Paige said, handing him a second sheet. "Mary found images of the handy man, Andrew Hammond, after he'd installed the cards. So he was definitely involved in the spy cam operation. She also found on the card from Zac's room the reason why he discovered that the smoke alarms were fake. He had a small fire in his room. When the smoke alarm didn't activate, you can see him opening it up to see why. Then the footage captures his surprise and anger as he realises what it is. After that there are images of him checking the smoke alarms in the other rooms and removing their cards."

"But no images of what happened to Mr Hammond?"

"No. And nothing to tell us who ransacked Zac's room."

Dom spoke up. "As you can see Alex, this footage doesn't help Zac as far as the handyman's death is concerned. What it does show is that there was a spy cam scam going on. What the police will need to find out is whether Andrew Hammond was acting alone or whether the letting agency is involved."

"I agree. I will accompany Paige to the police station now so that she can hand in the SD cards," Alex said.

"But not the letter, please" Paige pleaded.

"Not the letter," Alex paused and added, "for the moment."

"Thank you." Paige's face lit up with gratitude.

"Dom, can you stay here with the dogs while I run Paige to the station?"

"Of course. If she's with you they may go easier on her," Dom said with a wry smile. "But, Alex, don't mention that Mary copied the cards, will you? There's no need to cause trouble for her."

"Understood. We won't be long. Then we can work on a plan to address the issues in the letter." He stood up and stretched his long legs. Rafa looked at his master expectantly. "*Ahora, no. Quédate aquí.* Stay with Dom and Sprite." The Chocolate Lab settled back down next to Sprite.

"Okay, we'll be back soon Dom." Paige turned to the dogs and said, "Be good for *grandpère*," before following Alex out of the room.

The handover of the SD cards proved to be surprisingly straightforward. The duty sergeant took them from Paige and logged them as evidence in the Andrew Hammond investigation. He told them that he would leave a message for DI Denton, who would probably contact Paige tomorrow. Paige and Alex stepped out of the police station into the cold winter air. Their breath formed white wispy clouds as they walked to the car.

"Well, that was easier than I expected," Paige said.

"Yes, it was. I suspect that when they interview you about how you came to be in possession of the SD cards, it might be less easy," Alex said, shivering as he jumped into the car. "Brr, it's cold tonight."

"This is nothing. I'm going to have to take you to the French Alps and then you'll discover what cold is."

"Can we go in summer?"

"Ha, ha, very funny. No. Have you ever skied?"

"No. Will you teach me?" he asked with a twinkle in his eye.

Paige felt her cheeks flare like beacons as her imagination ran riot about what she'd like to teach him. "Of course," she stuttered.

"What's wrong?" he laughed, his gaze boring into her.

She felt as if he'd peeked into her mind and seen the film running through it. She coughed to cover her embarrassment. "Nothing. It should be fun to teach a sun-loving Spaniard how to glide down a snowy slope in freezing weather. I can picture it now." A grin of pure mischief lit up her face.

Alex's forehead crinkled into a questioning frown. "What? Is it such a strange idea?"

She bit her cheeks to contain her mirth as her imagination took flight again, this time picturing an out of control Alex barrelling into a snow drift. "You'd be a natural, Alex."

He turned on the ignition and pulled out of the car park. Both of them sat quietly with their own thoughts until the car arrived at Dom's house. Alex jumped out and, after reassuring Dom that all had gone smoothly, retrieved Rafa. He bid a quick farewell to Dom and Paige, explaining that he had an early start in the morning and disappeared out into the dark, chilly night.

Dom interrupted Paige's thoughts about where Alex could be going early on a Saturday morning. "So *ma chérie,* what's your next move?"

Paige scrunched her face up. "Not sure. I'm a bit stuck. I'm assuming that once the police view the SD cards they're going to be investigating the letting agency. There's not much point in me covering the same ground. Zac asked me to check on his grandma. She brought him up. There must have been a reason for that. It might help with finding out why Zac's been stealing jewellery. What do you think?"

Dom puffed out his chest. "Well, my dear, if you're looking for a sophisticated, debonair and respectable gentleman to escort you, I'm available. Apparently, I'm a real hit with grandmas."

Paige burst out laughing. "And incredibly modest with it," she said.

"I don't hide my light under a bushel," he replied grinning.

"No, you most certainly don't," she said, her eyes travelling over the lavender shirt, purple paisley cravat and burgundy cardigan. "Okay, I'll take you with me. What about Alex? Do you think he'd want to come?"

"I'm sure he would although he did mention being incredibly busy at work at the moment. You can always ask him though."

"I will. I'll give him a ring and see if he has any free time next week." Paige walked over to Dom and gave him a goodnight kiss. "*Bonne nuit, grandpère, dors bien.* Sleep well."

"*Bonne nuit, ma chérie.*"

Chapter 11

Saturday morning dawned crisp and bright. The walk to work with Sprite along the towpath was a delight as they both crunched through the frosty undergrowth. Of course, they could have kept to the gravel path but it was much more entertaining to hear the frozen grass pop and crackle under their feet.

"It's almost as much fun as swishing through piles of autumn leaves, isn't it?"

Sprite looked at her mistress as if to say, "Who's meant to be the adult here?" Paige laughed and leant down to rub behind her terrier's ears. "Come on, we've got a busy day ahead of us. It's Saturday and it's the holidays. I can't wait to see if our new window display for children encourages them to buy a book or two."

Paige and Sprite arrived in front of the shop door at the same time as Mary. "Hi, Mary. Isn't the frosty landscape beautiful? Just look at the delicate patterns on those leaves," she said, pointing to a small pile of leaves that had been blown into the doorway.

"I suppose so," Mary muttered. "I'm more concerned about how busy we're going to be today and whether I should have persuaded Harriet to come and help to cover Zac's absence."

"We'll cope, sis. I passed on the SD cards to the police last night. I expect that they'll contact me at some point today. Alex came with me and…"

"Did he indeed? How was he?" Mary arched her

eyebrow.

"Fine."

"Fine. Nothing more than fine?"

"No, just fine. Anyway, he left as soon as we returned to Dom's. He had an early start this morning."

"Did he? Where was he going? He can't have lectures. It's Saturday."

"I don't know," Paige muttered before lifting her chin and adding, "and it's none of my business."

Mary gave her little sister a gentle nudge in the ribs. "Ah. But you'd sure like it to be, wouldn't you?"

Paige grunted. "If you've finished winding me up, we need to get going or we'll be late opening up."

"Very subtle change of subject - not. But you're right," Mary said, glancing at her watch, "Time to turn the sign round."

Sunny was run off her feet all morning with orders for hot drinks, warming soups and toasties. Customers coming in from the cold lingered at their tables cradling warm cups in frozen hands. Numerous children were milling around the shop with brown moustaches on their faces, evidence of the popularity of the hot chocolate on the menu. Paige was thrilled that her new window display was working. There were more children in the shop today. Malik, his tall frame resembling a complicated origami sculpture, sat on a small chair reading aloud. Children sprawled on the carpet at his feet listening avidly to *The Gruffalo*. It was a story that still captivated young readers over twenty years after its release. Paige caught Malik's eye and gave him a thumb's up. He gave her a quick nod before focusing on his listeners again.

A group of older girls were huddled round a display of Jacqueline Wilson books while some boys were thumbing through copies of *Horrible Histories*. One boy had a copy of *Rotten Romans* in his hands and was talking to his mate. Paige's thoughts about whether he and his friend realised what a rich Roman history there was in Exeter were jostled out of her mind as the door bell jangled. Paige was surprised to see Professor Watkins. He'd presented the talk on the archaeological dig at the Cathedral Cloister Gardens with Zac. He pulled off his hat, unwound his scarf from around his neck and lifted his head to scan the shop. When his gaze landed on Paige, he made a beeline for her.

"Miss Harper, what a pleasure to see you. Are you well?"

Paige, who had no idea he knew her name, was taken aback by his friendliness. "Yes, thank you. And yourself?"

He gave her a dazzling smile and said, "Yes. Would you join me for a warming drink? It's wonderful to have some bright sunlight, isn't it? But the price we pay is the low temperatures." He rubbed his hands together and walked towards a free table. He gestured to Paige to sit down. "Now what can I get you? My treat."

"Err, thank you. Just a tea, please."

"Any particular type?"

"A cup of strong builder's tea should hit the spot. It's been a busy morning."

The professor took off his overcoat, stuffed his hat and scarf up a sleeve, and hung it over the back of his chair before joining the queue at the counter. Paige's mind went into overdrive. He definitely wanted something from her, but what? She hardly knew the man and he was acting as if they were bosom buddies. Obviously, it had to be something to do with Zac. She felt for her dream catcher. It wasn't there. Biting down the panic brought on by its absence, she forced herself to concentrate on when she'd last felt it around her neck. She remembered having it on last night when she got ready for bed, but not this morning. With any luck it was at home. She closed her eyes to use her photographic memory to locate it.

"Are you okay?"

Paige jolted and opened her eyes. Professor Watkins was standing next to her, concern written over his face. "Sorry, yes. Just taking a breather." She gave him what she hoped was a reassuring smile.

"Of course. I can see how busy it is and with all those children making so much noise, it must be exhausting." He waved his hand in the direction of the children's section.

"Do you have children?" Paige asked.

"No, thank heavens. Never wanted them. Happy to teach adults, if you can call students adults." He twisted his lips in distaste. "I do wonder at times if I'm not teaching kindergarten."

Paige decided to let the subject drop. Willow arrived with their drinks. Paige wrapped her hands round her mug and took a sip.

"So what can I do for you?" she asked.

Professor Watkins picked up his coffee before answering. "Well, as you can imagine, I'm worried sick about Zac's welfare." He dropped his voice and leant in towards Paige. "Have you heard from him?" he asked in a conspiratorial whisper. "I understand you found the body in his room. That must have been such a shock for you."

He reached his hand out. Paige continued to hold her mug in two hands. No way was she letting this man touch her, although... as she didn't have her dream catcher maybe she should let him touch her hand. She might get an intuition. Carefully, she placed her mug on the table and rested her hands on the table. His stubby fingers patted the back of her hand. A flash of heat scorched her flesh where his fingers made contact. Her vision blurred and she saw coins cascading all around him, but, unlike her vision of Zac, he wasn't drowning in them. Dressed like a Roman Emperor, he was standing tall and triumphant as coins ran through his hands. Paige gasped, withdrew her hand and wrapped her arms around herself.

"I'm so sorry. I didn't mean to upset you by mentioning the body," he said, taking in Paige's wretchedness.

Paige realised that he'd put her reaction down to her finding Handy Andy's body. "I'd rather not talk about it. As you can see, it still distresses me."

"Of course. I understand. And you must be worried for Zac," he said, still digging for information.

"I am. I have no idea where he is. It's an awful situation." She pulled out a handkerchief, dipped her head and dabbed at her eyes.

"Are you okay?" he asked, his voice uncertain.

"I will be." Paige lifted her head. "Can I ask you a question?"

"Err, yes. What do you want to know?"

"I heard that a TV crew had been at the Cathedral dig site and that there was a discovery that could change the history of Exeter. Is that true?" She raised her eyebrows questioningly.

The professor blustered, looked angry and a little embarrassed. "Actually, it was a huge misunderstanding. Apparently, local reporters received a call purporting to be from me saying that there had been a newsworthy development at the archaeology site. But I didn't make the call. Then a team member contacted me in a panic and asked me to get to the site immediately as the media were waiting for my announcement. When I arrived I had to explain that the whole thing was a hoax. Someone intended for me to look foolish. Of course, with the dig being in the centre of the city, plenty of people saw the news crew and rumours spread like wildfires."

"I'm so sorry that you had to go through that. You have no idea who would want to do that?"

The professor grimaced and shook his head. "No. A disgruntled colleague? A student? Anyway, I've taken up too much of your time. If you hear from Zac, please give him my regards. I must dash." He rose hurriedly to his feet, grabbed his overcoat off the back of the chair and headed for the exit as if he'd been fired from a rocket launcher.

Mary came over to her table. "What was all that about?"

"That was Professor Watkins, Zac's lecturer. That was one very embarrassed man. Remember Violet arriving the other day to say that something that could change the history of Exeter had been unearthed and that the local news team were at the dig?"

"Of course. She made enough of a song and dance about it."

"It was a hoax. Someone pretending to be Professor Watkins contacted the local media announcing an amazing find at the digs. They set him up to look like a fool."

"Poor man," Mary said. "I wonder who it was."

"He says he has no idea. It could have been a student prank. It wouldn't be the first time to happen in a university city." A brief smile passed across Paige's features as she remembered some of the scrapes of her student days. "But it was cruel. It was intended to humiliate him. Anyway, that wasn't why he came to see me. He wanted to know if I'd heard from Zac."

Mary's features clouded over. "You didn't tell him anything, did you?"

"No. But Mary he touched my hand and I had a vision of him as a Roman Emperor filling his coffers with coins. Something's not right. And it must have something to do with Zac. But what?"

Chapter 12

The first thing Paige did on arriving home was to search for her dream catcher. When she found it under her pillow a weight lifted from her shoulders. She'd be lost without this treasured link to the grandmother she hardly remembered. The clasp had broken. Maybe when she turned in her sleep? She carefully placed the necklace on her bedside table. She'd have to take it in to get it fixed. One of the Cellar retail units on the quay was owned by Gail, a jewellery maker. She'd pop in and see if she could repair it for her. Happy to have found her precious talisman, Paige returned downstairs to cook her meal. Tonight it was a simple dish of pasta with a cheese sauce. She told herself that on Saturdays, when she had no rugby match and had worked a busy day in the shop, she couldn't face complicated recipes. The reality was that she didn't enjoy cooking. For her it was a means to an end - giving fuel to her body. She ate in the kitchen. Feeling comfortably full, Paige sauntered into the living room and snuggled down on the sofa.

She was surprised that Saturday had come and gone with no contact from the police. She'd expected to be given the third degree as to how she came to be in possession of the SD cards. But so far, they'd left her alone. Meanwhile, she needed to fix on a day to go and visit Zac's grandmother. This week her day off was Monday. She knew that Dom was available then. Now she had to find out whether Alex could accompany them.

She picked up her mobile and pressed Alex's number. She was looking forward to chatting to him and finding out about his day. The call went straight to voice mail. Disappointed she sent him a quick WhatsApp message:

Planning to visit Zac's grandmother with Dom on Monday. Do you want to come?

For the next five minutes she stared fixedly at her screen waiting for the ticks to turn from grey to blue to show he'd read her message. She waited in vain. Over the next two hours, in between attempting to relax watching a romcom - who was she kidding? No way could she relax - and regularly checking her screen, she became more frustrated. There was still no sign of her message being read and she began to feel a little miffed. It wasn't as if he always answered immediately but this silence, combined with his mysterious early start this morning, was unusual. Wild thoughts ran through her head.

Maybe he's seeing someone. You haven't exactly given him clear signals, Paige Harper.

Paige gave herself a shake and said to herself, "Stop obsessing over Alejandro's whereabouts."

She needed physical activity to distract her. Getting up from the couch, she called to Sprite, "Come on. Let's go for our evening walk."

The Norfolk Terrier stretched and trotted to the door. Paige pulled on her thick pink jacket, wrapped a warm scarf round her neck and put on her mitts. She opened the door to the crystalline world outside where frost sparkled on the bare tree trunks and glistened on the path in the glow of the streetlights. Breathing in, her nostrils zinged as the fresh air hit them. Feeling revitalised, she strode out on to the pavement.

"How are you doing, little one?" she asked Sprite as the dog scampered alongside her. "Should I get you a doggy coat for this cold weather?"

Sprite glared at her mistress as if the suggestion that a hardy terrier would need a coat was an insult to her breed.

"I'll take that as a no then, shall I?"

Sprite ignored her mistress and continued along the pavement investigating compelling scents. Every so often she paused to leave her mark. Paige slowed her pace to accommodate Sprite's. She raised her eyes to the night sky. Stars shone brightly in the inky blackness. It wasn't often that a British winter sky was so clear. "If only I could see as clearly where my relationship with Alex is going as I can see the stars tonight." A small voice inside her head whispered, "What relationship?"

She turned to Sprite and asked, "What if he's with another woman?" Her dog paused as if to seriously consider the question. "Yes, that's what I'm really worried about. There, I've said it out loud. I'm so confused about what I want, Sprite."

The dog had no answer to give her.

Paige was still restless so she extended their walk into the city to nose around the archaeology dig site. As there was no sign of anyone patrolling the perimeter to disturb her, she peeked over the barriers to see how the work was progressing. The area had been staked out into grids that were each of a similar size. Remains of brick walls emerged at irregular heights from the dug trenches. She could imagine Zac down on his hands and knees gently scraping away at the rich, red Devon soil hoping to uncover some Roman treasure. Sprite growled menacingly. Paige became aware of a figure shrinking back into the shadows and felt a chill crawl down her spine. It could just be someone on their way home from the pub but her antennae told her otherwise. Whoever it was, they were moving stealthily in her direction. It was time to go. She and Sprite set off for home at a brisk jog. All thoughts of Alex had evaporated.

Sunday Paige spent the day with Mary and her family. They went to Exmouth and while the adults wandered along the beach in the bright, crisp winter sunshine, George, Mary's teenage son, ran up and down the sand throwing a ball for Sprite.

"So, are you going to see Zac's grandmother tomorrow?" Mary asked.

"Yes, Dom and I are off to Bideford first thing," Paige replied.

"And Alex?"

Paige shook her head. "Not heard back from him."

"That's unlike him, isn't it?" Mary looked at her sister.

"He can do what he likes," Paige said defiantly, crossing her arms.

Mary reached out and put her arm around Paige's shoulder. "Yes, he can, but normally he would have replied to you. It's alright to be upset, you know."

Paige shivered. "He's obviously so busy having fun with a friend that he hasn't got time for me," she said bitterly.

"Oh, is that the green-eyed monster talking?"

"I have no right to be jealous," Paige said, a grimace of anguish flashing across her features.

Mary gave her a hug. "Feelings aren't ruled by what's right or wrong, Paige."

Paige let herself be comforted by her sister's hug. "When did you get so wise?" she whispered.

Mary joked. "Don't get used to it, okay? You've still got the sibling exclusivity on emotional intelligence. Touchy-feely is *so* not my thing." Mary dropped her arms and continued walking alongside her sister.

After a morning on the beach the group returned to Mary's where the wonderful smell of the dinner she'd left cooking in the oven filled the kitchen. Everyone tucked in to the delicious meal of roast beef, roast potatoes, parsnips, carrots and fluffy Yorkshire puddings. Mary confessed to having bought the Yorkshire puddings ready-made.

"You're forgiven, Mary. Even a domestic goddess can't mix a batter when she's strolling along the sands," Paige said. "This is divine." She lifted her nose and sniffed loudly. "And if I'm not mistaken there's apple crumble for dessert. I think I've died and gone to heaven."

"You could learn to cook like me, you know."

"Maybe. There's not much motivation when there's just me, though."

"If you get together with the handsome, mysterious Spaniard, that should give you the impetus you need."

Paige held up her hand. "No mention of him. I still haven't heard back. Anyway, it could be my cunning plan to find a man who can cook so I don't need to."

"Can Alex?"

"I don't know. It's never come up in conversation."

"Then perhaps it should. If he can cook as well as being drop-dead gorgeous you'd forgive him anything."

"Mary, I'm not that shallow." Paige looked at her sister and winked. "Well, perhaps a little. Of course, if he turned out to be an ace at cake making then that would definitely seal the deal."

Mary laughed. "You and cake."

The rest of the afternoon passed with Paige watching a Six Nations rugby match with her brother-in-law and nephew. The atmosphere got quite tense in the final ten minutes of the game as the England team held on to their slim lead against Scotland. Mary, who was knitting a cable knit woollen jumper, concentrated on her pattern and seemed oblivious to the noise. Perhaps living with two sports crazy males she was used to it.

"Right Mary, I'm off," Paige said standing up and stretching.

Mary put down her needles. "Do you want Peter to drop you home?"

"No, it's fine. I need to walk off that Sunday roast and Sprite will enjoy a new route filled with different smells. It's cold but nothing a seasoned Alpine skier can't cope with. And, it's not raining, which is always a godsend in wet and windy England."

"True. Make the most of the dry evening. And have a safe trip to see Zac's grandmother tomorrow."

"I will along with my debonair bodyguard," Paige said in an amused voice.

"I don't think dear Dom could qualify as a bodyguard."

"He could always strike someone speechless with one of his vicious put-downs - they're legendary at the university." Paige giggled. "No, seriously, he'll be there to charm Mrs Jones. You know he has a way with the more mature woman."

"Well, I hope it goes okay and that you come back with some useful information." Mary opened the front door and waved Paige and Sprite off.

About fifteen minutes into the walk the hairs on the back of Paige's neck tingled. Sprite growled ominously.

"It's okay, girl. I can feel it too. Someone is watching us," she whispered.

Paige bent down as if to tie her shoe lace checking if she could see anyone. Was that a tall, dark shape skulking in that doorway? She couldn't be sure. No time like the present to find out.

"Let's run, Sprite," she shouted loudly. "It'll give us some exercise." They both sprinted along the pavement. Paige heard footsteps scurrying behind her. She didn't stop to look. She hit the turbo button and powered on. Eventually her ears picked up only her trainers hitting the pavement. Panting, she and Sprite turned into their street. Paige risked a glance behind them. If someone had been following them they hadn't managed to keep up. Perhaps she'd imagined it? No. Two nights running was too much of a coincidence. Sprite had sensed something too. Was the person that Zac suspected had been following him now stalking her?

Chapter 13

Monday

The morning started badly when Paige saw that those two little grey ticks on her WhatsApp message to Alex still hadn't turned blue. Why wasn't he answering her? Stifling her disappointment, she prepared for her day out with Dom. Sprite was coming with them. It would take approximately an hour and half to get to Bideford. The town was situated on the River Torridge estuary and in the 16th century had been Britain's third largest port when Sir Walter Raleigh had landed his first shipment of tobacco. Nowadays, the small town on Devon's north coast with a population of just over twenty thousand, was classed as one of the most deprived areas in the region. Paige was checking her phone again when the front doorbell rang. Dom was standing there looking as dapper as per usual. Today's outfit consisted of a green tartan suit, a pale lilac shirt and matching pocket handkerchief. A woollen fawn overcoat completed the ensemble.

"Morning, *ma chérie*. All set for our adventure?" Dom asked, animated.

"I think so," Paige replied.

"That didn't sound very enthusiastic. What's wrong?"

Paige shrugged. "Nothing. I'm all prepared. I rang Mrs Jones earlier just to confirm that she's expecting us.

She sounded quite excited. Apparently, Zac has spoken about us in glowing terms. Let's hope we live up to her expectations."

Dom gave her a shrewd look but didn't probe further. "Great. Let's get this show on the road, as they say in the movies."

His comment was rewarded by an exaggerated eye roll from Paige.

The route to Bideford wound its way through the rural Devon countryside. Sheep grazed the green undulating fields as the occasional cloud scudded across the wintry slate sky. As the car got closer to the coast, stark, leafless trees grew bent over, bowed into submission by the force of the Atlantic gales. On the outskirts of town, Paige gave the satnav her full attention. The housing estate was a warren of rows of drab houses. Following the electronic voice's instructions she eventually pulled up outside an end of terrace house whose paintwork had seen better days. *You have reached your destination* the disembodied voice said. The front door opened and a woman in her mid-sixties beckoned to them. Her face was that of a regular smoker, wrinkled and grey. She led them into a front room, its yellow stained ceiling and overpowering smell of cigarettes confirming Paige's assumption. Mrs Jones invited them to take a seat. Paige and Dom sank into the sofa.

"Now what can I get you? Tea? Coffee?"

Dom gave her a winning smile. "A cup of tea would be wonderful. Thank you, Mrs Jones."

Zac's grandmother blushed and patted her pewter coloured permed hair self-consciously. "Oh please Professor, call me Sheila." She then turned to Paige. "And for you, Miss Harper?"

"A tea would be great. And please, call me Paige. Do you need any help?"

"No, you sit tight and I'll be back in a jiffy."

When she'd left the room, Dom said to Paige, "I've sunk so low in this sofa that sitting tight is not a problem. I'm not sure I'm going to be able to extract myself from its marshmallow jaws."

Paige grinned. "Don't worry, old man, we'll help you, won't we Sprite?"

The terrier, who was on her best behaviour sitting next to her mistress, nodded. Paige slipped her a doggy treat.

Mrs Jones returned with a tray laden with a teapot, milk jug, sugar bowl, cups and saucers. A plate of digestive biscuits took centre stage. She served them their drinks.

"I'm so thankful that you contacted me. I wanted to tell you what a good boy Zac is. The police have got it wrong. He wouldn't hurt anyone." She wrung her hands. "You've got to help him." Her eyes pleaded with them.

"Sheila, perhaps you could start by telling us a little about Zac's background, if you feel comfortable sharing with us," Dom said.

"I cleared it with Zac. He said you can be trusted."

Paige's jaw dropped. "You've spoken to him?"

"Yes. He's in a safe place. He's very scared. I had that Professor Watkins sniffing round here. I didn't tell him nothing. Zac don't trust him."

Dom and Paige exchanged a look. The professor had been busy!

"What can you tell us about, Zac? I hate to bring this up but you do know that he stole some jewellery from one of our employees?" Paige said.

Mrs Jones took a sip of her tea then carefully placed her cup on the side table before saying, "Zac's mum used to give him coins when he was little. She worked at the caravan park and, when she got a tip, she'd give him a few 10 pence pieces or a fifty pence piece. She always gave him 'shiny' coins, never coppers or pounds."

"If I'm not being indiscreet, Mrs Jones, why did you bring up your grandson?" Dom asked gently.

"My daughter was killed in a hit and run on her way home from work. She was walking along an unlit lane. Police never solved it. Said it was one of those things. Country lane, no clues, no witnesses. Zac was eight at the time. He took it hard."

"Oh, I'm so sorry. It must have been a difficult time for him and for you," Paige said.

"Well, you just get on with it, don't you? Thing is," she paused, "when Zac gets stressed he takes shiny objects. At school he saw a child psychologist, like. The man said it was because they reminded Zac of his mum. He ain't done it for ages. When he was a lad his uncle bought him one of those metal detecting machines. That helped. He'd search for treasure on beaches and in fields. That's how he got into archaeology. He found a few old things and got interested in their history, like. And, he's a clever lad." She beamed with pride. "Me, I ain't got much schooling - stock shelves at the local Co-op - but Zac's clever. Must have got that from his dad."

"Where is his father?" Paige asked.

"Don't know. Never did. My daughter had holiday romances at the caravan site. Ended up pregnant with no idea who the father was." She wrung her hands. "We coped though. Then poor Charlene died. No, he's not had an easy life, our Zac. And now this." She fought to keep her voice steady.

Sprite moved next to Mrs Jones and gently put a paw on her knee. The woman stroked her. "Aren't you a beauty, little one? Zac always wanted a dog but there's no way I could cope with a dog as well. He's always talking about how lovely Sprite is."

Dom spoke quietly. "Mrs Jones, what has Zac told you about his problems?"

"He hasn't. He said it was better if I didn't know then I wouldn't have to lie to the police."

"That shows how much he cares for you. However, the longer he stays in hiding, the more the police are going to suspect him." Dom's brown eyes held Zac's grandmother's gaze.

"I know. But," she stopped and stared at Paige with eyes brimming with tears, "he said you'd solve the murder. When you've done that, he'll come out of hiding."

With a hollow feeling in the pit of her stomach, Paige said, "That's a lot of responsibility."

"He said you'd do it, Miss Harper. I'm begging you. Find out who the killer is and who's after my Zac. I can't lose another child." Tears ran down her wrinkled face.

"I'll do my best. I don't suppose Zac gave you anything for me?"

The woman shook her head. "No, he said he'd already gived yer something."

"Okay. If he does contact you again, please urge him to give himself up. In the meantime, I'll do what I can." Paige stood up and hauled Dom out of the sofa.

An upright Dom patted Sheila's hand. "Now dear lady, we will do our utmost to help Zachary. If he calls you do pass on our message, won't you."

"Of course Professor," she sniffed balling a tissue in her fist.

Once in the car, Paige said, "I need some fresh air. Let's park by the quay and take a walk. I'm feeling quite overwhelmed."

"That's a heavy weight she placed on your shoulders. I'm here for you, *ma chérie*. Let's get going. After our walk we can have a delicious pub lunch before we head back."

"Sounds like a plan, *grandpère*."

After a pub lunch and a bracing walk along the quay, Paige, who'd been mulling over what Zac's grandmother had said, turned to Dom. "Okay if we take a short detour before heading back?"

"Where?"

"I've been thinking about Zac's background and what Sheila said about his mum. What if he's hiding out at the caravan park where she used to work?" Paige looked directly at Dom.

"I admit it is a possibility. However, we don't know where this site is do we?"

"Actually, when we were at Sheila's there was a photo of a young woman who I'm assuming was her daughter, Charlene standing in front of a sign that said *Welcome to North Shore*."

"How will we find it?" Dom asked before slapping his forehead. "Of course, just Google it."

"Indeed, *cher professeur*. Not just a pretty face I see," Paige said, pulling out her phone and typing the name into the search engine.

Dom raised his walking stick at her. "Less of your cheek young madam. Now have you found it?"

"Sure. It's twenty minutes from here by car. Come on. Let's go."

The three of them piled into the Mini and Paige set the satnav for their new destination. Less than half an hour later they pulled up outside *North Shore*. It was a sorry sight to see. The caravans behind the high chain fences were covered in green moss and streaked with dirt.

"If Zac's in here, he's certainly not living the high life," Dom noted.

"I'm going to see if there's a way in. I won't be long. You take Sprite and walk the perimeter. If you see anything give me a ring."

Dom gave her a stern look. "No heroics, understood?"

"Of course," Paige said with her fingers crossed behind her back.

A wry smile quirked Dom's mouth. "And you can uncross your fingers now."

Paige grinned and brought her hands out from behind her back. "Busted."

Despite Paige's best efforts she didn't manage to find a way onto the site. For what looked like an abandoned ramshackle caravan park, it certainly was well protected. She'd called out to Zac. Nothing. Either he wasn't there or he didn't want to show himself.

"Oh well, it was worth a punt," Paige said as they got back into the car.

As Paige relaxed behind the wheel enjoying the tranquil drive through the north Devon countryside, Dom spoke up.

"Okay. I've been extremely patient, which you know is not one of the attributes that immediately comes to mind when people think of me, so come on, spit it out."

"There's nothing to spill," Paige said squinting at the road as if it needed all her attention.

"You seem to be forgetting who you're talking to. I know that something's not right. You've been quiet for most of the day and," he winked at her, "we both know that's not one of your natural qualities."

Paige screwed up her face. "Not very flattering, *cher grandpère*. What do you think about what Mrs Jones said?"

"Oh no you don't. I'm not being distracted. What is wrong?" He gently touched her cheek where a single tear rolled down her face.

"Mrs Jones has put a lot of pressure on me," Paige began only to be interrupted by Dom.

"Ah, ah. No you don't. This has nothing to do with Zac's grandmother. You were out of sorts before we even left Exeter this morning. Is it the fact that Alex was too busy to come with us today?"

"I wouldn't know if he's too busy. I haven't heard from Alejandro," she said looking dejected.

"Now we're getting to the nub of the matter. And your vivid imagination is creating catastrophic scenarios as to why."

"He hasn't even read my text," Paige whined.

"Oh please. You know there could be a million completely plausible reasons why he hasn't returned your call." Dom gave her a stern look. "He could simply have lost or mislaid his phone. He could be on a secret mission for our illustrious DI Denton."

A shadow of smile reached Paige's lips. "Now, you're just being silly."

"Is my suggestion any sillier than what you've been telling yourself?"

"Well, we both know that DI Denton couldn't organise a piss up in a brewery."

Dom gasped and dramatically laid his hand on his thin chest. "Paige Harper. Watch your language! Wash your mouth out with soap immediately child."

Paige giggled. "No soap on hand at the moment, *grandpère*. Okay, maybe I've been letting my imagination run away with me. As you say there are numerous reasons that could explain why he hasn't replied. Have you heard from him?"

"No. I've had no reason to."

She briefly turned her eyes from road and gave Dom a winning smile. "Could you send him a message?"

Dom arched a steel grey eyebrow. "No," he said firmly. "When we get back to Exeter you can sort this out. I'm not getting involved, *ma chérie*. It's between you and Alex." Paige puffed out her cheeks and pouted. "And," Dom added, "doing your best impression of a stroppy teenager, is extremely unbecoming of you."

Paige dropped Dom home before setting out for a walk with Sprite. Wrapped up warm in her fuchsia pink anorak with her matching bobble hat pulled down low over her brow, Paige was protected from the cold evening air. The night was drawing in and purple bruised clouds gathered on the horizon as the pair reached the park entrance. Slipping off Sprite's lead to let the terrier stretch her legs, Paige wandered along the path lost in thought. As she reviewed what Mrs Jones had said about Zac she felt a pinch of guilt. She hadn't really taken to the boy, having been put off by his falseness. However, now that she understood his background, his neediness made sense. Zac was a lad who'd been dealt a difficult hand in life. Being on the archaeology degree at the University of Exeter must have seemed like a dream come true. The fact that now that dream had turned into a nightmare was so unfair. He must feel that the odds were stacked against him. She had to help him. How? She wasn't sure. There were two trails to follow. The archaeology one. Professor Watkins' keen interest in wanting to know Zac's whereabouts was strange, but was it sinister? Paige felt an icicle run down her spine as she remembered her vision of the professor as a Roman Emperor. And she couldn't ignore the frequent visions of Zac drowning in coins.

Investigating the hidden spy cameras was the other route. Somewhere in the murky ether of the worldwide web were recordings from Zac's digs that might shed light on what he was so afraid of. Or so keen to keep hidden?

Paige and Sprite left the park. They'd almost reached home when all the nerves in Paige's body tingled on high alert. What was it? Hyper-sensitivity or something more sinister? The answer came swiftly. A dark saloon car that had been parked a hundred yards down the road turned on its full beam, revved its engine and accelerated towards her. Blinded by the headlights coming straight for her, Paige's instincts took over. She dived over the low garden wall to her right as the car swerved onto the pavement where she'd been standing.

Fear gripped her heart. "Sprite!" she screamed as she lay winded on the grass. A wet nose nuzzled her face. Paige trembled with relief. Her dog was alive. Gingerly Paige sat up. A quick scan of her limbs revealed nothing seemed broken. She gathered her terrier in her arms. Both of them were shaking. Out of the corner of her eye, Paige saw the house's front window curtains twitch. Seconds later the front door flew open.

"Oi! What the hell are you doing in my garden?" a deep voice bellowed. A large brawny man strode towards her.

She rose unsteadily to her feet. "I'm so sorry. A car tried to run me down. I dived out of the way." Her voice wobbled.

"A car?" His tone became less aggressive.

She nodded. "It was waiting for me. Had to be."

"I'll call the police."

"No. I didn't see what type of car it was - just a

dark saloon. The headlights blinded me. I'll call my friend to come and accompany me home."

"Come in and sit down. You've had a shock." He motioned for Paige to sit in the hallway. "I'm going to look at the pavement. See if they've left any evidence."

"Thank you." Paige collapsed on the bottom of the stairs and pulled out her mobile. *"Dom, it's me. Can you come and meet me? I'll explain later. I'm at,"* she paused and checked the house number, *"244, Topsham Road."*

"J'arrive."

The man returned from his inspection. "There are skid marks on the pavement and it looks like they might have scraped the side of their car on the wall. I'm calling the police."

Paige slumped. The last thing she felt like was getting the police involved.

Chapter 14

Tuesday morning dawned wet and overcast. The change in the weather was in keeping with Paige's mood. Not surprisingly, she hadn't slept well. She was tired and bruised from her impromptu dive over the garden wall. Fed up summed up her mood. Still no word from Alex. Someone had tried to run her over. Last night the police had interviewed her and taken her statement at the house whose garden she'd landed in. She'd reiterated that she hadn't seen anything. They took some scrapings from the owner's front wall and said that they would be looking at traffic cameras that might have filmed the car further down the road. Dom had fussed over her like a mother hen. He'd insisted on walking her to her door and checking the property before leaving her for the night. It was kind of sweet that a sexagenarian, who weighed little more than a narrow tail feather, imagined that he'd be a worthy opponent to someone intent on harming her. It made her feel warm and fuzzy.

In the kitchen, she let a reluctant Sprite out into the rain-soaked garden and prepared their breakfasts. A few minutes later a very soggy dog was back inside being rubbed down with a towel. Both girls then set about the serious business of eating. Paige couldn't function without her cereals and cup of tea. Feeling slightly more human after her stomach was full she got ready for work. With her dream catcher stowed safely in her handbag to give to Gail to repair, Paige picked up her car keys. Today was not a day to walk to work. There was no way she wanted to arrive like the proverbial drowned rat. That most certainly wouldn't improve her mood.

At River Books, Mary greeted her sister with a smile. "Hi little sis, how did your mission with Professor G go?"

"We found out that Zac has had a difficult life. And that he's so scared by what's going on he's refused to tell his grandma anything about it or where he's hiding."

"So he's been in contact with her?"

"Apparently. He rang her. Told her to trust me to solve the crime and no one else!" Paige ran a finger across the bridge of her nose.

Mary couldn't help but give a gape of astonishment at her sister's words. "What?"

"I know. Nuts, isn't it? And Professor Watkins had been to see Zac's grandmother."

"That's odd. Surely, that goes above and beyond a tutor's pastoral care role?"

"Hmm. There's something about him that doesn't sit right."

The shop door bell jangled.

"Talking about professors," she said, nodding towards the shop entrance. "Here's two for you."

Paige turned around. Dom, or Professor Emeritus Giraud to give him his full title, was accompanied by a round blubber ball of a man dressed in black.

"Well I never," Paige said, walking over to greet Dom and his companion. "*Grandpère,*" she said, kissing both his cheeks in the French style. "And, Bill, good to see you." She stretched out her hand and shook his clammy pudgy paw. "Or should I say Professor Williams?" The man preened. "Congratulations on your promotion."

"Thank you, Paige," he said with his Welsh accent.

There was no love lost between the pair. Bill, also known as Mr Blobby by his students, had wanted Dom to sell River Books to his wife, Penelope, and was full of resentment towards Paige who, in his eyes, had taken advantage of Dom's affection for her. It never occurred to Bill that he too had wanted to profit from Dom, his long-standing 'frenemy'. He also didn't like the fact that Paige had helped solve a murder for which he'd been a prime suspect. The tension between the two was palpable.

Sunny wafted over in a jingle of bangles. "Professors," she said, giving both of them a warm smile. "Are you here for coffee and cake?"

"Sunita, my dear. Yes, we will partake of your wonderful pastries. What do you have to tempt us today?" Dom asked.

Sunny's amber cheeks blushed pink. "You're such a charmer, Professor. We have your favourite lemon drizzle cake or if you are feeling a little more adventurous I've created an orange and raspberry sponge. Then there are the usual choices: rocky road bars, toasted teacakes, cupcakes…"

Bill licked his thick lips and said, "I'll certainly be adventurous and try the orange and raspberry sponge. And I'll have an americano, please."

"Make that two slices of the sponge cake and I'll have a cappuccino, please." Dom paused and turned to Paige. "You're joining us. What would you like?"

Paige tilted her head and met his eyes. "Surely, you and Bill don't want me to gatecrash your gossip session."

"Actually, it's you we came to see. Bill has information that might help us." Dom tapped the side of his nose conspiratorially. Bill's black currant eyes fixed on Paige as he nodded enthusiastically. His double chin bounced up and down long after he'd stopped moving his head.

Paige raised her eyes to heaven. "Okay, Tweedledum and Tweedledee. I'm intrigued." She grinned as Bill spluttered his annoyance at her use of Tweedledum, who was a fat, little man from Lewis Carroll's *Through the Looking-Glass*. One day she'd stop provoking him, but not today! "Sunny, I'll also try your new cake and have a cup of Assam, please."

The unlikely trio took their seats at the café table near the back. They waited until they'd been served their cakes and drinks by Willow, the regular waitress, before Dom began to speak. "Bill, as you know, is on numerous committees at the university." Paige dipped her head in agreement. Professor Williams was notorious for his penchant for committees, especially ones where he was the chair. "Well, he has been approached by student reps who are worried about the spy cameras that were found in Zac's student house. In particular, they are worried the police aren't taking their concerns seriously. The police have informed a female student, who lives in the same digs as Zac, that their priority is solving Andrew Hammond's murder."

Bill took over. "Paige, the university is a great institution but it moves at the rate of an elderly aunt on a zimmer frame. We will look into the student's concerns and make official representation to the police…" he trailed off.

"I sense a 'but' coming," Paige said and took a sip of her tea. The warmth travelled through her.

Bill fiddled with his coffee mug. "I was wondering if you could help," he said in a strangled voice.

Paige choked on her mouthful of tea. Bill Williams asking for her help. "Wow," she spluttered.

Dom laid a hand on hers. His eyes flashed a warning. "Paige, this isn't easy for Bill."

"I understand." She bit the insides of her cheeks to stop the laughter that threatened to bubble out of her mouth at the weirdness of the situation. "Bill, of course, I'll help. I'll need to meet with the student. Can you arrange that?"

Bill let out a sigh of relief. It was like watching a black air-filled balloon deflate. He pushed his shoulders back. The chair creaked ominously. "I appreciate it," he said as his hand reached into his inside pocket to extract a small notebook. Laying it on the table, he opened it and tore out a sheet. "This is the name of the girl and her details. I have her authorisation for you to contact her direct," he said, placing the torn page in front of Paige.

"Thank you. I'll see what I can do."

After they'd finished their refreshments Bill and Dom left the shop, bickering as per usual. It wasn't for nothing that Paige called them 'frenemies'.

Mary beckoned her sister over. "What was all that about? Did I hear right? The mighty Professor Bill Williams asking lowly Paige Harper for help?"

A victorious smirk lit up Paige's face. "Yep. That's a turn up for the books, isn't it?"

"Suspicious, if you ask me. So what are you going to do?"

"First, I'm going to ring," she paused and glanced down at the torn page in her hand, "Mica Murrel. We'll set up a meeting to find out how we can help her."

Paige went up to her office and rang the number Bill had given her. The girl picked up immediately.

Hello.

Mica, hi, it's Paige Harper. Professor Williams gave me your number.

Oh, thank you for ringing me. When can we

meet?

I'm in my shop, River Books, down on the quay most days. When would suit you?

I haven't any lectures this morning. I'll be there in an hour.

Great. See you then.

Paige hung up and skipped down the creaky stairs to the ground floor.

"Mary, she's coming in an hour," she called over to her sister.

"That's keen. I was going to say that I'll get the SD cards information ready to show her, but that's stupid. We're not meant to have them."

"No, we're not. Nevertheless, we should be able to find out who lives in which room. I know you already have a list of the tenants. That'll move our investigation along."

Mary pushed her glasses up her nose. "Strictly speaking we do not know who the tenants are and do not have an investigation."

"Semantics," Paige said waving her hands around.

"Says the woman who earns part of her livelihood finding the right words," Mary countered, nudging Paige in the ribs.

"Exactly. An expert manipulator of words in several languages," said Paige, who'd worked as a freelance translator in the past and who still did on occasions. The extra work helped bolster her finances.

The shop door swung open and Alex strode in with Rafa in tow. His gold-flecked eyes homed in on Paige and he rushed across to her.

"Time to use one of your languages, little sis," whispered Mary as she made herself scarce.

"*Cariño. Lo siento*," he said as he leant forward and kissed her cheek.

At his touch Paige felt herself light up inside like a bonfire. "*Por qué?* What are you sorry for, Alex?" she asked coldly, tamping down the flames inside. She wanted him to know she wasn't happy at being ignored.

He held up a mangled phone. "This."

At the sight of the chewed remains of Alex's mobile, Paige's voice softened, "What happened?"

Alex fixed his laser beam stare on Rafa.

"No, don't tell me Rafa ate your phone?" she laughed. "Alex, that's like telling the teacher your dog ate your homework!"

The look of incomprehension on the Spaniard's face made her realise that he didn't understand the connotation.

"*Es verdad.*" His eyes begged her to believe it was true. "Rafa chewed my phone. I've just got a replacement phone and sim card. Then I saw your message from Saturday and your missed calls."

"So where have you been since Saturday?" Paige demanded. She wasn't going to forgive him too easily.

His shoulders sagged. "The department organised a team building exercise. Paige, it was horrible." He looked at her with sad puppy eyes. "We had to hike on Dartmoor and sleep in youth hostels," he spoke the words in a low, pained voice.

Paige put her hand over her mouth in an attempt to smother the howl of laughter fighting to burst out. It didn't work. She convulsed into a fit of giggles. Alex gave her a hurt look. She gasped trying to control herself. "I'm sorry, Alex. I understand that for a Spaniard having to hike across Dartmoor in the middle of winter must be akin to a non-Catholic facing the Spanish Inquisition. Really scary." She cracked up again, dissolving into a heap.

Mary, who had been watching this exchange with a wry smile on her face, stepped in. "Alex, why don't you come and sit down over here while my sister tries to behave like an adult - which will be a challenge in itself!"

Alex allowed himself to be led to a café table. Sunny walked with her natural grace over to him and said, "Alex, what can I get you?"

"An espresso, please Sunny."

Sprite had magically appeared to say hi to Rafa. After an enthusiastic greeting both dogs sat on their haunches watching the young Nepalese woman's movements. Sprite raised a paw to Sunny. "And two doggy treats, is it?" Sunny asked. Sprite barked her agreement.

Paige came and sat with Mary and Alex, swiping a cuff across her face to dry the tears of laughter. "I'm not sure that Rafa merits a treat," she said. Sprite glared at her. Paige held up her hands in surrender. "Fine. Your boyfriend's forgiven."

The coffees, tea and doggy treats delivered, Paige filled Alex in on her visit to Zac's grandmother the previous day. Alex was particularly interested in the details about the boy stealing shiny objects when stressed.

"That's unusual behaviour. Fascinating. So you have no idea where he is?" Alex asked.

"No. I'm working on several avenues. I'll let you know if I find anything." Seeing the Spaniard's face scrunch up into a frown, no doubt about to launch into a lecture about not investigating on her own, Paige opted for diversionary tactics. "Actually, Alex, one of the girls from Zac's digs is coming in to speak with us. Her name's Mica Murrel. I don't know whether you want to meet her. She may agree to have you in our meeting," Paige said.

"How did she get in contact?" he asked.

"Would you believe it that it was Bill Williams?

Apparently, she approached him pushing for the university to ask the police to focus on the SD cards. Bill explained to her that university protocols and procedures take a long time. He offered me as an alternative."

"He must have been desperate," Mary muttered, which earned her a light punch on the arm from Paige.

"You know, you're probably right," Paige admitted. "He doesn't hand over power easily - and especially not to me! I wonder what it is about this girl that made him so keen to dump her on me?"

Chapter 15

The shop door swung open. A girl, who looked like a clone of the Jamaican model Grace Jones, whooshed in. She was tall, angular, ebony-skinned and strikingly beautiful.

"I think we're about to find out why Bill palmed her off on you," Mary said.

Paige stood up and went to meet the girl. "Mica?"

"Yes, hi. You must be Paige," the girl said, her voice deep and husky.

"Yes, that's me." Paige made the introductions, "This is Mary, my sister and shop manager and this is Dr Alejandro Ramos, a friend."

Mica stepped forward and smiled at Alex. His eyes didn't leave her face. It was as if he was mesmerised by her. Paige felt her hackles rise. She stepped between Mica and Alex to break the spell. Did she really want Alex in close proximity to this beguiling creature?

Mary cleared her throat. "Shall we go to my office? Mica, if you'd like to follow me," she said leading the way.

"Of course," Mica said, dragging her gaze away from the handsome Spaniard.

"I'll be with you in a minute," Paige said to Mary. Once they were out of earshot, she grabbed Alex's arm. "Do you think it's a good idea for you to join us? She's seems a little smitten. It might distract her from giving us her full attention."

Alex's face lit up with a grin of pure male satisfaction. "Ah, *cariño, estás celosa, verdad?*"

Paige glared at him. "Oh grow up, Alex. I'm not jealous!" she hissed before turning swiftly on her heels and stomping towards the office. "Come on, Mary's waiting for us." Behind her she heard a little laugh escape him.

Mary's room was small. She sat behind her desk and the three others sat in a semi-circle facing her. To spite Alex, Paige placed herself between him and Mica.

Mary began, "Mica, thank you for coming in. If you could tell us what we can do for you? All we know from Professor Williams is that you're concerned that the police aren't doing enough to find out who placed the spy cameras in your lodgings."

"Yes, I asked Professor Williams to put pressure on the police to move their investigation forward but, unsurprisingly," her lips twisted with scorn, "he quoted a litany of reasons why it would be difficult for the university to get involved. Owl is in my French class and I remembered her talking about how you'd solved murders. When *Monsieur Patapouf* answered in the negative..."

Paige interrupted, "Sorry, Mica, you said 'Owl'?"

"Yeah, Olivia. We all call her Owl." She waved her hand dismissively.

Paige bristled. "Okay. So you asked Professor Williams to contact me?"

"Yeah. Well, sort of. I asked for your phone number but he got on his high horse about data protection and said he would 'facilitate a meeting.'" She held up her fingers to draw imaginary inverted commas around the last three words.

"That sounds like Bill," Mary said. "Now that we've got that cleared up, what are you hoping we can achieve that the police can't?"

Mica placed a folder on the desk and opened it up. "These are photos of each one of us that is renting a room in the house. I've labelled the photos with their names, email addresses, phone numbers and which room is theirs. They've all agreed that you can contact them for any information that will help with your investigation. We're all worried sick. Worried that the killer will return. Worried about Zac, although he's a bit of a loser," she said scornfully. "I know he wouldn't have the balls to kill someone. I'm certain he didn't kill that creep Handy Andy. The police are on that trail. The thing is," she dropped her voice and gave Alex a conspiratorial smile, "there are things on those recordings that some of us would rather not have floating out there on the web for all to see. You're a man of the world, I'm sure you understand, don't you?"

Alex blinked his almond gold-flecked eyes as if blinded by the force of her gaze. He raked his fingers through his chocolate curls. Paige cursed the man. Didn't he realise how unbelievably attractive he looked when he did that? Mica was practically drooling.

Mary stepped in. "Mica, you do understand that what was on those SD cards has probably already been distributed on the web, probably to a site with paying punters?"

"Yes."

"And that the current recordings are most probably not the only ones in existence?" Mary added.

"Yes, I understand that." The young woman screwed her face up into an angry scowl.

Paige spoke up. "Mica, you called Handy Andy a creep. Does that mean that you had dealings with him?"

"He came to the house pretty frequently to deal with the small problems that rental properties inevitably have. I spoke to him a couple of times. Each time it felt like he was undressing me with his eyes. Of course, now I realise that if he'd seen what was on the recordings he knew what I look like naked." Her eyes flashed with anger.

"I'm sorry for that, Mica. It's an awful invasion of your privacy. A betrayal. Mary and I will get to work and see what we can find out," Paige said. "I don't suppose any of you have heard from Zac, have you?"

"No, sorry." Mica reached into her pocket and pulled out a handful of notes. "Here, we can't afford to pay you much. We had a whip round."

Paige shook her head. "No, keep the money. You're students, for goodness sake."

"But," Mica said.

"No buts. All we ask is that you cooperate. And understand that I may have to ask embarrassing questions to which I'd like truthful answers."

The young girl nodded. "Understood. Thank you so much. I'll report back to the others and let them know that you're going to help us."

Alex rose to his feet. "Let me show you the way out, Mica," he said, glancing at Paige.

Paige shot him such a fiery look he should have burst into flames. He didn't. His faithful dog seemed equally entranced as he followed docilely in their wake. Paige ground her teeth. "Even Rafa isn't immune to her charms," she said to Sprite. The terrier flicked her head and sashayed away as if to say 'I don't care'.

Once Mica had left Mary turned to Paige, "So now we know who the ebony model is Mica. I recognised her from the SD cards."

"Me too. At least, with Mica involved we have permission to question all the tenants."

No sooner had Alex and Mica left than Violet

bowled into the shop. Powering across the ground floor, she came to a halt in front of Paige. Today Riverside's President, dressed in a taupe fake fur coat and matching toque, resembled a tubby koala. Paige had read that koalas may look nice and cuddly but that they had very sharp claws.

"Paige, my dear. Who was that young African beauty being so friendly with Señor Ramos?" Violet's little currant eyes scanned the bookshop owner's face to see whether her question had hit home.

Paige swallowed, cursing the telltale blooms of colour she could feel spreading over her cheeks. Yep, koalas are definitely vicious. "Oh, that was a friend of Professor Williams," Paige said sweetly. Her whole being screamed to lash out at the interfering witch.

"Really? Bill?" Violet narrowed her eyes. "A friend?"

"Hmm."

"So why was she cosying up to Alex?"

Good grief, the woman was persistent. "Maybe she's got personal space issues?"

A mocking smile played on Violet's scarlet-painted lips. She reached out a chubby hand and patted Paige on the arm. "Very droll. Of course, I'm sure there's a perfectly valid reason why they were so engrossed in each other." Content that she'd won the skirmish, Violet waddled over to the café and plonked herself down at a table.

Paige was in a sulk. She'd let herself be played by Violet. She was worried about Mica's designs on Alex. Mary had been right to be suspicious of Bill. Paige really didn't get a good vibe off that girl. Thinking of vibes, her fingers instinctively reached for her throat. She had a good excuse to get away from Violet, who continued to give her pitying looks over the rim of her coffee cup.

"Mary?" Paige called.

"Yes?" Mary said poking her head above the counter under which she'd been searching for a new till roll. "What do you want?"

"Okay, if I just pop out to pick up my dream catcher? I took it into Gail to be repaired."

"Sure, it's quiet. I can cope."

Paige hurried upstairs and fetched her coat. Sprite roused herself from her basket on seeing the signs of an outing. "Come on, girl. Let's get some fresh air."

Together the two of them walked briskly along the quay. The rain had stopped but grey clouds hung heavy in the leaden sky. Inside Gail's workshop the acrid smell of hot burning metal reached Paige's nostrils.

"Gail. Hi."

A large, middle-aged woman in a floral smock was sitting at a workbench. She glanced up from the delicate piece of jewellery she was soldering. "Give me two minutes, Paige. This bit's tricky."

"Sure. No problem." Paige wandered along the shelves admiring the delicate silver pieces on display. "You're so gifted. These dream catcher earrings are absolutely fabulous," she said picking up a pair and holding them up against her ear in front of the mirror.

Gail put down her soldering iron and heaved herself up. "They'd go well with your necklace, wouldn't they?"

"You know what, I'll take them. I love the tiny turquoise beads you've threaded into the weave."

"Great. I'll wrap those for you. Your necklace is ready."

"Thanks Gail. You're a star. How much do I owe you?"

"That'll be £35 altogether." She motioned to the card reader. Paige swiped her card. Gail handed her the receipt and said, "Paige, I saw Alex earlier with a very striking woman."

"Not you too, Gail. Violet's already been winding me up about Alex."

Gail gave Paige the stink eye. "I was going to say," her voice curt, "if your fragile ego can handle it, that I know the girl."

Paige flinched. She'd forgotten just how abrasive Gail could be. "Sorry, Gail. I'm all ears."

"That girl, Mica, is trouble. I've done some custom metalwork for her."

"Custom metalwork?"

"Handcuffs, collars. Look, I wouldn't normally share information about my clients, but then she should pay me what she owes me."

"Hang on, Gail. Are you saying she works as a dominatrix?" Paige asked, her eyes as wide as saucers.

"I just know what I made for her - cuffs, keys, collars, leashes, masks - you can reach your own conclusions."

"Well, I never. This puts a very different spin on things. Must rush. Thanks Gail. Really appreciate it." Paige sped out of the shop towards River Books.

Chapter 16

Back at the shop, Paige related what Gail had told her. Mary's expression darkened and then brightened. "This should make her far easier to track on the web. There are lots of things about Mica that don't add up though."

Paige nodded. "I know. Why, if she's working this sideline business, would Mica want to get the university involved in the search for the SD cards? Surely, she'd hope to keep her extra activities secret from them? Why approach Professor Williams? The way she spoke about him, it was obvious she doesn't respect him, so why go to him? To get our contact details? But she's already admitted that she knows Olivia and could have got her to put us in contact. And why get us involved? What is she hoping we'll uncover? I don't like it, Mary."

"Me neither. Maybe she is genuinely afraid that the SD cards and the killer are linked. Let me set my magic fingers to work and see what I turn up." She gave her little sister an absent look as she disappeared into her office. Her mind was already on the challenge awaiting her.

Paige spent the rest of the day manning the till and the ground floor. Unfortunately, the shop was quiet and gave her far too much time to ruminate on what her sexy Spaniard could be doing. She tried busying herself with arranging and rearranging the shelves to distract herself from thoughts that were running wild like a bush fire. When five o'clock arrived and Paige closed up for the day, Mary was still closeted away in her office. Paige poked her head round the door. "Don't stay too late or Peter will be sending out a search party."

Mary lifted her head as if she were resurfacing from a deep dive and coming up for air. "I've texted him and told him to get takeaway for him and the kids. I think I'm on to something." Paige opened her mouth to ask "What?" Mary ignored the question and waved her hand towards the door. "Now, off you go. See you tomorrow." She turned her head back to her screen. Paige was forgotten.

On her way to the car, Paige called Dom and invited herself over to his house for later that evening. They agreed she'd organise an Indian takeaway. At six thirty Paige and Sprite set out from their Lodge House to Dom's imposing mansion. The rain had started again and they sprinted along the gravel drive. Sprite stopped for a quick squat before catching her mistress up as they bundled through the back door.

"Hello. We're here," Paige shouted as she shook off her raincoat. She grabbed the roll of kitchen towels and pulled off a few sheets to wipe down Sprite's soggy fur.

Dom strolled into the kitchen and Sprite wriggled out of Paige's grasp to greet her friend. Dom bent down and rubbed behind the dog's ears before giving her proffered tummy a stroke. "Hey, little miss. You're still a bit wet under here. Paige pass me some towels, will you?"

Paige handed over the roll and watched as Dom dried Sprite's belly. Sprite basked in the attention.

"*Chérie.* So what's wrong? I know that look," Dom said, wrapping his thin arms around Paige.

She let herself be held in his embrace and breathed

in deeply the familiar scent of Aramis. "*Grandpère*, I'm so confused. I need your razor-sharp brain to help me see clearly. I feel like I'm trying to fight my way through a tangle of roots that are determined to trip me up."

"Sounds like you need a machete rather than a razor," he said. "One jungle explorer to the rescue." He raised his arm and pretended to chop through imaginary branches.

"Very funny. *Merci grandpère*. Right so shall we order and then I can tell you all my woes?"

"Indeed. Have you got your credit card ready? You did say this was your treat."

Paige pulled her wallet out of her pocket. "*Voilà!* I've the menu here on my phone. Choose what you want and I'll ring it through."

Half an hour later the food was delivered by a scrawny youth on a moped. The poor kid was drenched to the skin. Paige took pity on him and gave him a generous tip. She carried the bag into the kitchen and emptied the containers into serving dishes while Dom laid the table. Dom was a stickler for propriety. There was no dishing up food direct from plastic containers in his house. The pair ate in companionable silence whilst Sprite looked on longingly. After they finished, Paige cleared up and they retired to the living room with a cup of tea. It was lovely and cosy with a fire burning in the grate.

"Nothing beats a real fire," Dom said, settling himself in his favourite armchair on one side of the fireplace. Paige curled up in the chair opposite him and Sprite spread out on the rug between them.

"The flames are mesmerising. I could sit and watch them for hours."

"Me too, but I believe you have need of my superior brain?" he said, a teasing quirk at the corner of his mouth.

Paige let a sigh escape. "Yes. The more I learn about this case the more confused I become. However, the first person I need to ask you about is Bill."

"Bill? What about him?"

"Do you know why he was so keen for my help?"

"No. It did surprise me. You're not exactly his favourite person."

"No, I'm not. He put me in contact with Mica Murrel and I'm starting to believe that he purposely wanted to offload her. She's a problem."

"How do you mean?"

"She came to meet me and Mary at the shop. Alex was also there."

"So he's resurfaced has he?" His eyes twinkled with amusement.

Paige huffed. "Yes, I'll fill you in on that later. This girl looks like Grace Jones. Do you remember her? A model with long ebony limbs and chiselled cheekbones?"

Dom shook his head. "Can't say I do."

"Never mind. Let's just say Mica looks like a high-class model. That's not the problem - well not too much." Her lips twisted in distaste. "Basically, Mica's not very nice. She's bitchy and snide. She's arrogant and dismissive."

"She's rattled your cage, that's for sure."

Paige glared at Dom. "Not at all," she snapped. "She was rude about Olivia - she calls her 'Owl'. She said that Zac was a loser. And," Paige paused for dramatic effect, "she's a dominatrix!"

Dom's eyebrows shot up. "Is she now? How interesting. And how did you come by this information? I'm assuming she didn't say to you, *Oh and by the way, Paige, I'm a dominatrix.*"

"No she didn't share that nugget. It was Gail."

"Gail? The woman who runs the jewellery shop on Riverside? How would she know?"

"She's made metalwork accessories for Mica - cuffs, collars, masks."

Dom wrinkled his nose in disgust. "I find Gail rather an abrupt, coarse individual. I can imagine her working in a forge bashing the life out of an anvil with a hammer and terrorising the horses. But I wouldn't have put her down as someone who gossiped about customers."

"In her defence, Mica owes her money for work that she's done for her," Paige added hastily.

"I see. I'm assuming that you're puzzled that this girl contacted Bill to get the University involved if she has this exotic activity?"

"Yes. And why would she want to contact me? She must have known I'd find out about her other life."

"Troubling. The pieces don't stack up." Dom scratched his chin thoughtfully.

"No they don't. Also, I haven't told anyone else this…"

"Please don't tell me you've put yourself in danger again." Dom drew in air between his teeth.

When Paige finally spoke, her voice was hesitant, "On Sunday evening when Sprite and I walked back from Mary's it felt as if someone was following us." She decided to omit telling him about her late night visit to the Cathedral on Saturday and the feeling of someone stalking her. If she admitted to that her refusal of a lift home from Mary's would seem foolhardy.

Dom jolted. "Oh Paige. Who was it?"

"I don't know. I didn't actually see anyone. Just a tall, thin shadow melting into a doorway. But Sprite started growling."

"I don't like the sound of that."

"No. Anyway, we ran like the wind. The person

gave chase but all the sprint training I do came in handy." She gave him a brittle smile. "Whoever it was didn't keep up with us for long."

"Your bravado doesn't fool me, *ma chérie*. I can see it shook you up, especially after last night."

Paige butted in, "When someone tried to run me over. It can't be a coincidence, can it? I have no idea who I've upset - again."

"The police did say they would try and trace the car. If they do, we'll at least know who is targeting you."

"True. It would be good to know if the attack's connected to the death of Andrew Hammond aka Handy Andy, if it's linked to the archaeology dig or to Zac. Zac did say in his letter that he was sure someone had been following him. It seems they've turned their attention to me." A sense of dread rolled through the pit of her stomach. "If only I could figure out what's going on."

"Then it's a good thing you have me and my superior brain to help you, isn't it?" His face wore a sudden formidable look that reassured Paige. No, he couldn't fight a physical adversary but his intellectual acuity was a force to be reckoned with.

Paige stood and wrapped her arms around his shoulders. "What would I do without you, *grandpère*?"

Chapter 17

River Books was surprisingly busy for a wet Wednesday morning. Just as Paige was preparing to ask Olivia about Mica, a coach party of the grey-rinse brigade piled into the shop to shelter from the rain. The tour manager bustled over to the café and enquired if they could provide her elderly travellers with hot drinks and cake. From the upper floor Paige peered over the banister to see what the noise was. She watched as Sunny gave the tour manager a warm smile and say, "We'd be pleased to help if you are willing to be patient with us. We're a small team. How many are there in the group?"

"There's thirty-six of us. I realise we're springing this on you." She lowered her voice. "We had a walk along the river planned but there was a rebellion in the ranks. No one wanted to get soaked in the downpour when they saw this bookshop and its café looking so welcoming and dry. I can't blame them. This is a delightful place." The woman in her fifties opened her arms expansively to take in the higgledy-piggledy shelves piled high with books, the literature related displays and the café's inviting spread of food.

Taking in the situation, Paige skipped down the stairs and called out, "Welcome to River Books everyone. If you'd like to find yourselves tables we'll get your drinks and cakes sorted. This is our chef, Sunny," she said, pointing to her café manager.

Sunny bowed to the group and said, *"Namaste."*

"Her delicious pastries are legendary in these parts. Of course, do feel free to browse the bookshelves, as well. We've a book for every taste." Paige added.

She hurried over to the café to help Sunny and Willow with the orders. The next hour was manic but such fun. Gales of laughter rang out from customers clustered round the tables. There was no mistaking how happy they were to be inside in the warm and not outside traipsing along the river bank in the driving rain. 'Oohs' and 'aahs' sprinkled conversations as people bit into Sunny's cakes, savouring the delicate flavours and textures. Sunny's violet cupcakes proved to be a winner with several women buying some to take with them. The Nepalese woman glowed with happiness as compliments on her patisserie skills poured in.

Members of the party wandered around the shop examining the offerings on the shelves. Mary manned the till ringing up a regular flow of sales. Even those who didn't buy a book bought a bookmark or a notebook. Finally, the tour guide told the group that the coach would be waiting for them in fifteen minutes so if they wanted to make last minute purchases now was the time to do so.

"Thank you so much for allowing us to shelter in your shop and café. We've had a wonderful time and you've been so welcoming.

Mary smiled and said, "Hopefully, we'll be seeing you again."

As the group trooped out Dom came in shaking off his umbrella.

"Dominic Giraud as I live and breathe," boomed a deep voice.

"Alfie? Alfie Jeffreys. Well I never, old chap, what are you doing back in my part of the woods?" Dom asked.

"Came to see the archaeological digs. You know

me, never could resist an ancient relic," he guffawed slapping Dom on the back.

"Careful old boy. No damaging precious artefacts," Dom joked as he rubbed his shoulder.

"Look. Do you fancy doing lunch? I'll have a word with our tour guide and tell her I'll catch up with the group later." Alfie looked expectantly at Dom.

"Excellent idea."

Alfie disappeared to talk to the tour leader before returning looking exceedingly pleased with himself. "Done and dusted. Now where are you taking me?"

"How about The White Hart?"

"Perfect. It's not far from here. We shouldn't get too wet."

Paige had been following this interaction. "Dom, I could drop you both off, if you like?"

"Paige. That would be great. Let me introduce you to an old acquaintance. Meet Dr Jeffreys. He used to teach Ancient History here in Exeter before moving north. He's a keen amateur archaeologist for all things Roman." He turned to Alfie, a short and rotund man with gingery, grey hair, and said, "Alfie meet Paige Harper. She's the owner of River Books."

Paige stepped forward. "Pleased to meet you Dr Jeffreys. I couldn't help overhearing that you're interested in the Roman digs at the Cathedral. One of our student staff, Zac, is studying archaeology at the uni and has been involved in the work."

Alfie's eyes widened. "Lucky lad. He's not in today, is he?" he asked, his voice hopeful.

"Unfortunately not. Dom knows him though. We attended a lecture that Zac took part in about the Roman finds. Do you have any contacts within the university these days?"

Alfie's brow furrowed as he replied, "Not anymore.

It's been a while since I've been back down this way. Anyone I may have known has long since left. I did request a special visit with Professor Watkins hoping that my status as a former university employee might grease the wheels. Didn't work. Too busy apparently."

"That's a shame. Maybe Dom can pull some strings?"

Dom raised his eyebrows at Paige as if to say *'What are you playing at?'*

Paige mouthed 'Zac'.

"Ah, I'll make some calls. Now let's get to the pub."

"Just let me grab my coat and car keys." She cantered up the stairs and returned a minute later. "Right, let's go, gents."

In the car Dom asked, "How's Pat? Is she on the trip with you?"

Alfie's whole body slumped. "She died eighteen months ago. I really miss her. It's lonely without her. That's why I joined this tour. The opportunity to chat to people and with the added bonus of not having to worry about driving myself. I don't see as well as I used to."

"I'm sorry to hear about Pat's passing, Alfie. You know you're always welcome to stay with me if you fancy a break down here."

"Thanks. I may hold you to that. If you could wrangle a site visit for me at the Cathedral, I'd be down here like a shot."

"I'll see what I can do, old chap."

Paige pulled up in front of The White Hart. Dom and Alfie, climbed out of the Mini as best as two older gentlemen can with muffled huffs and puffs. They hurried into the fifteenth century inn dodging the rain. "Enjoy your lunch," she called out before pulling away.

Back at River Books Paige caught up with Olivia after lunch.

"Olivia, can I ask you about Mica Murrel?"

A shadow of wariness clouded the young girl's face. "I'm not sure what I can tell you. She's in my French class at uni. We don't have much to do with each other."

"Having met her, I'm not surprised by that in the least and I mean that in the nicest possible way. Nevertheless, I'd value your insights. You're a wise young woman. She's approached us to ask for our help with the SD cards."

"Can I be perfectly frank?" Her voice faltered. "I don't want you to think I'm being unkind."

"Dive right in, Olivia. I respect your opinions."

Olivia fiddled nervously with her cardigan buttons. She took a deep breath. "She's not a nice person. She's mean to most of the class - making up nicknames and ridiculing what we wear. I know she's beautiful, but that's not an excuse to belittle those of us who are less physically perfect." The young girl wrapped her hands protectively over her plump stomach. "The way she talks to the lecturers, you'd think she was in charge. The younger ones are afraid of her. She's made several complaints about their teaching methods to superiors. Even senior managers tiptoe around her as if she has something over them. I wouldn't be surprised if she's involved in blackmail. Oh sorry, that sounds rather far-fetched, doesn't it?" she raised her eyes and looked at Paige questioningly.

"Hmm. Maybe. What about Professor Williams?"

A smile curled the edge of Olivia's mouth. "No disrespect, but he's a master of manipulation, isn't he?"

Paige blinked in surprise. She hadn't thought the girl was that perceptive. Or rather, she hadn't thought she'd voice her observations.

Olivia continued, "Mica failed to get him to do as she wanted. Whatever she's holding over other senior lecturers doesn't include him. Mica discounted him because Mica despises physical imperfections. That's her blind spot. Just because Professor Williams looks like a barrage balloon doesn't mean he doesn't have a fine and acute brain."

"I'm impressed, Olivia. Bill has fooled many a student, but not you."

Olivia blushed. "Thank you, Paige."

"Bill passed Mica on to us. She wants us to investigate the spy cam SD cards at her digs. Any thoughts on that?"

"Professor Williams wouldn't want to deal with her. She should come with a health warning. Sending her your way gets her out of his way. And, I don't want to speak out of turn, but I imagine that he would get a thrill from passing trouble on to you." She glanced up nervously at Paige.

Paige burst out laughing. "Oh, I've no doubt that Bill would indeed get a rise out of handing me a poisoned chalice. But why would Mica ask to be put in contact with me?"

"It's got to be linked to Zac. She knows that Zac worked here. Maybe she's hoping you'll lead her to him."

Paige slapped her forehead. "Why didn't I think of that. I should recruit you to our investigation team.

"It was nothing," Olivia said abashed.

"Mica told me that Zac was a loser. What did Zac think of her?"

Olivia rubbed her brow. "You know how Zac always tried to say the right thing? Well, I once mentioned that Mica was in my class and his mask slipped. He blurted out that she was pure evil.

Afterwards he tried to backtrack until I reassured him that I agreed with him. When I asked him what she'd done, he clammed up." She shrugged her shoulders. "That was Zac. I'm really worried about him," she added.

"We all are. I'll do all in my power to find him and make sure he's safe." Paige wrapped her arm around Olivia's shoulders and gave her a squeeze. "Come on, time for cake."

Olivia laughed. "Is there ever a time that isn't for cake?"

"Don't be silly! Not in my universe!"

Later that afternoon Paige shared Olivia's insights into Mica with Mary. The sisters agreed that they wouldn't give Mica any information directly related to Zac.

"How has your hunt among the dark depths of the web gone?"

"Great," Mary said. "I've found quite a few images of Mica and others who live in the same house."

"And?"

"From what I can establish most of the spy cams in other buildings were installed at the beginning of the university term, around mid-September. What's bizarre is that there aren't any recordings from Zac's digs until later - around mid-October I think. I can't pin the date down exactly. I wonder why the delay in setting them up?" Mary's brow furrowed.

"Does seem a bit weird. Maybe they were there but nothing was uploaded until later?" Paige said.

"Unlikely. Anyway I've tracked the students that Mica gave us photos of. They're in various states of undress, completely unaware that they're being filmed. Nothing in the showers. Thank goodness for small mercies. But there are sex scenes with the girls.

Someone has edited them to show the most detail possible. It's disgusting. Nothing posted about Zac or the other male student. Maybe they don't have a love life."

Paige felt her stomach clench with revulsion. Voyeurism was something that she'd never understood. "I hope the police come down hard on the people behind this racket."

Mary continued, "I've been scouring the web to see what there is about Mica. That's where it gets interesting."

"Go on."

"There's a recording of Mica preparing for her other job. She's dressed in a skin-tight black catsuit. She packs a small case with her equipment - collars, whips, etc - and a video recorder. If she records her sessions that could tie in with Olivia's suggestion that she was into blackmail."

"Indeed. Anything else of interest on her?"

Mary smiled like the cat who'd got the cream. Paige bounced up and down on her toes with impatience. "Come on, Mary. What is it?"

"Our Mica had a distinguished visitor." Mary paused. A minute ticked by.

"Do you want me to get down on my knees and beg?" Paige spluttered.

"That would be fun," Mary giggled. "Okay, I'll put you out of your misery. It was Professor Watkins."

"Well, that is an interesting turn of events. I didn't realise they knew each other. How were they with each other?"

"I don't think he's one of her dominatrix clients. This looked like an argument. There's no sound on these recordings - it would take up too much memory on the SD cards. I imagine the police will be using a lip-reading specialist to decipher the conversation. What was even more interesting was a coin that Mica gave to the Professor. He didn't seem happy with it. He held up his index finger as if to say 'only one?'"

"Wow. Do you think she'd been stealing from Zac? Maybe it was Mica who knocked Handy Andy off his stool and ransacked Zac's room. Oh, Mary. What have we stumbled into?"

Chapter 18

Thursday morning Paige was restocking the shelves upstairs when she heard the scratchy tones of DS Brown asking Mary where Paige was. "About time they turned up," Paige muttered under her breath. She heard wooden steps creak and groan as the female sergeant and DI Denton lumbered up to see her.

"Miss Harper, can we have a word?" DS Brown asked.

"Of course. How can I help you?"

"We'd like to ask you how you came into possession of the SD cards."

"As I explained to the duty sergeant on Friday of last week, an envelope addressed to me was posted through one of our customer's letterbox. She contacted me and I went to fetch it. Inside I found a pouch with SD cards inside it."

"Was the pouch the only thing inside?" asked Brown sharply. "You didn't 'forget' to give us anything else?"

Paige threw back her shoulders, lifted her chin and glared at the woman. "Are you calling me a liar?" she snarled.

DI Denton held up a placating hand. "Paige, I'm sure that DS Brown meant no such thing. However, I must ask whether you looked at the cards before you handed them in?"

"Inspector, hand on heart, I can swear that I did not

look at the cards before handing them over to the police," Paige said firmly. She'd looked at the copies Mary had made but not the originals.

"You're not known for your restraint. How did you resist the temptation?" Brown sneered.

"I don't have to listen to your insinuations. I did my civic duty and gave the police the cards in the forlorn hope that perhaps they would help the authorities to solve the handyman's death." Her voice dripped with sarcasm.

Brown bristled. "We're working hard. We've tracked down the letting agency owner who is now helping us with our inquiries into the fake smoke alarm spy cameras."

Paige's eyes flashed with victory before lowering her gaze but not before DI Denton noticed. Paige had managed to provoke his DS into giving out information. DI Denton rubbed his lined forehead.

"So the smoke alarms were spy cameras, were they? That's awful. The poor students. Is there anything on the recordings that show what happened to Zac? Or who ransacked his room?" Paige asked chancing her arm.

"We can't divulge that information," said DS Brown primly.

"I'll take that as a no then."

"Have you heard from Zac?" DI Denton asked.

"No. We're worried sick for the poor boy."

"He could be the killer," Brown stated.

"I'd prefer to believe that he's not."

"Another of your 'feelings'?" Brown taunted.

"DS Brown," DI Denton snapped. He turned to Paige. "Our apologies, Miss Harper. We won't keep you any longer. Of course, if you do hear from Zac, please urge him to give himself in."

"Before you go, have you made any progress with the jewellery found in Zac's locker?" Paige asked.

"Actually your employee, Beth, came in with her friend Malik to identify her bracelet. She gave us a statement about how she believed it came to be in Zac's possession. She said that she would not press charges against him although we advised her otherwise," DS Brown said in a disgruntled voice.

"And have you traced any other owners?"

"No. The fact that it's costume jewellery and of little financial value means that people are unlikely to report the loss."

"Perhaps Zac found the others. Maybe he didn't steal them?" Paige asked hopefully.

"I shouldn't think so," growled DS Brown.

"But, it's not impossible," insisted Paige.

"No, not impossible. Improbable, but not impossible," admitted DI Denton.

"Understood. Now let me show you out," Paige said, leading the way down the stairs to the shop door.

As soon as the door had closed behind them Paige stomped over to the till where Mary was arranging bookmarks in the display.

"Eeerrr. That woman," Paige exploded.

"What did they want?"

"To know whether there was anything else in the envelope from Zac and if I'd looked at the SD cards before I passed them on. I said no."

"So you lied to the police?" Mary said, fixing her with reproving eyes.

"No I didn't. For the first question I used that well-known interviewing tactic of answering a question with another one. And for the second question I answered honestly that I hadn't looked at the cards because I only looked at the copies you made on your computer." Paige beamed smugly at her sister.

"Hmm. Clever, I suppose in a sneaky sort of way."

Paige bowed with a flourish, "Thank you, sister dearest. I also asked them about the jewellery. It seems that Beth has been into the station to make her statement with Malik in tow."

"Ah, is romance in the air?" Mary asked.

"Who knows. He seems very protective of her. Anyway, Beth refused to press charges for theft, much to the sergeant's displeasure."

"Good. So what next?" Mary asked.

"Time to line up interviews with the students from Zac's digs. We'll invite them to come here and tempt them with free cake and drinks."

"Sounds good. Do you want me to ring them?"

"No, you've already put in a lot of time on the internet searches. I'll do it."

Paige skipped up the stairs with a jaunty step. Now that the police had officially told her about the spy cameras, even if she'd known about them before, she now felt within her rights to talk to the students as requested by Mica.

During the afternoon she made a stream of calls arranging for the young men and women to come into River Books on Saturday.

Two days later on Saturday afternoon the group of young people were looking decidedly uneasy. They huddled round one of the café tables. Drinks and pastries were spread out in front of them. Paige joined them.

"Look Miss Harper, we're here but to be honest we're not sure why," said a young woman who'd been elected as their spokesperson.

"Mica told me that you were all happy to speak to me about the spy cams and Zac." Paige's eyes scanned the disgruntled faces in the circle.

"Yeah, well you don't say no to Mica. Not if you share a house with her," muttered a beanpole of a boy with lank, greasy hair. Paige checked the list and identified him as Kevin Stevens.

"Let me get this straight," Paige said, "you aren't worried about the spy cam footage or about the man found dead in Zac's room?"

"Of course we are, but the police are investigating. They've interviewed us. They've arrested the landlord. They've promised us that they'll get the videos taken down from the websites. They've told us that they think Handy Andy's death was probably accidental; that he fell off the chair." The spokeswoman sat back and folded her hands on top of each other on the table in front of her, a satisfied expression on her face. The others nodded their agreement with her summary.

"But what about Zac? He's missing. His room was turned over," Paige said.

"Zac's a bit weird. Maybe he tossed it himself?" replied one of the girls.

Paige gaped at them. None of them seemed concerned about their housemate. "Okay. So you're here because Mica bullied you in to coming, is that it?"

They all shrugged. "Pretty much."

A surge of anger stormed through her body. Her voice shook just a little, betraying her true feelings. "I won't take up too much more of your precious time. I've a few questions for you and then you can be on your way."

"You'll tell Mica we were helpful, won't you?" asked a mousy-haired girl, who Paige identified from the information Mica had given her as Ivy.

"Of course," Paige said through gritted teeth. "I've

prepared a small questionnaire for you each," she said handing out the papers. "Questions such as when you last saw Zac; odd things you might have noticed in the weeks leading up to the incident; how often you saw the handyman; unusual behaviour from any of your housemates." The mousy-haired girl looked startled. Paige continued, "I'll treat all of this information in confidence. If you prefer to spread out on to other tables for more privacy while you fill them in, feel free."

The beanpole boy stood up and sauntered to another table. Once he'd made a move, the mousy-haired girl got up and scurried across to a table on the opposite side of the room. The spokeswoman and the three girls, who were obviously her mates, looked pointedly at them. "We'll be fine here," they chorused loudly before picking up the pens Paige had laid out for them. It didn't take long for them to fill in the forms, swallow down their drinks, munch their cakes and leave. The mousy-haired girl and beanpole boy took a bit longer before leaving together.

Paige shook her head in disbelief as she collected the completed questionnaires. A frown creased her forehead as she flicked through them. "So much for looking out for your mates. No wonder Zac didn't talk about them. What a bunch of self-centred brats. I wouldn't want to be friends with them either."

"What are you prattling on about?" Mary asked. "You look angry."

"I am. The bottom line is that the students only agreed to come and speak to me because they're afraid of Mica. They believe the police have got everything under control and see no reason why I should get involved. No concern for Zac's well-being. Nothing. At least they did agree to fill these in," she said, waving the sheets of paper in front of Mary. "I'll read through them and see if anything pops out. I don't hold out much hope."

"Mica didn't come then?"

"No, I thought she would. Apparently not."

"If they're so afraid of her, perhaps it was better she didn't," Mary said.

"I had to reassure them that their responses would be confidential. I'd bet that the mousy-haired girl and beanpole boy are the most likely to take this opportunity to spill some venom about Mica. The other four were toeing the party line." Paige sighed and grasping the sheaves of paper in both hands turned to take them to her office. Her eyes lit up as she saw who was entering the shop. Her heart skipped a beat.

"Alejandro, how are you?" she asked as the long-limbed Spaniard clad in tight black jeans and his signature cowboy boots moved towards her with the stealth of a black panther.

"Hola, Paige. Bien, gracias. Y tú?" he asked, warm chocolate curls falling over his brow. He swept the chaotic hair from his eyes.

Paige's insides spun like a Catherine wheel. "Yes, I'm fine."

Mary snorted loudly, "Really?"

"Okay, maybe not fine. Frustrated, angry and tamping mad."

Alex's almond eyes flickered with amusement. "Ah *cariño*. That's more like you. Will you have calmed down by 7pm?"

"Why?"

"I've come to invite you for dinner this evening and don't want to be shot down in flames by my fiery friend - this is the English idiom, no?" he said chuckling to himself.

"Perfect," Mary answered. "You're a brave man, Alex taking on my sister."

Paige flushed crimson. "Mary," she hissed.

"Oh sorry, did I overstep?" Mary said with a grin of pure mischief.

Paige ignored her sister. "Thank you, Alex. I would love to have dinner with you."

"I will come and pick you up at a quarter to seven. I'll book a table at The Smugglers. *Hasta pronto, cariño.*" Giving his strange little heel click, Alex strode out of the shop.

Chapter 19

Paige was all of a flutter. She wasn't a vain person and, under normal circumstances, didn't spend much time on her appearance. However, this wasn't a normal circumstance. Alex had asked her out to dinner. She wanted to look her best. Sprite lay down on the bedroom floor watching with amusement as her mistress pulled clothes out of the wardrobe and piled them on the bed.

"Ugh! What am I going to wear! Do I do casual? Do I dress up? Oh, for goodness sake, it's only a meal at The Smugglers. Casual it is."

She picked through the pile on the bed and chose navy jeans, a pink roll neck jumper and a long navy cardigan which had some delicate bead work down the front.

"There we are Sprite. Casual with a touch of class. What do you think?" she asked whirling in front of the mirror. Her dog gave a yap of approval. "Just my earrings to add and I'm ready to go." Paige selected a pair of studs with aquamarine stones that brought out the blue of her grey-blue eyes.

Sprite barked and rushed off to greet the visitor she'd heard arrive. Paige pulled a brush through her hair and declared herself presentable. Downstairs she opened the front door to let Alex into the entrance hall.

"Paige, *cariño, qué guapa!*" Alex said his eyes drinking her in.

Paige could feel her face blushing. Alex had never told her she was pretty before. "*Gracias, Alejandro. Y tú tambien, Alejandro.* You as well."

"*Yo guapa?*" he said, his eyes sparkling with mischief. "You think that I am pretty?"

Laughter bubbled through her lips. "Very funny. No, you're not *guapa* - pretty, you're *guapo* - handsome. Having masculine and feminine versions of adjectives in Spanish is just plain annoying."

"Most languages have different gendered words. English is one of the odd ones."

"But it does make it an easier language to learn." Paige turned to Sprite. "Now, young lady, off to your basket. No double date for you and Rafa tonight."

Sprite huffed and sauntered reluctantly towards the kitchen. Paige put on her coat, wrapped her scarf round her neck and picked up her handbag. Locking the door behind her, she followed Alex down the path and slid into the front seat of his BMW estate car. He turned on the car stereo and they sat listening to the Spanish group Amaral as they made their way along the Topsham Road. Paige was doing her best to concentrate on the music but she was failing. Her mind kept returning to the fact that Alex had called her pretty. She could feel a smile playing on her lips.

"What are you smiling at?" Alex asked interrupting her thoughts.

"Nothing. Just happy."

He reached out and stroked her cheek. The look in his eyes made her skin quiver. *Deep breaths,* she told herself as every nerve ending sparked. The atmosphere in the car crackled with tension.

Alex parked and they walked along Riverside to The Smugglers. Paige breathed in the frigid air. It helped to calm her.

As they pushed open the pub door Judd called out,

"Evening," from behind the bar. "I've put you over there by the window." He lifted his ham-sized arm to wave in the direction of a table for two in a bay. "No dogs, tonight?" he asked. The landlord loved dogs and was particularly fond of Sprite and Rafa.

"Not tonight, Judd," Paige said. "We're out on our own without our chaperones," she joked. "Like grown-ups," she added.

"You a grown-up, Paige?" He laughingly shook his head. "That'll be the day."

"Cheeky," she replied, waggling her finger at him.

The couple took their seats at the table. Paige looked out at the lights along the quay reflecting off the river's rippled surface as the water continued its unhurried journey to the sea. Was tonight going to be choppy or smooth? Jen, the pub's grumpy cook, made Paige jump out of her skin when she appeared behind her and said, "Right so what's you twos having?"

"Hi Jen," said Paige recovering from the shock of Jen coming to take their order. The woman very rarely ventured out of her kitchen. "I'll have the traditional fish and chips with mushy peas, please. Alex, have you chosen?"

"*Si*. I will have steak and chips, please Jen." He gave her a winning smile.

Paige could have sworn she detected the tiniest hint of a blush on Jen's cheeks before she turned her back on them. Did Jen, the woman whose granite-like personality made grown men quake in their boots, have a soft spot for Alex? Well, that was a turn up for the books. Mind you, Paige could understand it. He was a devastatingly handsome man. Feeling his eyes on her, she looked up to see him watching her intensely. Mary's words came to mind. What did she know about Alex's past? Tonight she was going to find out.

Their meals arrived. While they ate they chatted about rugby and how the Six Nations tournament was going. Both Alex and Paige played the game. It was a safe topic. After they finished their main meal she'd steer the conversation to his past.

Paige held her cup of tea in her hands and took a delicate sip. Alex picked up his espresso and looked at her over the rim of the tiny cup. She hugged her drink a bit tighter and launched into her questions.

"Alex, how did you end up in Exeter? It's quite a way from Valencia. What made you decide to move to England?"

A flicker of darkness momentarily dulled his gold-flecked eyes. "My wife died."

Paige gulped. "Oh, I'm so sorry, Alex." She put down her cup and covered his hands with hers. "I shouldn't have asked. Let's change the subject."

"No, *cariño*. You shared with me your sadness about your friend being murdered in your flat in France. It's time I told you my story." His voice held a tremor. "I met Inés at university. We were both on the same course. Both passionate about psychology. Both convinced we could change the world for the better. After we finished our undergraduate studies we married. Our families thought we were too young. We were in our early twenties, full of plans for the future. Inés worked in a centre for troubled teens. She loved the job. She had a big heart, Paige. Too big." He paused and gave her a wistful smile. "I'd decided to continue with a post-graduate degree at the university. It was a Tuesday in November and I had a late lecture. We'd arranged to meet in town for a pizza when I'd finished." His voice cracked. "I waited and waited for her at the restaurant. I tried ringing her mobile. It went straight to voice mail. In the end I went home leaving a message with the pizza restaurant owner in case she turned up."

Paige felt a cold shiver run all the way down her spine. "Where was she?" she said softly.

Alex continued as if she hadn't spoken. His eyes were glazed as he travelled back in time. "When I got home there was a policeman waiting outside our apartment block. Inés had been giving extra tuition to one of the teenagers in her unit after hours. I'd been worried that he'd become obsessed with her, but she'd brushed off my concerns saying that he deserved a chance. I found out later that he'd made sexual advances to her which she'd turned down. Unknown to us, that rejection led to him stalking her. He attacked her on her way to the pizzeria. She fought back but in the ensuing scuffle he stabbed her. She died. Why?" he demanded, his voice almost savage.

"Alex. I'm so, so sorry. I didn't mean to rake up such raw emotions," she said in an almost inaudible voice.

"No, Paige, I want you to know. After Inés died I changed to a course in criminal psychology. I need to understand what pushes people to commit horrendous crimes." He raised his almond gold-flecked eyes which shimmered with unshed tears. "Our parents were wrong. We were right to get married young. We had a very happy, if short, marriage."

"And by coming to Exeter afterwards you distanced yourself from where it happened."

"I stayed in Valencia to finish my PhD and worked in the psychology department for a few years. But I couldn't escape Inés. I'd walk into a café and get flashbacks of when we'd shared a coffee, almost expecting to see her at our favourite table. I'd smell her fragrance in the perfume section of *El Corte Ingles*. I'd hear a song and think of her. I couldn't get past her death. In the end, I decided I needed to move away from Valencia where memories were waiting to trip me up around every corner. Give myself a fresh start. I was offered a good lecturing post at the University of Exeter with the option of helping the police in complex psychological cases."

She tilted her head and met his eyes. "I'm glad you chose Exeter, Alex."

"Me too. You, Paige Harper, have certainly shaken up my world."

She touched his face and slowly traced her fingers over his features. "Glad to be of service, Señor Ramos."

He held her fingers and kissed their tips. Her stomach turned to molten lava. "*Vamos*. Let's go," Alex said rising suddenly to his feet. He strode over to the bar and settled up their bill.

Behind the counter Judd gave Paige a wink. "Have a good evening," he said a wide grin splitting his face in two.

"I intend to," she said, as the flush deepened in her cheeks. "Night, Judd."

"Night, Paige, Alex. Be good and, if you can't be good, be careful, eh!" he chuckled.

Chapter 20

On Sunday morning Paige woke up groggy after a troubled night. The dinner with Alex had been wonderful. They'd made steps in getting to know each other better. She now understood why he was so hard on her when she bent the rules and put herself at risk. In his mind, Inés, had died because she'd ignored protocol and given one of her students unsupervised extra tuition. She'd believed that the kid needed another chance but, by misreading his state of mind, her actions had led to her death. Alex's fascination with the psychology of a killer made sense. It was his way of attempting to impose control on an unpredictable world. Because the Spanish police quickly apprehended his wife's assailant, he equated the police with good crime solving. Paige did not. Her experiences had been very different with the French police after the death of Élodie. They'd dismissed Paige's concerns that she herself had been the intended target. Had refused to take seriously the threats she'd received from her ex, Xavier, and, in the end, she'd had no alternative except to run away. Élodie's murder had never been officially solved.

So why had Paige's sleep been so disturbed? Was it because of the past being raked up again or was it because after a passionate kiss on the doorstep Alex had left? Her body had been bubbling like a volcano about to erupt. It had been screaming out for more than just a kiss. Yet, her inner voice acknowledged that if she and Alex had shared more than a passionate embrace she would have felt guilty. It would have felt like she was taking advantage of him. He'd been vulnerable after telling her his story. Her logical brain had recognised that. Her body hadn't.

An empty Sunday stretched in front of her. The forecast was for dry and windy weather in the morning with rain moving in from the west in the afternoon.

In the kitchen Paige let Sprite out in the garden for her morning patrol of the perimeters and began preparing their breakfasts. Once the meals were ready she called Sprite in and they set about the serious business of eating. Paige finished her bowl of porridge, wiped her mouth on her serviette and leant back in her chair.

"Sprite, we'll go out this morning while the weather's okay. We went to Exmouth last week. I fancy somewhere different. How about Sidmouth?"

Her dog ignored her and continued to root around in her bowl for the last remaining crumb of food.

"I'll take your disinterest as a tacit agreement. Sidmouth it is."

Paige went to get ready. She dressed in warm cord trousers and a thick jumper. She picked up her fuchsia pink jacket and matching bobble hat. After chucking a towel in the car's boot in case Sprite got wet in the sea, Paige attached the terrier in her harness and they set off for the coast. They passed Crealy Adventure Park on their way out of Exeter and then the Mini cruised along the A3052. Paige enjoyed driving the windy road bordered by fields and hedges, feeling the car respond to her touch. Two hours walking and running on the Sidmouth beach in the brisk wind was enough exercise for both of them. Paige felt refreshed. Even if it was too cold to swim, the ocean always worked its magic on her.

Back at the house Paige made herself a warming soup for lunch. After she'd finished her meal, she spread out the questionnaires that Zac's housemates had filled in. Connecting her phone to a speaker via Bluetooth, she brought up a country music album and pressed play. Don William's comforting voice filled the air helping her to concentrate as she collated information from the sheets. As she'd suspected the four girls' answers gave her little to work with. They'd obviously copied each other. Each one claimed to have only rarely encountered Handy Andy in the house and when they had, he'd seemed polite and pleasant. None of them could remember when they'd seen him last. Each of them thought his death must have been an accident. As for Zac, they'd had little to do with him. He kept himself to himself. He didn't move in their social circles. He wasn't on the same course as them. They didn't really know him. They had no idea who could have ransacked his room. Each one believed the police's assurances that any video footage from the spy cams had been removed from the web.

"Can they really be that naive?" Paige asked out loud.

She picked up the greasy-haired boy's questionnaire next. His name was Kevin Stevens. Surely he'd be able to tell her more. His dislike of Mica had been obvious yesterday. Had he used this opportunity of anonymity to vent his spleen about her? Paige read through his answers and felt a wave of disappointment. If she were to believe what he'd written, he lived a hermit's life and never interacted with his housemates. He claimed that he barely knew Zac. He couldn't remember ever seeing Handy Andy in the house. Paige ran her fingers through her hair in frustration. She'd been banking on him giving her some leads and now felt cheated.

"Okay, so let's see if the mousy-haired girl is more forthcoming," she said, laying the questionnaire out in front of her. The girl's name was Ivy Hargreaves. She was studying statistics. Her answers were neatly set out in detail. "This is more like it," Paige muttered. Ivy had often seen the handyman in the house. She'd once asked him why he needed to change the smoke alarm batteries so frequently to which he replied that the landlord was a responsible person who liked to keep his properties safe. She'd talked to Zac when they bumped into each other in the hallway or the kitchen but she'd never had an in-depth conversation with him. He'd seemed shy to her. The clique of four girls in the house normally ignored her, which was fine with her. She thought they were vacuous airheads. Ivy confirmed that Mica was feared by all. Mica had nicknamed her 'Creeper' which she thought showed Mica's limited intelligence. However, if it meant that the girl left her alone, so be it. Mica seemed to have some hold over Kevin, who she'd nicknamed 'Cheese string'. Ivy said Mica had explained that the nickname suited him because he was tall and thin and smelt bad. Kevin disparaged Mica and women in general all the time. Ivy had witnessed Kevin arguing with Zac when he'd called him 'teacher's pet'. Paige underlined this and turned to her laptop.

She inserted the USB stick that Mary had given her that was filled with her notes about the SD cards and the web searches she'd conducted. Her sister had also added the names of all the students on archaeology degrees at the university. Opening the list of students on Zac's degree, Paige was surprised to see that Kevin was on the same course. "Barely knew, Zac!" she sputtered. The boy had been in the same lectures as Zac. What was he hiding? And why had he accused Zac of being the 'teacher's pet'? Prickles ran up her spine. Was this the breakthrough she needed? She was going to crawl all over this liar's life. Why had he professed to hardly know Zac? Why was he afraid of Mica? Paige felt at last she had a trail to follow. She sent up a silent prayer of thanks to Ivy.

Paige's head was so full of Mica that she did a double take when her phone rang and Mica's name flashed up on the screen as if she'd conjured her up.

"Mica, great to hear from you. How are you?"

"Fine. How did the meeting with my housemates go?"

"Not too bad. Thank you for orchestrating that."

"Did you learn anything?" Mica's voice rose a notch betraying her nervousness.

"I've a few leads to follow," Paige replied deadpan.

"I should have warned you that Kevin can't be trusted. He's a nasty little weasel."

"In what way?"

"Well, you've seen how physically repulsive he is. I think he's part of that Incel movement."

"What's that?" Paige asked.

"Incel is short for 'involuntary celibate'. People who define themselves as incel complain about not being able to get a sex life despite the fact that they want to be in a relationship," Mica explained.

"Thank you for the tip. I'll look into it. Sorry, I've got to go. I'm meeting someone shortly," Paige lied.

"Fine."

"Oh, by the way, would you mind filling in one of the questionnaires that the others completed for me? I can forward it to you if you text me your email address," Paige asked, crossing her fingers that

Mica would agree.

"*If you insist,*" Mica huffed.

"*Please.*"

"*I'll text it to you now and you can send me the form,*" Mica said, abruptly before hanging up.

Paige did a little fist pump. Mica's phone call was an interesting one. One thing was certain; there was bad blood between Mica and Kevin. So what was that all about? Paige's fingers felt for her dream catcher and rubbed it. Things were warming up. A shiver of excitement zinged down her spine.

Paige's brain was buzzing. She spent some time chasing down information about Incels. What she found was disturbing. There was some serious hate against women out there on the web. She could imagine that Kevin would absolutely hate Mica, who was sexuality personified. Her viciousness towards him would reinforce his women-hating views. As she trawled the web Paige learnt the term 'keyboard warriors' meaning people who hid behind the anonymity of their computers to post their heavily biased comments. Having met Kevin, Paige could easily imagine him sitting in his digs spewing out venom via his keyboard. Yet, before she got too carried away, she needed to find out if Kevin really was part of this movement and was it relevant to the case. Or was Mica trying to play her?

Chapter 21

Monday was Mary's day off. Paige was enjoying a guilt-free mid-morning break at the café without her sister's disobliging comments about her cake eating capacities when River Books' bell jangled and the door crashed open. A pink-faced Violet powered across the shop floor and plonked herself on a chair next to Paige holding a hand to her ample bosom. It was an entrance worthy of the stage.

"Violet, what's wrong?" Sunny asked, her chocolate drop eyes wide with concern.

"It's the archaeology dig," Violet gasped. "They've found a body."

"Is it a Roman skeleton?" Paige asked.

Violet waved Paige's question away like an annoying fly. "No, you don't understand. A fresh body. A recently killed body," she enunciated. She turned to Sunny and said in a sugary sweet voice, "Sunita, my dear, could I trouble you for a glass of water?"

Sunny sprang to her feet. "Of course." She disappeared into the kitchen.

Paige felt a twinge of guilt for what now seemed like a crass comment about a Roman skeleton. The shop door swung open and a pale-faced Dom strode across to where she was sitting. "Violet," he said stiffly, nodding in her direction. Sitting down next to Paige, he gently held her hand and said, "I wanted to be the first to tell you face to face, although I may be too late," he said, glowering at Violet. "They've discovered a man's body at the Cathedral dig."

Paige searched his face. "Zac?" she asked.

"We don't know yet. Alex is on his way there. As soon as he finds out who it is, he'll let me know."

Sunny returned carrying Violet's glass of water. She beamed at the elderly academic. "Dom, lovely to see you. What can I get you?"

"I need a strong brandy but I'll make do with a black coffee please, Sunny."

"What's wrong, Professor? Have you had some bad news about the body?" she asked noticing the worry etched across his distinguished features.

"No. Or not yet anyway. We're waiting to find out if the body discovered at the Cathedral is Zac's," Paige said. "Let's pray it isn't."

It was Sunny's turn to slump in a chair. "Oh, I hope not. He's a sweet boy."

Violet regained some of her composure. "If it is him, it will look bad for the Riverside community and especially for River Books who employed him," she said, giving Paige a laser-like stare that should have reduced her to dust.

Paige shook her head in disbelief. "You really are incredible," she hissed.

Dom, sensing a spat in the making, stepped in. "So, Violet, how did you find out about the body?"

Surprisingly, Violet flushed and dipped her head. "Dominic, you know I can't reveal my sources."

There had always been a suspicion in Paige's mind that Violet had an informant inside the police force.

"Is that because it's a police officer?" Paige asked.

Violet theatrically placed a hand against her bosom once more before replying, "My dear, that's absurd."

"Is it though?" Paige retorted.

Dom's phone ringing cut off the riposte that had formed on Violet's waspish lips. All eyes were glued to his anxious face as he answered. "Alex. Yes, right." He nodded to himself. "Okay. Thank you. Yes, I'll let her know." His tone gave nothing away. He hung up and his shoulders visibly relaxed. "It's not Zac," he told the assembled group who heaved a collective sigh of relief. "Unfortunately, it is someone known to us." He paused. "It's Professor Watkins." A stunned silence greeted his announcement.

Violet was the first to recover her voice. "He seemed such a charming man," she simpered. "Who could want to harm him?"

"I'm confused," admitted Paige. "I was convinced that he was in some way responsible for Zac going missing. Now he's dead, that doesn't make much sense."

"Or, it makes even more sense," said Dom.

"How?" Sunny asked.

"If Professor Watkins was involved in something unsavoury that young Zachary had discovered and had been told to silence his troublesome student, a task at which he, as far as we know, has failed, his partners in crime could have decided that he was a loose end that needed tidying up."

"That's a lot of conjecture," Paige said.

"It is. However, if I'm correct then this means that…"

"Zac is in even more danger," Paige interjected, interrupting Dom.

"Yes. Hence tracking him down becomes imperative."

"If he's still alive." Violet's mouth turned down. She seemed genuinely sad.

Paige stood up and beckoned to Dom to follow her upstairs. Once inside her office away from Violet's prying eyes and ears she said, "Dom, we should ring Zac's grandmother immediately. There's a possibility she can find a way to get a message to Zac before it hits the news."

"Indeed. Do you want to try?"

Paige picked up her phone and scrolled through her contacts until she reached Sheila Jones' name. She pressed the ring icon. It went to answer phone.

You've reached the mobile of Sheila. Sorry I can't take your call right now. Please leave a message.

Paige said, "Sheila, this is Paige Harper. Please ring me as soon as you can." She turned to Dom. "Shall I send her a text as well? She's probably at work and can't answer the phone. She may be able to read messages."

"That would seem prudent," he said.

Paige typed out a quick text. "Done."

"I'll be off, *ma chérie*. Why don't you and Sprite come round for dinner tonight? I may have more information. I'm going off to pay old Bill a visit."

"If there's any gossip about the recently departed Professor Watkins, I'm sure that Bill will have sniffed it out." Paige grimaced in disgust. "Although, isn't it too soon even for Bill?"

"There will be rumours circulating around the university like an out of control bush fire and Bill will be there fanning the flames. I understand your dislike of him Paige but he's very useful in these sort of circumstances," Dom said, defending his frenemy.

"Fine. What time will you be expecting me?" she asked changing the subject. She and Dom would never agree over Professor Bill Williams.

"Let's say seven. That will give me time to go on my reconnaissance mission and for you to get home after work and walk Sprite before you come over." He bent towards her and kissed both her cheeks in the French style. "*Au revoir, ma chérie. A ce soir.*"

"Bye *grandpère*. See you this evening," Paige said, giving him a hug.

The rest of the day in the shop passed quietly. Paige spent her time behind the till and restocking shelves. Beth was in to work on a new window display for the video game section as an avidly anticipated new game was about to be launched. Beth sang quietly to herself as she stuck up posters and laid out video game cases in the window. Saturday was the release date and the shop was expecting a large crowd. Beth had overseen the order. It had seemed a lot of copies but Beth had assured Paige and Mary that they would fly off the shelves. Beth had a wide local network of fellow gamers who would buy from them.

Paige frequently checked her phone but there were no messages from Zac's grandmother. She'd tried ringing her again but the calls had gone straight to answer phone. It was frustrating. Not only was Sheila not answering her calls, neither was Alex. He'd sent her a quick text saying that he would catch up with her when he had a moment. She assumed he was busy at the crime scene. Patience wasn't her strong point. To counteract her impatience, Paige did what she always did - physical activity. She couldn't leave the shop and go for a run but she could reorganise the stock room and bring books up from the basement. Making sure Beth kept an eye out for the till, Paige ran up and down the stairs with armfuls of books for Olivia to arrange on the shelves. When 5pm came she felt the glow that came from having had a good work out. The last half hour of the day was taken up with making sure everything was in its place for tomorrow when Mary would be back. Paige still struggled with the fact that she was the owner of River Books. That she was her big sister's boss didn't feel real. Mary was far more competent and efficient than she was. A part of Paige suffered from 'impostor's syndrome'. What had Dom been thinking when he'd sold her his family bookshop? Perhaps, whispered a little voice, he trusted you and your people skills to make River Books a welcoming and friendly place in the community? Maybe she should believe that he saw something in her that she herself didn't?

Chapter 22

That evening at 7pm Sprite and Paige walked across the grounds to Dom's house, went round the back and let themselves in.

"Dom, we're here," Paige called out as Sprite sprinted through the kitchen in search of their host.

"Coming," Dom replied, his voice coming from the hallway. Sprite found him first and promptly laid on her back, legs up in the air as Dom bent his tall, thin frame to stroke her ginger belly. "Hello, young miss. You want a tummy rub, do you?"

"I'd rather have my tum filled with food than rubbed," Paige joked as she joined the pair.

"*Très drôle, ma chérie.*" He stood up, his long body unfolding like a piece of cardboard, and gave her a hug.

"Yes, I thought I was quite funny." She sniffed loudly. "If my nose is to be believed there is no food being cooked. Are we ordering takeaway?"

"Ah," said Dom just as Sprite scrambled to her feet and rushed barking towards the back door. "I think your answer has arrived."

Alex pushed his way into the kitchen through the melee of dog paws valiantly holding onto a plastic bag from which the mouthwatering aromas of Chinese takeaway emanated. Paige's heart hammered in her chest.

"Alex, so lovely to see you," she said, "and the

food."

"Cariño," he said, placing the bag on the table. He stepped forward and gave her a kiss on both cheeks. She breathed in his familiar citrus fragrance. It set off a tingling in her arms that ached to wrap themselves around his muscular torso.

Whatever current had been passing between them was broken when Dom yelled, "Rafa, no!" batting the Chocolate Lab's nose away from the bag full of tantalising aromas.

"Time for food. We'd better be quick or a certain young dog will eat it for us," Paige said, regathering herself.

"Indeed." Dom picked up the place mats from the centre of the table. "I thought we'd slum it here in the kitchen." He laid down three. "Paige, get out the crockery and cutlery, please. Alex, what would you like to drink? I've a rather nice Spanish Rioja."

"I could not refuse such an offer," Alex said with a smile. "Just one glass, though."

"Paige?" Dom asked.

"Fruit juice, thanks, Dom."

"Help yourself. There's some in the fridge."

Dom busied himself with opening the bottle of red wine. Alex guarded the food from Rafa while Paige laid the table. The food was as ever transferred onto serving dishes. When the drinks had been poured the three of them sat down to eat. Nearby the dogs lingered with intent just in case a morsel of food fell to the floor. Judging by their positioning the odds were on Dom to 'accidentally' drop something. At the end of the meal their patience was rewarded when Dom gave each of them a sliver of chicken.

"Okay, Alex," Paige said, putting down her cutlery and wiping her mouth. "I've been incredibly restrained during the meal, now what can you tell us about

Professor Watkins' murder?"

The Spaniard's gold-flecked eyes twinkled with amusement. "I'm impressed c*ariño*. You are improving," he said, looking pointedly at his watch. "Thirty-five minutes."

Dom clapped his hands gleefully. "I do believe he's getting the measure of you, *ma chérie*."

"When you two have stopped ganging up on me..." She let the silence lengthen as the two men smirked at each other. Her heart did a little jig to see them getting on so well.

Dom was the first to crack. "Actually Alex I'm rather curious to find out what you discovered. Obviously, only what you're allowed to tell us," Dom added gamely.

A grin tugged at the corner of Alex's mouth as he watched Paige and Dom trying to act as if they couldn't care less. He nonchalantly leant back in his seat and ran his fingers through his hair, pushing rebel curls back from his forehead.

"Oh for goodness sake, Alex, get on with it," Paige erupted, tearing her eyes away from the spectacle that was causing all sorts of weird and wonderful sensations inside her.

"Ah, maybe not improving, no?" he laughed.

"You've had your fun now tell me what you found out." Paige's eyes flashed.

"Professor Watkins was murdered with a blow to the back of the head. It probably occurred yesterday evening but until the autopsy has been done we won't know for sure. The police have no idea why he was there at that time as work on the archaeology site finishes at 5pm. One theory is that he was meeting someone there."

Paige interrupted, "Duh! You think!"

Dom lifted a hand and placed it on her arm. "Let

the man explain," he said calmly.

Alex ignored Paige's interruption and continued. "The other theory is that he wanted to take something from the site without any witnesses."

"You mean steal something?" Dom asked.

"Not necessarily. Maybe borrow it. There are strict rules about logging each artefact found at the dig and where it should be stored. Perhaps he wanted to examine a particular item in detail?"

The image of Professor Watkins dressed as a Roman Emperor with coins running through his fingers flashed into Paige's mind. Her dream catcher felt warm against her throat. "Did he have any coins on him?" she asked.

"Why do you ask that?" Alex said, slowly releasing his breath. "How could you know?" He eyed her suspiciously.

"Know what?" she countered.

"About the coins. Who have you been talking to?" His voice was low and tense with a threatening edge.

Paige slumped. "No one. Alex I could tell you how I know but you wouldn't believe me," she said, her voice suddenly empty.

Dom intervened. "I think what Paige is intimating Alex is that she had a vision. Is that not so, *chérie*?"

Suddenly her head felt as if it was being held in a vice. It squeezed tighter and tighter. She saw coins whirling as if caught up in a tornado. Paige pressed her fingers to her forehead. The men watched motionless as she stumbled to her feet, fetched some ice cubes from the freezer and wrapped them in her serviette. With the cubes against her brow the pain began to ebb. The vision of the coins disappeared.

"Are you okay?" Dom asked, concern written all over his face.

"I will be. Give me a few moments." Gradually the tightness loosened. "Sorry, Alex. Carry on, please."

Alex had been staring at her, a worried frown creasing his forehead. He took a deep breath. He eyed her uncertainly. "What I'm about to tell you is confidential and only known to the chief investigating officers. Both Andrew Hammond and Professor Watkins were found with a Roman coin in their mouths. When the police found the first coin they contacted me. My psychological profiling skills can help when there is a signature or quirkiness to a murder. They thought maybe the first coin was a warning. Perhaps to keep quiet? Now with a coin placed in the mouth of each body, they are anxious to understand the significance."

"But did the Professor also have coins in his pockets?" Paige asked.

"His pockets were empty. They'd been turned inside out. His wallet was lying on the ground next to him. It still had his credit cards and £40 in cash inside it."

"Whoever emptied his pockets wasn't intent on stealing money then, but they could well have taken something else. Maybe an artefact," Dom said.

"Or coins," Paige added. She scratched her head. "If my memory serves me right, wasn't it a custom in Roman times to put a coin in a corpse's mouth to pay Charon, the ferryman, to carry the body across the River Styx to the underworld?"

"Yes, it was. Both for the Ancient Greeks and the Romans. I'm sure if Alfie was here, he'd be enthusing about the subject. It was great to catch up with him the other day. His fascination with Exeter's Roman history knows no bounds."

"If I need any clarification on the rituals connected with death and bodies in Roman times, do you think he'd help?" Alex asked.

"My dear boy, he'd bite your hand off." Dom paused noticing Alex's confused face. "It's an idiom which means to be very keen to do something."

"Okay. I'll let you know if I need his expertise. Obviously for the moment the information about the coins is not being disclosed to the public."

"Understood. My lips are sealed," Dom said with a grin.

"Mine too," said Paige pulling an imaginary zip across her lips.

Alex burst out laughing. "More strange English idioms, no? In Spanish we say *soy una tumba*."

"Literally that means being a tomb, doesn't it?" Paige asked.

"*Si, cariño.*"

"This linguistic tooing and froing is wonderful children but we should refocus," Dom said. "Alex, the coin signifies that the murders of Andrew Hammond and Professor Watkins are linked. Does this mean that Zac has moved further up the suspect list?"

"Yes. The police are still searching for him."

"Alex, I've been trying to reach his grandmother all day. Do you know if the police have contacted her?" Paige asked.

"I don't but I will find out. Do you think she could be in danger?"

"Maybe. Could the police do a welfare check on her?"

"*Ma chérie,* it's possible that the reason she's not answering her phone is that the police are questioning her." Dom added, "If she is in custody it may well be the safest place for her."

"If they are holding her and they access her phone, they'll see the texts and missed calls from me. Bummer," Paige muttered. "I'm sure DS Brown will only be too happy to interrogate me about that." A shadow of dismay crossed her face.

Chapter 23

The following morning Paige arrived at River Books to find Mary already there and tapping away at her computer.

"Morning. You're in early. Where's the fire?" Paige asked as she entered Mary's office.

"I've been checking the local news feeds and they're full of Professor Watkins' death."

"Sounds reasonable."

"What's not reasonable is that there are several articles claiming that Mica and the Professor were in a relationship. The headlines are *'Respected university professor linked to student dominatrix'*."

"Wow. That's going to stir things up a bit."

"And look," Mary said, pointing to images that showed Mica in her dominatrix outfit and the Professor together.

"Has that been photo-shopped?" Paige asked.

"Probably. However, the articles say that sources close to the student say that she boasted about being in a relationship with him."

Paige scratched her head. "Umm. We do know that Mica and the professor knew each other because we've seen the images of them together. We also know from those images that the professor received a coin from Mica and didn't seem too happy about it. From the footage we saw it didn't look like their connection was through Mica's work as a dominatrix. What we need to find out is who could have known about them meeting. And who wants the police to investigate Mica for the murder."

"The whole thing smells off," Mary said. "Unfortunately, from our rare dealings with the woman, we know that she has made a lot of enemies. The suspect pool of who'd do this to her is the size of the Atlantic ocean."

"Yep." Paige's phone began to ring. She pulled it out of her jacket inside pocket. "Speak of the devil," she said before answering. *"Hello, Mica. How are you?"*

"On my way to see you. Have you seen the headlines?" the girl shrieked. *"It's character assassination. You have to help me."*

"I'm not sure what I can do. You need to go to the police," Paige replied.

"Too late, I'm here," she said, as the door to the bookshop slammed opened and a swirling vortex burst in.

"Mica. Come and sit down," Paige said, as the young woman stormed across the floor.

Angry Mica was even more beautiful when her sculpted features were animated than normal Mica. Was there no justice in the world? Paige wondered.

"I'm being set up," Mica declared sitting down at a café table. I don't understand why the press would insinuate that Professor Watkins and I were in a relationship. I hardly knew the man."

Paige and Mary exchanged a fleeting look. The girl was lying. "As I said on the phone, you need to go to the police. They should be able to help."

"Yeah right. Like they helped with the videos?"

"Mica they have helped with the videos. They brought in the landlord who confessed to rigging up the spy cams. He gave the police the account passwords and they have disabled the site that was broadcasting the images on the web," Mary said, pushing her glasses up her nose as she spoke.

"But we're still in danger. That's two murders now connected to Zac. He's got to be the killer. Maybe he's behind this fake information?"

"Do you honestly believe that?" Paige asked. Mica shrugged her shoulders. "No one knows where Zac is. I imagine the police are putting all of their resources in to finding him," Paige said. "Why would Zac want to kill Professor Watkins? I thought that he got on well with him. Kevin even called him 'teacher's pet'."

Mica's face became a grotesque mask. "Him," she said with repugnance. "Don't trust a word he says."

"Why?"

"Because Kevin's got a chip the size of the Roman Empire on his scrawny shoulders. He was jealous of Zac being chosen instead of him to help with the cataloguing of finds at the dig. He lies about everything. If he said that Zac and the professor got on well I wouldn't believe it. It was probably the opposite." She snorted with disgust.

"Listen, Mica. Forget Kevin for the moment. How well did you know Professor Watkins?"

The girl's eyes flickered with indecision. "Not that well. I saw him around campus occasionally."

Mica's lie made Paige's choice easier. "I'm sorry, Mica. I can't help you anymore. You must go to the police."

"So much for you being a super sleuth," the young woman spat as she rose from her chair and stalked out of the shop.

Mary watched her go and turned to her younger sister whose face had darkened.

Paige said with a wince of distaste, "Can't stand liars, Mary. Did you see the precise moment when she chose to lie to me? It was written all over her face."

Mary nodded. "It's best we don't get involved with her, Paige. She's bad news or is it fake news?"

"Ha, ha." Paige applauded. "Good one. We tried to help her. We met with her flatmates but she didn't bother to turn up. And she never filled in the questionnaire I sent her. There's something about why she wanted us to get involved that I've missed." Paige stared off into space waiting for a light bulb moment. It didn't come.

Mary broke the spell. "Now let's get some work done and forget about that troublesome person."

"Agreed."

The sisters split up to get on with their tasks; Mary to the till and Paige upstairs to tidy the shelves in the foreign languages section.

Paige was walking home along the riverside footpath. Sprite was investigating the bushes with a hopeful air. With the night closing in, nocturnal creatures were emerging. The river flowed swiftly by as if in a hurry to reach the sea.

"Come on, Sprite. Let's get a move on," she said, as the terrier stopped yet again.

Sprite huffed her displeasure before trotting behind Paige who broke into a jog. A little bit of exercise always helped when she was feeling stressed. Riverside had been buzzing with news of Professor Watkins' death. Over the course of the afternoon she'd heard whispers about likely killers. Zac and Mica were the odds-on favourites. The main generator of these rumours was Violet, who'd been only too thrilled to let drop that she'd seen Mica angrily exiting River Books earlier that day. Contrary to what Violet had perhaps intended - that customers avoid River Books - there had actually been more customers than usual. Sales had been particularly brisk in the real crime section. Sunny had been run off her feet in the café and the food counter was seriously depleted by closing time. Paige, who always enjoyed getting one up on Violet, put on a little spurt.

As her phone began to vibrate inside her jacket, Paige slowed to a walk. She pulled it out and saw it was Alex.

"*Buenos tardes. Que tal?*" the Spaniard's rich voice asked. "*You sound out of breath.*"

"*I'm fine. I'm jogging home. Almost there. Can I ring you when I get in?*"

"*I can come round. I have news.*"

"*Perfect. Give us half an hour.*" Paige hung up and pocketed the phone again.

"Looks like we're going to have company, little one. I wonder if Rafa will be coming?" she said to Sprite.

Sprite gave her mistress an appraising look and then set off at pace towards home. Paige scrambled to keep up.

Chapter 24

Sprite danced in the doorway as Rafa entered the kitchen followed by Alex. The two dogs rolled around on the floor in a frenzied greeting as if they hadn't seen each other for years instead of days.

"Come in Alex," Paige said as he scrambled over bouncy canine bodies.

"I didn't think to ask whether you were staying for dinner," Paige said.

"Sorry, I can't this evening. I'm seeing someone at 8pm. However, I wanted to let you know the latest developments before the police contacted you."

Paige's heart beat raced. "What? Is it bad news?"

"Zac's grandmother has been taken into custody for refusing to divulge where her grandson is hiding."

"Maybe she doesn't know."

"They've got phone records proving she's been in regular contact with him. They had a tip off from a member of the public who saw Zac's photo on the local news that they'd seen him near a caravan park. Apparently, there are many sites in the area for tourists but obviously at this time of year they aren't open. The person became suspicious when they saw an older woman entering the park and talking to a red-headed youth. They reported that the woman seemed upset and they were worried for her safety. When they approached her the man ran off."

"I did wonder if he was hiding out where his mother

used to work. It's a place called *North Shores*." Paige omitted to add that she'd tried to enter the site illegally on her trip to Bideford. There was no point antagonising Alex.

Alex blinked. "How did you know the name of where his mother used to work?" His hands flapped away his question. "Oh, never mind. He wasn't there. He was staying at a site belonging to a friend of his grandmother."

"I tried ringing Zac's grandmother on several occasions," Paige said.

"I know. So do the police. They'll be coming to talk to you about that. That's why I came round. I wanted to warn you so that you wouldn't be surprised when DS Brown and DI Denton turn up."

"Thanks Alex. I'd sort of guessed that Sheila was being held by the police when she didn't get back to me. I suppose they think that Zac killed Professor Watkins?"

Alex nodded. Her shoulders slumped. She looked dejected. He wrapped an arm round her. "Hey, you're not going to give up, are you?" he said, giving her a squeeze. "Where's that feisty woman I like so much?" He looked pleased with himself.

A shadow of dismay crossed her face at the use of 'like' rather than 'love'. She brushed it aside. "Feisty? Where did you learn that word?" she asked intrigued.

He glowed. "It is good, no? One of my colleagues used it to describe one of his students. When he explained what it meant, I thought that is a good adjective for Paige."

She laughed. "It is Alex." Straightening her spine, she hooked a strand of hair behind her ear and said in a voice that sounded far more confident to her ears than she felt, "I'm not going to abandon my belief in Zac's innocence. I will continue to be feisty."

"*Estupendo*. Perfect. Now, I must go. I don't want to be late," he said, giving her cheek the lightest of strokes.

"I won't keep you. You don't want to be late for your friend or he'll wonder where you are."

"She, not he," Alex corrected her as he walked out the door followed by a reluctant Rafa who was unhappy to be leaving his playmate so soon.

Paige's body absorbed the feminine pronoun as if she'd been sucker punched. "Bye Alex," she whispered to the handsome Spaniard's retreating back.

Sprite sat in her basket, her amber eyes watching her mistress close the door behind the visitors. It was as if she picked up on Paige's confusion. Paige asked out loud, "Why did Alex call round? He could have told me about the police over the phone. Was it to see me or was it to let me know he was going out with a woman this evening?" She felt a knot of nerves in the pit of her stomach. Chastising herself for questioning his motives, she muttered to her terrier, "This is why I don't want a relationship. I begin to doubt myself. That man is my kryptonite. I'm not going to let him weaken me. Let's focus on the positives."

She paced the kitchen speaking out loud to her pet. "He's right, Sprite. I am feisty, curious - or just plain nosy - and adventurous - some would even say reckless. And what have I been doing? Nothing. Being passive. That's not me. I've let Mary do the internet searches. Yes, I know that's what she's good at but even so, I could have done more background digging. I thought that Zac's grandmother was keeping things back but I didn't press her on it. Yes, I checked out the caravan park but that was a quick once over. I've let Mica stomp all over me. I don't like the girl. I don't trust her. The normal me would have been following her, questioning those who know her but, apart from interviewing her housemates who are all petrified of her, I've done nothing. I should have been back to the house to snoop. I should have been up at the university to talk to her classmates. The same with Professor Watkins. He was acting suspiciously and I didn't find out why. Now I never will. I haven't even been to the dig in the Cloisters Garden - well, not in the daylight. I mean what has happened to me? Have I been trying to be a model citizen and play by the rules, so that Alex will like me more? Good grief. How pathetic." Paige straightened her spine and shouted, "Will the real feisty Paige Harper step forward!" Sprite gave an encouraging bark.

"Decision made. I'm back. I'm going to poke around at the dig, not just peer over the fence. It's late so I should be able to sneak around in the dark," she announced to Sprite and the empty kitchen.

Paige, dressed in her black rugby tracksuit, black beanie and black gloves, jogged along the pavement. This wasn't the time to be wearing her fuchsia pink jacket and matching bobble hat. For this occasion she needed to be dressed like an invisible ninja not a bright beacon. The evening air was crisp in her lungs as she covered the two miles to the centre of Exeter with a loping, long stride. She felt the thrill of being on a mission. Her heart did a little drum roll when she reached Cathedral Green. Extra fencing had been erected around the dig. Blue and white police tape with '*POLICE LINE DO NOT CROSS*' was draped round the site entrance. Paige glanced around her. The area was quiet. In the summer the place would have been heaving but it was winter and most people were wrapped up warm at home. Stealthily she toured the fencing looking for gaps. Near the back of the site away from prying eyes two fence panels had been pushed apart. Paige squeezed through. Immediately a sound to her right made her crouch down. Was it an animal? Urban foxes were often out at night, even in the city centre. Focusing on where the noise had come from, Paige saw a dark figure on their hands and knees with their back to her. Definitely not a fox. This was a human. A torch flicked on. The person picked up a trowel and, focusing the beam on the earth in front of them, began scraping. What were they doing? What should she do? She wasn't meant to be here and the other person digging illegally certainly wasn't. Should she challenge them? And say what? Call the police? How would she explain why she was trespassing at a crime scene? No, no police.

Silently she watched as the person plucked what looked like some sort of pouch from the ground, brushed off dirt and placed it in a clear plastic sachet before cramming it in their pocket. Shoving the trowel in their jeans' back pocket the individual stood up and turned around. As they swung round the beam of their torch caught Paige full in the face, dazzling her. Temporarily blinded she felt more than saw the figure begin to sprint towards her. This wasn't the moment to hang around. She sprang up and zipped through the gap, taking a few seconds to pull one of the panels closer to the other behind her to narrow the exit. The fence panels clattered when the pursuer crashed into them as they grappled to get out of the reduced gap. Paige ran like her life depended on it. Conscious of the pounding steps behind her, she hotfooted it down through Southernhay, raced across Western Way and disappeared into the side streets of St Leonards. No way was she going to run along Topsham Road where she'd be in full view and easier to follow. In Bull Meadow she allowed herself to stop for a breather.

Leaning against a tree trunk in the shadows she scanned the area to make sure she'd shaken off her hunter. With ears on high alert she picked up nothing except for her laboured breath. She relaxed a little. Still keeping to the back streets Paige hurried home. She'd escaped. The big question was whether the person with the flashlight had recognised her. She hadn't been able to see their silhouette clearly enough when they were kneeling with their back to her to work out if it was someone she knew. And when they shone their torch in her eyes she'd been blinded by the light. And, of course, she'd needed to get the hell out of there and quick.

    Later, sitting in the living room curled up on the sofa with a warm cup of tea in her hands, Paige closed her eyes and visualised the scene at the archaeology excavations. The figure had been tall and slim. She hadn't been able to see whether it was a man or a woman. The form had been a black androgynous silhouette. Her nose twitched as she remembered a scent that triggered a faint olfactory memory. It was vaguely familiar. She'd definitely smelt it recently. But where? She knew better than to force the memory to the surface. The answer would come to her eventually. She refocused on her visualisation. Everything had happened quickly. The hand holding the torch had been wearing a glove. The individual's face had been covered with a balaclava, giving her no clues as to skin colour. The trainers popped into her mind. Being sporty, Paige was an expert on trainers. She could spot the difference between brands from fifty paces. The individual had been wearing Solar Glide trainers with Gore-Tex written in orange across the top. It was a breakthrough of sorts. Unfortunately, those particular sports shoes were available for both men and women. Placing her tea on the table next to her, Paige jotted down the details in her notebook while they were still fresh in her mind.

"Sprite, I need to find someone who is tall and thin, wears Solar Glide trainers with orange lettering and whose scent is familiar," Paige said.

When Paige had returned, Sprite refused to acknowledge her. She'd been in a sulk. First, Rafa had come round and left almost immediately and then Paige had abandoned her to go off on an adventure on her own. Now finally Sprite sauntered out of her basket to come and sit next to her mistress. Paige decided that this was a break in hostilities and gave her a doggy treat from the stash in the table drawer. "Are we friends again?" she asked. Her pet paused mid-chew as if seriously considering the question. "Hey, I did explain why I had to leave you behind and I've just given you a treat. Surely I'm forgiven?" In response Sprite finished chewing her treat and flopped onto her back to offer up her belly for a rub. "Okay, that's a fair price to pay for your forgiveness," Paige said, bending down to give her a stroke.

Chapter 25

Paige arrived at River Books with Sprite the next morning. She'd decided not to mention her previous evening's reconnaissance mission to Mary. Her big sister would only give her a hard time about being irresponsible and reckless whereas Paige liked to think of her excursion to the site as showing initiative and daring. Oh, she'd had enough of playing safe. Paige was going to turbo-charge her investigation. Her first task this morning was to talk to Olivia.

"Good morning, Olivia. How are you today?" Paige smiled at her most responsible and hard-working employee.

"Fine, thanks, Paige. And you?"

"Great. Listen can I ask you when you next have a lecture with Mica?"

Olivia blinked at the question. "This afternoon at 5pm."

"That's quite late. Does that mean that some students skive off?"

"Not normally. We're not first years. I'd like to think we realise how valuable lectures are."

"That's me told," Paige joked.

A faint blush rode up the young girl's neck. "I didn't mean..." she stuttered.

"Hey, just winding you up." Paige winked.

"Oh, okay. Can I ask why you want to know?"

"Sure. In view of recent developments in the news I

was hoping to catch up with some of her classmates. I imagine that the rumour mill will be running at full speed and loose lips are manna from heaven for an investigator."

"I thought you and she had fallen out. She was mouthing off about you being worse than useless." Olivia lowered her gaze as she said this.

Paige shrugged her shoulders. "Sounds like Mica," she said in a quiet voice. "Anyway, could you spread the word that I'll be in the student cafeteria after your lecture ready to buy a coffee for anyone who'd like to chat with me?"

"Okay. Should I tell them not to tell Mica?" Olivia twitched nervously.

"Be discreet but don't worry if she overhears. I can handle her. I'm doing this for Zac. After Professor Watkins' murder the police are convinced he's the murderer. Any information I can pick up that gives me a better understanding of Mica's interactions with Professor Watkins could be useful."

"Do you think she had something to do with his death?" Olivia's eyes widened to owl-like proportions.

"Honestly, I don't know. What I am convinced of is that there was more to her relationship with the deceased Professor than she's letting on. Tell your fellow classmates that I'll be easy to spot. I'll be wearing pink Converse and my fuchsia pink coat will be hanging over the back of my chair."

"I will, Paige. You can count on me."

"Thanks, Olivia. Now we'd better get back to work before the manager has a word with us," Paige said, grinning as Mary made her way across the shop floor towards them.

"What are you plotting Paige?" Mary asked as Olivia scurried away.

"Nothing. Just filling Olivia in on the new stock

we've ordered."

Mary nudged her glasses up her nose and fixed her younger sister with a stare that was screaming *I don't believe you*. "Good. The books should arrive tomorrow." She turned and walked back towards the till where a customer was waiting to pay for their purchase.

At 6pm Paige was seated in the student cafeteria at a table facing the entrance. At five past the hour Olivia walked in with a small group. She gestured in Paige's direction. Paige waved.

Olivia came over. "You're lucky. Mica wasn't in class today so more people are willing to talk to you knowing that she's not here to bully them afterwards for speaking with you," she said.

Paige stood up and greeted the small group of four girls and two boys with a "What can I get you all?"

"It's easier if we go and order ourselves and you pay," a vivacious girl said.

"Deal. Olivia if you can guard our table, I'll go to the counter with the others. What can I get you?"

"Okay. I'll have a hot chocolate, please."

"Any snacks?"

"No, just a hot chocolate."

"The whole works? Chantilly cream? Marshmallows?" Paige asked.

Olivia licked her lips. "Yes to both. Thank you."

The students draped their coats over chair backs and trooped after Paige. Once their orders for coffee combinations that made the mind boggle had been magicked up, the group settled round the table.

Paige began. "Firstly, thank you all for agreeing to speak with me. I'm the owner of River Books down on the quay. As some of you may know, my employee,

Zac Jones, has disappeared. He shares a house with Mica in Heavitree. He's also on the archaeology course with Professor Watkins. And he was working at the cathedral Cloister Gardens dig. At the moment, the police are convinced that he killed the man found dead in his room and Professor Watkins. I won't believe that Zac is a murderer until I have solid evidence."

"I don't know Zac," a girl said. "I thought you wanted to know about Mica?"

"I do. However, lots of things in Zac's life overlapped with Mica's. That's why I'm interested in any gossip you have about Mica and Professor Watkins."

"Because she's not here today people are saying that she's been arrested. I think that Miss *'I'm better than you'*, just doesn't have the b…, oops sorry - courage to face us," one of the young male students sneered.

"Mica's a piece of work. She acts all high and mighty as if she's superior to us mere mortals. Yes, she's stunningly beautiful on the outside but inside she's ugly," said a girl with short, blonde hair. "Did you know that she works as a dominatrix? I mean, how awful is that?" Her voice squeaked with exaggerated outrage but the spark of curiosity in her eyes told a different story.

"Yeah, and I heard she's been hired by some of the lecturers," added a boy who looked about fourteen but had to be at least twenty. "That's why she gets away with handing in her essays and translations late."

"Can you give me the names of lecturers who are more lenient with her than others?"

The boy hesitated. "Err. Well…"

"We all know who they are," piped up the Asian girl with straight long black hair. "Dr Fulbright and Dr Havers. Both men seem to go out of their way to help her. The women lecturers are afraid of her too but with them if they challenge her she plays the race card," she said, a note of contempt in her voice.

"Thanks. I'll look into Dr Fulbright and Dr Havers." Paige held up her hand as concerned looks were exchanged. "Don't worry, I know how to be discreet - contrary to what my vibrant fashion choices may convey," she added with a laugh. The tension among the group dissipated. "Now what about Professor Watkins?"

The girl with short blonde hair spoke up. "The other evening I was visiting my friend, Ivy. She shares the same student digs as Mica."

"I know Ivy," Paige said encouragingly.

"We were getting ready to go out when we heard raised voices coming from Mica's room. We decided to listen. Ivy and Mica hate each other and Ivy wanted to collect any ammunition she could use against Mica." The girl paused.

Hearing this Paige was reminded of the nickname that Mica used for Ivy - creeper.

"You've got to understand that Mica was really mean to Ivy," the girl insisted in justification of their snooping.

"I understand," Paige said in an appeasing tone. "What did you overhear?"

"They were shouting at each other. The man was saying where had she found it. Mica was saying it was left outside her door. He asked who left it there. She said she didn't know. It could have been either of the boys on his course. That's when we realised it must be a lecturer she was arguing with. We waited to see who the man was. We didn't recognise him at the time but we found out later it was Professor Watkins. He stormed out of Mica's room slamming the door behind him."

Paige soaked up this information. Mica had been

talking about the boys on Professor Watkins course living at the digs. The problem was that both Zac and Kevin lived there. "They didn't mention the boy's name or his nickname?"

"No."

"Did you get the feeling the argument was about Mica's job as a dominatrix?" Paige asked, changing the direction of her questioning.

"I don't know. If they were acting out a scenario with Mica being the dominatrix wouldn't the professor have been playing a subservient role?"

"I don't know. It's not my specialist subject," she said which earned her a collective guffaw. Paige had a good idea that the argument had been about the coin she'd seen Mica handing to Professor Watkins on the recording.

"Oh, by the way," the girl added, "We weren't the only ones listening in. I saw Kevin quickly shut the kitchen door as we left the house."

Paige filed that snippet away for later. "What about Zac? Was he there?"

"I couldn't say. I didn't see him." The girl shook her head.

"You've been very helpful. Has anyone else got anything to share?" Paige asked.

The following half hour was filled with general grumblings about Mica and her hold over their lecturers but no extra information about her relationship with Professor Watkins came to light.

Paige thanked them all and the group broke up to go their separate ways.

As she made her way home, Paige reflected on what she'd learnt. She needed time to digest it all and work out her next plan. Things were hotting up.

Chapter 26

The news broke on the national news early on Thursday morning. Zachary Jones had been named as the prime suspect in connection with the murders of Andrew Hammond and Professor Marcus Watkins. His face was splashed all over the newspaper headlines. The news item urged the public to get in touch if they saw him, but not to approach him as he could be dangerous. A cold shiver ran all the way down Paige's spine. Could she have read him so wrong? Was Zac a ruthless killer? The news bulletin had called Andrew Hammond's death a murder. Did that mean then that the police finding a coin in his mouth had become public knowledge? She'd have to find out. The worst thing was that River Books was mentioned as being Zac's place of employment.

As she prepared for work Paige thought about the implications of Zac being named as a murder suspect for River Books. Her stomach cramped at what lay ahead for her shop. Could their reputation survive this latest assault? It was going to be a media circus there today. She picked up her phone and rang Mary.

"Hi Mary, have you heard the news?"

"Yes. We're going to have a difficult day. Which of us is going to manage the media?"

"I can. You know I've got the interpersonal skills."

"But you've also got an impulsive and unpredictable character. Will you be able to keep

your cool when they ask you uncomfortable questions?"

"Call me ice cube." Paige joked.

"Paige," Mary warned. *"I'm serious."*

"Mary, I've got this. Do you want me to bring Dom along?"

Mary said,*"Why that poor man took it upon himself to become your protector, I'll never understand."*

Paige laughed and replied, *"My natural charisma?"*

Mary snorted and ended the call.

Paige and Sprite walked over to Dom's. Going round the back of the house, Paige tapped on the door. She heard the click of Dom's walking stick on the kitchen slabs. The key turned in the lock and the door swung open.

"Chérie. Bonjour. Lovely to see you." His dark brown eyes scanned her face with concern. "Not that I'm not delighted to have this early morning visit from you both, but what's wrong?"

"Dom, Zac's photo is on all the front pages. The police have issued a statement naming him as the main suspect for the murders. Unfortunately, the articles mention River Books as being where he worked. We're going to be overrun with media types. Mary and I wondered whether you'd come to give us moral support. I'll be handling the reporters." Paige paused as a barely concealed grin flashed across Dom's face. "Mary felt that you would add some gravitas. I'm sure she thinks that you being there will rein in my - and I quote - *'impulsive and unpredictable character'.*"

"She can always dream," he said with a wry smile. "However, I will rise to the challenge and ride to your rescue, *ma chérie.*"

Paige watched this man, who was so precious to her, as he moved gingerly leaning hard on his stick to take a seat. "Dom, is your hip playing you up?"

"Just a niggle. I've taken some painkillers. They'll take effect shortly," he snapped, his hawk-like features challenging her to disagree.

"If you're sure," she said.

"I'm certain." His gaze brokered no argument.

Stubbornness was a trait they both shared and Paige knew when not to insist. "Lovely," she said. "I'll come and pick you up at 8.30."

"Perfect. Now off you go and get yourself ready," Dom said, shooing Paige and Sprite out the back door.

At five minutes to nine Paige, Dom and Sprite made their way across the quay to the bookshop. Riverside was heaving with reporters. Gathered outside River Books was a local TV crew. The sound man was carrying a long mic that looked like a furry grey animal was impaled on it. Another man was shouldering a camera. A young woman presenter was practising her live broadcast smile. Paige and Dom nodded politely and asked to pass. A mic was shoved under Dom's nose.

"Sir, what can you tell us about your employee Zachary Jones being hunted by the police for a double murder? Are you shocked?" the young blonde-haired woman with impeccable make-up asked, her voice squeaking with excitement.

"We will be making an announcement at 9.15," Dom said, as they squeezed inside the door that Mary was holding ajar for them.

"Thank goodness you're here. I managed to scramble inside but I don't know how Sunny is getting on," Mary sighed.

"There she is," Paige said, spotting the petite

Nepalese woman weaving her way through the media crowd. "I'll get the door." She swiftly opened it and let Sunny pass inside before slamming it firmly shut behind her.

"We need to establish what we're going to say," Mary said, regaining some of her control. "Dom, any ideas?"

Dom pulled out a pale blue sheet of Basildon Bond writing paper. "I've noted down a statement." He unfolded the paper covered in beautiful script that had obviously been written with his Mont Blanc fountain pen and said, "We, the staff at Rivers Books, were saddened to learn that our employee, Zachary Jones, has been named as the main suspect in connection with the murders of Andrew Hammond and Professor Watkins. Professor Watkins was a respected academic, whose contribution to the field of archaeology will be sorely missed. We extend our condolences to both families. We believe in the innocence of Zachary. Nevertheless, we will continue to support the police in their efforts to solve these two murders, which have shocked our local community."

Paige gave him an encouraging smile. "Sounds good to me. Mary?"

"Yes. That's good. But, I don't think we should state that we believe in Zac's innocence. We could end up looking foolish if he turns out to be the killer."

"Mary, do you really believe that?" Paige asked aghast.

"Honestly, I don't know. He's a strange lad. You admitted that yourself. And there were those incidents of theft." Mary crossed her arms. Paige understood her sister's body language. She was still angry about Zac stealing from Beth.

"*Chérie,* Mary is correct. It would be stupid to publicly nail our sail to the mast." He held up his hand as Paige opened her mouth to protest. "I'm not saying that we can't still believe in his innocence, just not announce it to the world. If we proclaim that we don't believe he's guilty, I'm sure that DS Brown would see it as a declaration of war. It wouldn't help the poor boy in the long run."

Paige raked her fingers through her long blond hair. "You've both got a point. So I won't say anything about him not being guilty. I'll speak about him being a good employee and an enthusiastic archaeology student. Okay?"

"Perfect. Now," said Dom, checking his wristwatch, "Time to face our audience." He brushed imaginary fluff off the shoulder of his green tweed jacket, readjusted his mauve pocket handkerchief, checked that his trouser cuffs were sitting just so atop his brown Oxford brogues and walked purposefully to the shop's main entrance. At the door he and Paige walked out together and stood side by side. Light bulbs flashed in their faces. The young TV woman approached. The camera man took up position. The sound man waved his furry animal mic near their faces.

"Good morning. I'm Professor Dominic Giraud and," he paused and turned to Paige, who said, "I'm Paige Harper, owner of River Books. We have prepared a statement. We will take questions afterwards."

Dom gave a commanding performance reading out their communication. As he finished, Violet, dressed in a kingfisher blue coat, pushed her way through the crowd to the front. Her hair was immaculate. Paige would wager she'd had it done especially for this occasion, which would explain why she hadn't been here earlier to greet the Press. Paige had been surprised by her absence. Violet's pale pink face powder and vermilion lipstick had been expertly applied. She wriggled her beach ball-shaped body between the professor and Paige. Opening her arms so wide that she almost took out Paige's eye, she began her speech.

"Good morning. I'm Violet Tucker, President of the Riverside Association. First, may I extend my condolences to the families of both murder victims. I can assure the Press that the members of our close-knit community are shocked and upset that a part-time employee is implicated in a double murder. We will do everything in our power to assist the police with their investigation." She beamed at the camera.

The TV reporter smiled at Violet. "Thank you, Madam President. I'm sure that the police will be grateful for any help your members can offer them. Now if I may, I'd like to ask Miss Harper about her employee," the woman said.

Violet was not going to give up her place in the spotlight easily. "You may ask me questions. I know everything that happens on Riverside," Violet insisted.

"Mrs Tucker, I really do need to talk to Miss Harper," the TV presenter said. She angled her body towards Paige, turning away from Violet.

"If you're certain, dear," Violet said. "I'm the Outreach and Liaison Officer for the Custom House." She waved a chubby bejewelled hand in the direction of the ancient white building with a cannon standing proud in front of it. "When you've finished with Paige, you come over to see me." This last line was delivered as a command by Violet before she swept away on her shiny court shoes towards her place of work. The crowd parted like the Red Sea before her.

The TV woman blanched and muttered under her breath something about interfering busybodies. Gathering herself together she said to Paige, "Sorry about that. Miss Harper what can you tell us about your employee, Zachary Jones? Did you suspect he was a murderer?" Her eyes glittered with a flash of malice.

"Zac is a good employee. I am not prepared to comment on an on-going police investigation."

"But surely, there were signs? Wasn't he a thief?"

Paige counted to ten. Someone had been running their mouth off. She wouldn't be baited. "I repeat, he's a good employee. He's been with us for just over six months on a part-time basis."

"I heard he was employed to cover for you when you play for the local rugby team. Is that true?"

"Yes. I play for Riverside Ladies."

"Oh, you were involved in a murder there, weren't you?" An excitable buzz fizzed off the reporter.

"Unfortunately, there was a death at the club," Paige replied.

"You're a murder magnet..." the woman began before Paige cut her off.

"Show some respect," she growled. "Now, if you have any other questions, Professor Giraud will be happy to assist you." Paige turned her back on the presenter and strode into the shop.

Inside River Books was crawling with reporters and the curious. She caught Mary's eye. Her sister gave her an imperceptible nod and motioned to the one free table in the café. At least the café was doing a good trade Paige thought as she slid on to a chair where Mary stood guard. Sunny appeared from the throng, her progress traceable by the jangling of the bangles she always wore on her wrists. She placed a large mug of Assam tea and a plate containing a raspberry and almond slice on the table.

"Here you are, Paige. This will help," she said. The young woman was dressed in a turquoise and yellow kurta sawal today.

"Thanks, Sunny. You're a saviour. I just managed to

keep my cool. I thought I was going to thump that reporter when she called me a murder magnet. That would have looked good on the lunchtime news, wouldn't it? Thank goodness Dom was there. He diverted the reporter's attention with, '*May I have a word?*' in that imperious voice that has seen many an adversary crumble to dust. Then he moved towards her swinging his walking stick slightly more than was strictly necessary. She shrank back as if he were waving a sword around."

"I'm glad that he had your back," Mary said. "The last thing River Books needs is its owner flattening a local TV celebrity live from the quay." She tapped Paige's arm. "I'm proud of you."

"Wow. Thanks. Once I've drunk my tea, eaten my cake, I'll take questions sitting here. Oh, it looks like my knight in shining armour has finished defending my honour," she said, as Dom made his way towards her a victor's smile stretched wide across his face. She patted the chair next to her and said, "Come and take a load off those plates of meat, Guv."

Dom shuddered. "At times, *ma chérie*, you have an appallingly eclectic choice of vocabulary. Since when do you use Cockney rhyming slang?"

"Just lightening the mood, Dom. Thanks for stepping in there. That reporter was trying to provoke me. I did the right thing. I walked away."

"You did. She's with Violet now. The tenacity of that woman is something to behold. As soon as she saw the crew making their way towards the car park Madam President swooped in and ushered them into the Custom House."

"There is some justice in the world after all," Paige said with a satisfied smirk.

Chapter 27

The media circus had moved on by midday. Paige was surprised to see Zac's flatmates, including Mica, sitting in the café having lunch. They hadn't seemed to her to be a group who chose to socialise together, yet here they were. Why? There was only one way to find out. Paige walked over to their table.

"Hello. Good to see you all again," she said a welcoming smile glued to her face.

"We'd bargained on the media being here. We decided to come and see if there were any developments. Fortunately, the press didn't recognise us as being Zac's housemates so we were able to observe them without being pestered with annoying questions," Kevin said.

Paige looked at the boy she knew Mica called 'cheese straw'. There was a difference in his demeanour. Today he looked more confident, less cowed by Mica's presence.

Mica glared at him. "Speak for yourself. One of the gutter press reporters tried to corner me. I told him to get lost, although I may have used slightly stronger language than that." Her mouth tilted up at one side in a smirk of malicious amusement. "He didn't budge. However, once I'd threatened to chain him up in my torture chamber he legged it."

"Do you have a torture chamber?" Ivy asked with bravado.

Mica sneered. "What do you think?"

"I don't know," she answered.

"Well, when you do want to find out, let me know and I'll give you a guided tour." Mica glared at her with antagonism.

Ivy dropped her gaze.

Suddenly the shop bell clanged loudly. Paige twisted round to see DI Denton and DS Brown marching into the shop followed by a posse of constables. The group headed in her direction. "Here we go," she whispered under her breath. The inspector, a big bear of a man, looked like an angry grizzly whose hibernation had been disturbed. He came to a halt in front of her. Paige braced herself. Surveying the table he said, "Mica Murrel, I'm arresting you in connection with the deaths of Andrew Hammond and Professor Watkins. My DS is going to read you your rights. Do you understand?"

As Mica looked wildly around her as if searching for an escape route, Paige caught a glimpse of Kevin's triumphant face before he forced himself to lower his gaze. His eyes had been gleefully drinking in the downfall of his arch nemesis. DS Brown was reciting, "Mica Murrel I'm arresting you on suspicion of...."

Paige zoned out. How had the police known to come to River Books at this precise time to arrest Mica? Had it been a tip off from the gutter press reporter that Mica had threatened? Or did Kevin have something to do with it? He'd certainly looked pleased with himself. But that just might be because Mica was in trouble. Something didn't stack up.

The afternoon dragged after the excitement of the press free-for-all and the arrest of Mica. At closing time Paige and Sprite set off for the car park to make their way home. Dom had left River Books after eating lunch in the café, heading in the direction of the Custom House. Paige imagined that he was going to try and find out what Violet had said to the TV news reporter. She wished him luck. Violet, like Dom, was a gossip. Both of them prided themselves in outwitting the other. She'd ring him later to find out who had won that particular battle.

Once she was home Paige rang Alex.

"*Alejandro, que tal? How are you?*" she asked.

"*Paige, I'm currently searching Mica's accommodation. I'll call you back later, yes?*"

"*Yes, please.*"

"*I must go. Speak later.*" He hung up.

Feeling thwarted Paige slumped in front of the television. The news was full of the search for Zac and of Mica's arrest. The reporters were offering theories. One of the more outrageous was that Zac and Mica had been working together. That couldn't be true, surely? Not unless both of them were very good actors.

There had to be a connection between Zac and Mica. The obvious one was that they both lived in the same house. Could it be that simple? Paige had been side-tracked by Zac's disappearance. Once the police had arrested the landlord, charged him and then released him, she'd put the landlord out of her mind. She leaped up from the sofa and fetched her laptop. Scrolling through the information Mary had prepared she found his name and address. Dave Allen, 10, Cludens Close. Surely it wasn't too late to call round? What excuse could she use for turning up on his doorstep unannounced? Grabbing an SD card similar to those that had been hidden in the spy cams, she stuffed it in her pocket and picked up her car keys.

Sprite eyed her from the comfort of her basket. Paige bent down and stroked her pet. "Won't be long," she cooed. The dog grunted in appreciation of the caress and then laid her head back down in her snug bed. Paige grabbed her phone and put in her pocket.

Stepping outside the front door, she had a moment's hesitation before saying to herself, "This is a good idea." She imagined the little imp on her right shoulder giving her a thumbs up while the angel perched on her left one shook its head in dismay.

The drive to Alphington was relatively straightforward at this time in the evening. Twenty minutes later Paige pulled up in front of a detached house in Cludens Close. Lights shone from inside the immaculate building. Its condition was in sharp contrast to the exterior of the student house the man owned in Heavitree. Paige climbed out of the Mini. Her palms felt clammy. She rang the doorbell and heard it chime inside. Her heart hammered in her chest. As the door began to swing open she put her hand in her pocket and pressed the record option on her mobile phone.

A stocky man in his mid-fifties opened the door. "Yeah? Can I help you?" he said with a strong Devon accent.

"Good evening. I'm sorry to bother you but I think I may have something of yours," Paige said, pulling the SD card out of her bag.

The man's eyes shifted nervously. "Don't know what you mean," he said.

"Oh, I think you do. Heavitree student house. Spy cams. SD cards. Ringing any bells yet, Dave?" Paige asked.

He snatched at the SD card. Paige pulled away sharply. "No, you don't," she said, amazed that her voice sounded calm.

"What do you want?" Dave asked in a resigned tone. "Look, I've had enough trouble from the police. I never should have done what I did. It was dumb." His head drooped. "How much do you want?"

"I don't want money. I want information."

He slumped. "What do you want to know?"

"Why did you set up cameras in that student house in Heavitree?" A pulse quickened in her throat as she waited for the answer.

"I set cameras up in several of my houses. Do you know how hard it is for landlords these days? Mortgage rates through the roof. More regulations added every day. Not to mention more demanding students than in the old days." His body folded in on itself. There was no fight left in him.

"I know, but was there a specific reason for choosing the Heavitree house?"

"Oh, I'm fed up with all of this. I wish I'd never accepted that bloody money," he said raking his fingers through his thin grey hair. "I was contacted and offered lots of cash if I recorded everything that went on in that particular house."

Nervous prickles ran up her spine as Paige asked, "Who paid you?"

"I don't know. Honest," he said, as Paige looked at him in disbelief. "I don't know how they knew about my scam. They approached me and asked me to install the cameras in that house."

"You put them in later? Not at the beginning of the academic year?" Paige asked.

"No, a few weeks later. Mid-October maybe."

"How did it work?"

"Andy left copies of the recordings in the cupboard under the stairs next to the meters and collected the money in cash from there in brown envelopes."

"That sounds too convenient. You really have no idea who it was?" Paige stared at him hard.

He shook his head. "Nah. Had to be someone who

lived in the house or was connected to one of the tenants though. Otherwise how could they put stuff in the cupboard?"

"Did you suspect anyone?"

"That black girl. She's loaded and she seems the type to me who wouldn't shy away from a bit of blackmail."

Paige drew a hand across her forehead. "If it was Mica, the police will find out. They've just arrested her. Did you tell the police about the money?"

He paled. "Don't be daft. I was in enough trouble, weren't I? And with Andy being killed, I thought his death might be connected to it all. We've been mates since school. I was the brains and he was the muscle. Good with his hands. Could fix anything could Andy." His eyes glistened with unshed tears. "We made a good team." The man looked genuinely heartbroken.

"I'm sorry for the death of your friend. Thank you for speaking with me," Paige said.

"Does me good to get it off my chest, like. So, you gonna give me that SD card?"

"Of course, although it's blank." Paige waited for an angry reaction.

Instead the man smiled sadly, defeat emanating from every pore. "Got me. Why are you so interested anyway?"

"I found your friend's body. And I don't believe Zac Jones killed him."

"If it wasn't him, who was it?"

"That's what I intend to find out," Paige said.

"Let me know when you do," he said. "I'll kill the bugger." With that he turned round and shut the door firmly behind him.

Chapter 28

That evening when Paige returned home from visiting Dave, the landlord, she'd convinced herself that Mica must be the murderer. She felt invigorated and confident that she would be able to prove Mica's guilt and Zac's innocence. Tomorrow she'd go over all the information she had collected during these last three weeks. Now though she needed to take Sprite out for her last walk before settling down for the night.

Sprite had roused herself from her basket and was waiting impatiently by the door as Paige unhooked the lead and attached it to her collar.

"Okay, young lady, let's get going. I'm buzzing after my daring mission, which much to my astonishment actually paid off. I need to walk off the adrenaline before turning in for the night or I won't sleep a wink."

The pair set off down the road. The street lights glowed a misty yellow in the gloom. Cars passed sporadically, their headlights washing over Paige and Sprite triggering memories of the attempted hit and run. The police had come up empty. There had been no trace of the car on traffic cams and the paint scrapings from the wall had turned out to be from a popular model of black Mercedes. They turned down a side road and completed the walk round the block in half an hour. Paige felt more relaxed and ready for a restorative sleep. As she was locking the back door a taxi turned into Dom's drive. Unable to see who the passenger was because of the high fence, she resolved to ask Dom tomorrow.

Friday morning Paige set off for work armed with renewed positivism. She was going to solve this case and get Zac cleared.

"Morning, Mary, how are you?" Paige asked, fairly skipping into the shop.

"You're very chirpy this morning. What's up?" Mary asked, eyeing her sister suspiciously.

"Well, now that you ask, I've got some news. Last night I paid Zac's landlord a visit."

Mary's eyebrows shot up. "You what! What on earth possessed you? You called on a man who's been involved in a murder investigation. Please tell me you took Alex with you?"

Paige studied her shoes. "Not exactly," she said.

"But you told him or Dom where you were going, didn't you?"

"Err, not quite."

"Give me patience." Mary spoke the words in a low, pained voice.

"It was fine, honestly Mary. He was quite nice with me actually," Paige said quickly.

"Oh, that's alright then! A murderer is on the loose and you go waltzing off in the middle of the night on your own to speak to a man who owns the house where one of those murders took place. And you didn't let anyone know what you were doing but he was nice to you," Mary snapped.

"When you put it like that, it might seem a tad irresponsible."

Mary exploded. "A tad irresponsible? It was a lot more than a tad. It was…"

Paige interrupted her sister's tirade. "Look we both know that if I'd told anyone they would have tried to stop me…"

"With good reason. Have you got a death wish? In the last few weeks, you've had someone follow you and someone try to run you over with their car. Have you no concept of danger?"

Paige zoned out. Thank goodness she hadn't told Mary about going to the Cathedral dig the other night and being chased.

"Are you listening?" Mary shouted.

Paige fell back to earth. "Yes. Sorry. I did find out some facts from Dave which point to Mica being the killer."

"Dave? You're on first name terms with the man now?" Mary's normal pale complexion was turning an alarming shade of puce.

Paige's heart pinched with guilt. She hadn't wanted to upset her sister. Trying to placate her, she said, "I'm truly sorry. It was unimaginably stupid of me."

"Yes it was." The tension in Mary's shoulders relaxed a little. "Let's get to work. You can tell me over lunch. We've been putting on quite a floor show for our customers," Mary said quietly, nodding towards a suspiciously large number of people who just happened to be browsing the shelves nearby.

Paige grinned widely at the curious faces and performed a bow. "That's all for now folks. Our mini drama is over."

Mary hung her head and covered her eyes with her hand. "You're incorrigible," she sighed and made a beeline for her office.

Sunny beckoned Paige over, her bangles singing a tune as she motioned to her. "Paige, remember you promised us all to not put yourself in danger?"

"I'm sorry Sunny. I did learn useful information."

Sunny pinned her dark, chocolate gaze on Paige's

face. "That is no excuse. I'm disappointed in you, my friend."

Paige felt herself shrink. Sunny was always her cheerleader. Paige turned away ashamed of herself. Her earlier bravado evaporated like an early morning mist on the river.

At 11am Dom strode into River Books with Alfie Jeffreys in tow. Paige rushed over to say hello.

"Dom, it's lovely to see you and you too, Dr Jeffreys."

"*Ma chérie*, Alfie heard of Professor Watkins' death and wanted to be here to help if necessary. He's staying with me," Dom said.

"Ah, that explains the taxi last night then," Paige said.

"That's great deduction, dear Watson," Dom said, doffing an imaginary cap.

"I aim to please, Sherlock." She gave a curtsy.

Alfie roared with laughter. "You make a wonderful double act."

"Well, thank you, Dr Jeffreys. How long are you staying?" Paige asked.

"Paige," Dom remonstrated. "The poor man has only just arrived and you're already asking him when he's leaving."

Archie held up his hand. "Dom, it's a perfectly natural question." He turned to Paige and said, "I intend to offer my services to the police as an expert in all things Roman." He puffed out his portly chest like a courting pigeon.

"Come on, let's see what gastronomical delights Sunita has for us today," Dom said, ushering Alfie towards a table.

"Catch you later," Paige said.

Customers kept Paige busy so that she was surprised when Mary came to ask her if she was ready for lunch. She hadn't noticed the morning pass.

"I thought we'd go the Smugglers. We can speak there without being overheard," Mary said.

"Good idea. I'll fetch my coat and I'm all yours." Paige bounded up the stairs to her office and fetched her coat and scarf. Sprite rose to her feet and shook herself. "Come on," Paige said, "Judd's always happy to see you. You can charm him into giving us a good table."

As they entered the pub, Sprite sashayed up to Judd, who bent down to stroke her proffered belly. "Hello, gorgeous," he cooed. Standing up he smiled at Paige and Mary and said, "And how are you two beautiful ladies?"

Paige lightly punched his arm. It was like hitting an iron anvil. "Flattery will get you everywhere, Judd Petherick. We're hungry and looking for a quiet table to have a sisterly *tête à tête*."

"Hi Judd, it's a working lunch. Could we have that table over there?" Mary said, pointing to a table in the far corner of the dining area.

"Of course. If you go and take a seat I'll get you some drinks. What would you like?"

"A sparkling apple juice for me, please Judd," Paige said.

"And a bottle of mineral water, please."

"Understood."

The sisters waited until their drinks had been delivered and they'd given their food orders before getting down to business.

"I'm still angry with you," Mary said. "Your foolish jaunt better have been worth it."

Over a lunch of a Ploughman's for Mary and burger and chips for Paige, the younger sister explained what she'd learnt from Dave. That he'd been paid to install spy cams in that particular house. That he'd given copies of the recordings to an unknown person. That Andy carried out the exchanges by leaving the SD cards in the cupboard under the stairs and retrieving the envelopes of cash. And that whoever was behind the arrangement had access to the house. Paige shared with Mary how Andy and Dave had been best mates since school and that she was sure if she needed more help to solve Andy's murder, he'd give it to her. At this point Mary reminded her that it was the police who were meant to be doing that.

"You do realise that what you've told me could implicate Zac even more, don't you?" Mary asked.

"Agreed. But it also implicates Mica," Paige said.

"Did Dave tell the police about this arrangement?"

"No, only me. I'm not going to tell them. If he wants to come clean, that's up to him."

"Paige that's withholding evidence in a murder investigation," Mary snapped.

"Mary, if I told the police I'd have to explain why I'm sticking my nose into their investigation, which incidentally, they've told me to keep out of. And I'd be a sitting duck for DS Brown, who'd love nothing better than to take a pop at me."

"Okay. We'll both go back over the evidence we've collected so far and, taking this new information into account, formulate a theory as to who had a motive and the opportunity to commit both murders."

"Agreed. We're going to crack this, Mary. This time tomorrow Zac will be cleared of all involvement in the murders," Paige declared.

"I admire your optimism," Mary muttered.

Chapter 29

Saturday morning Paige set off for River Books. Her list of evidence pointing to Mica as the killer was in her bag. Knowing she wouldn't be able to have some time with Mary before lunch, Paige, in an attempt to keep her mind off the murders, set about sorting out the children's corner for Saturday morning story time. The initiative had proved popular with young families. Paige had a sneaky suspicion that part of its success was down to the fact that Malik ran it. Many of those who Paige called 'yummy mummies' fawned and fussed over the handsome young employee with his dark Eastern Mediterranean looks.

"Malik," Paige said as he walked towards her. "I've put out the cushions and tiny chairs. Can you remind me which book you're reading from today so that I can check we've got enough books on display?"

"An old favourite, *The Hungry Caterpillar*. There's a box of extra copies under the counter and I've put bookmarks next to the till. I've got activity sheets of 'Hungry Caterpillars' to colour in," he said holding up a sheaf of papers in one hand and a large pot of crayons in the other. "No need for you to do anything. Everything is under control.

"Perfect. I'll leave you to it, Malik. You've got it all under control," Paige said giving him a pat on the back. Blast, she'd have to find other tasks to distract her.

When lunchtime arrived Paige was straining at the

leash to show Mary her list and set out her theory as to why Mica had to be the killer. The morning had been a typical manic Saturday. Paige wasn't complaining because Saturdays were their most profitable days. The video game section was always heaving with teenagers comparing notes on gaming techniques and vying for Beth's attention. Beth with her numerous piercings and Goth-like clothes was extremely knowledgeable but perhaps most importantly for the young customers - cool. Paige waved to her as she slipped into Mary's office. Sitting at her desk Mary unwrapped her sandwiches and Paige took a seat opposite her and did the same.

"Let's see what we've got that builds a case against Mica," Mary said as she opened her laptop and scrolled through the files on her desktop.

Paige opened her laptop and clicked on the folder titled 'Evidence'. "I've noted the following:

- Mica is wealthy. She can afford to pay for the SD cards to be copied and given to her. She was familiar with Handy Andy. She told us she'd seen him several times."

"Hang on," Mary said. "Didn't Gail say Mica owed her money?"

"Yes. You've checked Mica's finances. She's wealthy from a privileged background. I suspect not paying Gail is some sort of power play," Paige said, returning to her list.

"She works as a dominatrix. Based on my dealings with her, I'd say that she's narcissistic and likes being in control. Having copies of everything that goes on in the house would fit that profile."

Mary interrupted, "But, if she had been in complete control wouldn't she have made sure that recordings of herself weren't broadcast over the internet?"

"Perhaps she saw them as being free publicity for

her sexual services," Paige answered.

"Then why did she go to Professor Williams and ask him to intervene and then ask for you to get involved when he refused?"

"Double bluff," Paige said. "To paint herself as being as much of a victim of the illicit recordings as the others in the house."

Mary screwed up her nose. "I'm not buying that. She doesn't strike me as the victim type."

"I'm not saying she sees herself as a victim. I'm saying she's intelligent enough to realise that if there were recordings of others in the house flying around the internet but not her, she'd attract the attention of the investigating officers immediately. Also, another reason that she could have contacted Bill was because of his power in the university. I managed to catch up with two of her lecturers that other students said were giving her an easy ride. They refused to say one way or the other but I got the feeling that she had some hold over them. When I mentioned Bill to each of them, they clammed up completely."

"Okay. We both know that Bill is not a person to mess with, especially if you're a junior lecturer in the French department." Mary stroked her chin thoughtfully.

"Agreed," Paige said. "Returning to the SD cards, if Mica had copies of previous ones perhaps she saw something in Zac's room that she wanted."

"Such as?" Mary asked.

"What about the jewellery that Zac had stolen?"

"That was in his locker at work."

"It was after he ran away but he could have had it in his room before then," Paige said. "And they were sparkly pieces. That could explain the ransacked room."

"You can't have it both ways, Paige. You've said

that she's rich. Why would she want cheap costume jewellery?"

"She wouldn't have known it was cheap from the recordings. They're not exactly HD quality. And being rich doesn't exclude wanting more."

"Point taken. What else makes you think she's the murderer?" Mary asked.

"She could've had an argument with Handy Andy and knocked him off his stool, then ransacked the room. Maybe she heard Zac coming back and hid in the toilet on that floor. Maybe Zac saw her and that's why he fled."

"That's an awful lot of 'maybes'. Let's just for argument's sake say that Zac did see her, why did he run?"

"Because she threatened him about the thefts," Paige said.

"In his note to you he said that someone was trying to frame him for the handyman's death."

"He could have meant Mica, Mary."

"Hmm." Mary looked far from convinced.

"Zac could have seen Mica with Professor Watkins. Zac had discovered something suspicious - maybe at the dig. Remember I found the note he'd made in that book *Studies in the Roman and Medieval Archaeology of Exeter*, which said *check coins from the dig*?"

"Yes. What about your vision of Professor Watkins with coins running through his fingers?"

"Before his death I would have said that it signified he'd been stealing coins from the site. Now I'm not so sure. In my vision he was dressed as a Roman Emperor. Most Roman Emperors were murdered, perhaps what my vision meant was that getting involved with the coins would get him killed. Interpreting visions is not a science." Paige stared off into the distance lost in thought.

"Earth to Paige," Mary said.

"Sorry. Where were we?"

"We saw Mica give him a coin and them have an argument over it. What if he was trying to find out who'd been taking the coins? That would explain him popping up all over the place asking questions about Zac, wouldn't it?"

"It would. The last thing he'd have wanted was to have to publicly admit that coins had gone missing from the site where he was in charge of the university's involvement. He'd already had the embarrassment of that hoax call to the local media to deal with."

"But why are you so convinced it's Mica?" Mary's puzzled expression portrayed her confusion.

Paige felt a nervous tightening in her throat. She took a sip of water. "Well, there is something else I haven't told you. Or anybody."

Mary's eyes almost disappeared in a narrow squint behind her glasses. "Go on," she said disapprovingly.

"I think it might be Mica because the person who followed me from your house was tall and thin as was the person who chased me the other night when I caught them digging something up at the Cloister Garden excavation site," Paige's voice faltered as she saw the flash of anger in her sister's eyes.

"So last night's dangerous escapade wasn't your first one then?" Mary snarled menacingly.

"No," Paige mumbled.

Mary threw her hands up in the air. "I'm so angry with you now. Immediately after closing today, I'm going to march you to the police station and you are going to tell them everything. Do you understand?"

Paige nodded. Her heart drummed against her ribs.

"Now leave before I say something I truly regret,"

Mary said, pointing to the door.

Paige gathered her belongings and hastily scuttled out of the room. Keeping her gaze lowered she walked as serenely as she could across the shop floor and up the stairs to her office. Once inside, she collapsed in a heap next to Sprite's basket. Sprite nuzzled her neck. Paige wrapped her arms round the warm ginger bundle and buried her face in the soft fur. "I've messed up with Mary big time, little one," she murmured.

Later that day Paige sat in the grotty, puke-green painted interview room feeling as sick as the decor looked. Mary had been true to her word and had bundled Paige into her car and driven her to the police station as soon as they'd closed up. Her sister had made sure Paige had been signed in by the duty officer. Then she'd waited until Paige had been taken through to an interview room before leaving with Sprite.

The door swung open and DI Denton lumbered in looking like a crumpled grizzly. Behind him DS Brown strode in, her body quivering with barely contained excitement. She resembled a piranha that had smelt blood and was impatient to move in for the kill. Paige's heart sank. She wished the ground would open up and swallow her whole. Unfortunately the concrete below her feet refused to cooperate. DS Brown licked her lips. Her eyes gleamed with steely resolve. Paige's fingers reached for her dream catcher as she prayed for protection from this vindictive woman. Immediately she realised her mistake. DS Brown's eyes narrowed as she watched her movement.

"Still believing in all the woo woo nonsense, Miss Harper? What are the spirits of the dead telling you today?" she mocked.

DI Denton cleared his throat noisily. "Let's begin. For the purpose of the tape today is Saturday 9th

March. The time is 18 05. Present in the room are DI Denton, DS Brown and Miss Paige Harper. Now Miss Harper…"

The interview had begun.

Chapter 30

The interview lasted an hour. Paige exposed her theory about Mica's guilt. Against her better judgement she admitted to having made a clandestine visit to the archaeological site on Tuesday evening. DS Brown looked as if all her Christmases had arrived at once. Here was an opportunity to prosecute Paige for interfering with a crime scene.

"Boss, we will have to charge Miss Harper for this," Brown said, her eyes glinting with triumph.

"Later Sergeant," he replied in an irritated voice. "Miss Harper can you recall anything particular about the intruder?" he asked in a mellow voice.

Paige replied, "The person was tall and slim like Mica and completely clothed in black. Their footwear was distinctive. I'm an aficionado when it comes to sports trainers. The individual was wearing Solar Glide trainers with Gore-Tex written in orange across the top. Unfortunately, those particular sports shoes are available for both men and women."

"It's something we can follow up. Thank you," the inspector said. "Anything else you'd like to add?"

Paige shook her head. "No. I've told you all I know. So are you charging Mica with the murders?"

DS Brown's gloating expression made ice run down Paige's spine. "Actually, we released Miss Murrel earlier today. She has a solid alibi for the time of the murder of Professor Watkins."

"But," Paige spluttered, "she had an argument with him about a coin."

She'd barely finished when DS Brown jumped up and almost fist-pumped as she exclaimed, "I told you boss that she wouldn't have been able to resist looking at those SD cards. We can charge her for interfering with evidence too."

The inspector, a thoughtful frown drawing his eyebrows together, sighed and said, "I think an unofficial warning is enough for now, sergeant." He focused his weary eyes on Paige and said, "Miss Harper, you are pushing my patience to the limit."

"I'm trying to help Zac," Paige said. "Have you found him yet?"

"You know full well that I am not going to disclose any information pertinent to an ongoing investigation. DS Brown if you would like to accompany Miss Harper and fill in the necessary paperwork before she leaves."

DS Brown grinned from ear to ear. The inspector said, "This interview is terminated at 19.22."

Paige had been well and truly played. Basically she'd confessed to her illegal sleuthing for nothing. She felt a fool. All she'd achieved was to put herself firmly on the police's radar - again. The police had let her incriminate herself while all along they'd known that Mica was innocent. DS Brown gloated at her predicament as Paige signed the forms. Paige scowled. This battle wasn't over. Payback time would come.

During the walk to Mary's house, Paige came back time and again to the evidence that pointed to Mica. She should have listened to Mary about Mica. There had been too many holes in her theory. However, listening to her sister and confessing to the police her illegal entry to the archaeology site hadn't turned out to be such a good idea. When Paige reached Mary's place and explained about Mica's innocence, Mary had the good grace not to say *I told you so.* A wave of discouragement overwhelmed Paige as she confessed to her big sister about the warning.

"Do you want me to drop you off at home?" Mary asked, realising that her sister was upset.

Paige shook her head. "No thanks. Sprite needs an evening walk. Bye."

Sprite, sensing her mistress' sombre mood, limited sniffing lamp posts to a minimum.

Sunday morning Paige decided to walk along the quay with Sprite. Weekends were busy at the Cellars, retail units built into the side of the quay. She needed a boost and Cassie, her artist friend who ran Cellar 7, would do the job.

"Cassie, morning," Paige called out as she entered the Aladdin's cave of beautiful canvases that were her friend's creations.

A small petite woman with white hair in a pixie cut and warm brown eyes emerged from behind an easel. A streak of blue paint highlighted the right side of her nose. Paige laughed. She'd rarely seen Cassie without paint on her face.

"Blue, is it?" Paige joked.

"Ha, ha. How did you become such an amazing sleuth?" Cassie said, her tone light.

Paige's face collapsed and tears leaked down her cheeks. "Not such a great detective after all, Cass."

"Hey, what's wrong. Come on. Sit down. I'll pop along to the café and get us some warm drinks. They're not as good as Sunny's but as you're closed today, they'll have to do," Cassie said, steering Paige to a chair in the far corner of the shop.

"A hot chocolate would be lovely. Thanks."

Cassie pulled on her colourful patchwork coat. "Hold the fort. I won't be long," she said rushing out the front.

Returning with two steaming cups of hot chocolate, Cassie sat next to Paige. "When you're ready to tell me, I'm here for you," the older woman said.

"I made a mess of things. I was convinced that the murderer was Mica - you know that girl who looks like an ebony beauty? - and I went to the police with my theory. Strictly speaking Mary forced me to go. I let slip I'd been doing some clandestine investigating that could have been dangerous." Paige paused as Cassie drew in a breath. "And yes, I know I promised my friends and family that I wouldn't put myself in danger and that I'd be a team player. What can I say? In the heat of the moment I forgot and in my headstrong way charged in where angels fear to tread, as Dom would say. Mary was furious with me and insisted I tell the police what I'd been up to. The upshot was that last night Mary hauled me to the police station where I told them what I'd discovered during my snooping. They gave me an unofficial warning."

"Oh, Paige, that's awful. Was it that horrid woman who is all sharp edges?"

"Yep. At least the inspector made her tone it down a bit or it could have been worse. She was hoping to charge me with obstructing a murder investigation. But do you know what's the most frustrating part of this fiasco?"

Cassie waited.

"The police had already cleared Mica of the murder and she'd been released before I even got to the station. So I confessed to my wrongdoings for nothing."

"Oh Paige. Poor you."

"I'm dreading tomorrow at the shop. You can bet

your bottom dollar that Violet will have heard all about my downfall and will be there to crow."

"Don't let her get to you, Paige. Now changing the subject completely I saw Dom in town yesterday with a portly gentleman. Do you know who he is?"

"That's Alfie Jeffreys. He used to be at the university. He's an expert on Roman history. Dom bumped into him in River Books when Alfie was visiting with a coach tour. He lives up north somewhere."

Cassie scrunched up her face. "That's strange."

"What?"

"On the day the coach group sheltered in your shop, I saw him earlier. He certainly wasn't with the group."

"Are you sure?"

"Positive. He was browsing in here. Every so often he checked out the window and when he saw the group pass and double back towards your shop he followed them."

"How odd. Maybe he'd come ahead and was waiting to rejoin them. Otherwise he was lying. Why would he? He said that he was part of the group because he didn't drive anymore," Paige said, scratching her head. "He's staying with Dom. He arrived by taxi Thursday evening. I happened to be returning from a walk with Sprite when the car drove down Dom's drive."

"Bizarre," Cassie muttered. "Anyway, I'm sure we've just got our wires crossed."

Paige felt her pulse spike. She was going to do her damnedest to uncross them.

Chapter 31

Monday dawned grey and miserable which pretty much reflected Paige's mood. After their morning routine of breakfast and strong cups of tea for Paige and garden patrols for Sprite, the pair set off for work. The Mini chugged along Topsham Road in the rush hour traffic. The car stereo blasted out *'Human'* by The Killers, one of the anthems that Paige used to get herself into an upbeat mood. By the time she'd parked the car and walked towards River Books she was ready to take on the world.

Inside the shop, Mary was standing chatting to Sunny, who by some miracle, had arrived before Paige. By the way they abruptly stopped talking as she entered, Paige realised that she must have been their topic of conversation.

"Morning, Mary, Sunny," Paige said, waving casually to them as she made her way upstairs to drop off her coat and bag in her office. She heard Sunny making a fuss of Sprite and Mary saying that it was time to open. Paige closed the door of her sanctuary behind her and took some deep steadying breaths. "You can do this," she told herself before stepping out briskly onto the shop floor. Holding her head high she'd made it halfway down the stairs when the door's bell clanged. Violet charged in. Her beady raisin eyes searched for her target and settled upon Paige.

"Paige, my dear. How wonderful to see you at work," she gushed with false bonhomie. "I did wonder whether the police had released you. Interfering in a murder investigation is a serious offence after all," she clarioned. Violet swept her eyes around the shop eager to see the impact her statement had made, but she'd mistimed her entrance. There were only two customers milling around who barely gave her a second glance.

Paige continued sedately down the stairs until she was standing in front of Violet. The President of the Riverside Association was decked out in what Paige thought of as her koala outfit - furry coat and toque. The vicious claws that came as part of the package had yet to be fully extended. As she'd descended the steps Paige had kept a welcoming smile plastered on her face.

"Violet, thank you for your concern for my welfare. It's so kind," she said benevolently.

The older woman blinked in surprise at Paige's measured reply. But she wasn't one to abandon an attack at the first hurdle. "I'm so glad Mica has been cleared of the murders. I understand that you were certain of the poor girl's involvement." A smug smile played on her lips. "Of course, I understand how jealousy can be a strong motivator. That girl and your Alex did seem particularly close the other day."

The venomous arrow pierced Paige's heart. She flinched as she took the hit hard. Sprite, sensing her mistress' distress, trotted beside her and gave her an encouraging yap. Paige straightened her spine and fixed her grey-blue eyes on Violet's expectant face. "I don't know who your source is within the police department Violet, but they are mistaken. I was merely helping with inquiries. Of course, I'm happy that an innocent woman has been cleared. I would not wish for an *innocent* person to be falsely accused," Paige paused for effect, "Zac and myself included."

Violet brushed off Paige's implied slur. "Where is

Señor Ramos? I haven't seen him with you recently."

"He's a very busy man. He's a lecturer and a police consultant. It's not exactly surprising he doesn't have time to drop in for a social visit in the middle of a double murder inquiry. Now if you'll excuse me, I have to fetch some stock from the basement."

With that Paige turned away from Violet and strode across the shop to the stairs leading down to the storeroom. She forced herself to maintain a calm demeanour even though inside she was raging. Once inside the stockroom Paige let out a scream of frustration. "It would have taken so little for me to snap and strangle the poisonous gossip," she muttered to Sprite who had followed her down the stairs. "I'm proud that I held it together under such a sustained attack. Yet, the truth, despite what I said to Violet, is that I haven't heard from Alex recently. I rang him when he was searching Mica's room. He said he'd ring back, but didn't. Do you think it's because he shared his wife's death with me? Sometimes after sharing such personal and sensitive information a person withdraws. Do you think that's what happened with Alex?" Sprite cocked her head to one side as if seriously considering what Paige had said. She jumped up on her hind legs placing her front paws on Paige's legs. Paige crouched down and gave her a hug. "What would I do without you?"

Paige hid down in the basement for most of the morning. Supposedly she was reorganising stock but in reality she was avoiding being exhibit Number One. Violet had spread the news around Riverside about Paige wrongly accusing Mica of the murders. Several of the retail unit owners happened to drop in for a coffee over the course of the day trying to sniff out what had been going on. Mary was polite but non-committal. Some customers tried to wheedle information out of

Sunny but she just smiled her gentle smile and asked them what they'd like to order.

A few hours later when Paige had finally emerged from her self-imposed exile in the basement she heard the shop bell jangle. Her heart skipped a beat when she saw who it was.

"Alex, how lovely to see you," she said, walking quickly over to greet him with a kiss on both cheeks. He stood as wooden as a statue.

"Paige," he said, in a glacial tone. "I hear that you have had some trouble, no?"

"I suppose that horrid DS Brown filled you in. You shouldn't take any notice of her Alex. You know she hates me," Paige said in a low fierce voice.

"It was DI Denton who spoke to me. He was telling me how you crossed the police tape cordoning off the site of Professor Watkins' murder. And how you disturbed someone else there." His voice matched the hardness of his gaze. His gold-flecked eyes bored into her.

"Look Alex, I may have acted hastily…" Paige began, her voice sounding strained all of a sudden.

His gaze didn't waver. "Paige, why do you break your promises?"

"I didn't exactly," she said, as she shot him what she hoped was a winning grin.

He snapped back his head. "Yes, you did," he said through pursed lips. "You promised us - your family and friends - that you would not take unnecessary risks. You promised that you would not act irresponsibly on your own. But you did. You went at night to a place where a murder had already taken place without informing anyone of where you were going. This is true, no?"

Paige's insides crumpled. There was no denying she had done these things. "I was convinced that Mica was the murderer, Alex. I wanted to help Zac."

"But you did not help Zac. You helped the police build an even stronger case against him."

"No, that can't be true." Paige wrapped her arms round her middle in an involuntary attempt to protect herself.

"Please stay out of the police investigation. I think that until the case is solved we should not see each other again," Alex said, his tone brittle.

"But Alex, please. I thought we were friends," Paige pleaded.

"Paige I explained to you what happened to my wife. I cannot be involved with someone who puts herself in danger. *Adios, cariño*," he said sadly. He smiled at her briefly but his eyes were empty. He clicked his cowboy boot heels and hurried out of the shop.

In a state of shock, Paige stood dumbstruck watching his retreating figure. Moving as if she were walking through treacle, she made it to her office without having to interact with anyone. Fortunately for her, Mary had been in her office when Alex had come in and Sunny had been in the café kitchen. Neither one of them had witnessed her humiliation. She slumped into her chair. "I knew he was my kryptonite. I've just crashed and burned. When will I ever learn?" she muttered to herself. "I'm so sad. But I can't change who I am. I'm even more determined now to solve the murders."

Paige decided that she wasn't going to tell anyone about Alex ditching her. If anyone asked why they hadn't seen Alex with her, she'd use the same excuse she given Violet - he was a busy lecturer and police consultant. Pinching her cheeks to give herself a bit of colour she ventured back out into the shop. She repeated the mantra from William Hillary, founder of the Royal National Lifeboat Institution: *With courage, nothing is impossible.*

Finally it was time to turn the sign on the door from *Open* to *Closed*.

"Well, we made it through without you losing your cool," Mary said to Paige.

"I'll admit it was a close call with Violet," Paige said. "I never thought that I'd think of my least favourite room in the shop as a sanctuary, but today the stockroom was my haven. At least our turnover was up on a usual Monday. Between extra teas, coffees, lunches and cakes and what I call 'guilt buys' by those who'd come to be nosy we had a good day at the till."

"We did. Right now off you go. Don't get into any mischief, please," Mary said.

"No probs, sis," Paige said, waving as she made her way to the car park. Somehow she'd managed to keep it together after Alex's visit, even if she was dying inside. "I'd make a good actress," she said to Sprite. The dog gave an eye roll.

Chapter 32

Paige drove home and walked Sprite before preparing to go out again. She hadn't shared her plans with anyone. After her conversation with Alex today she was less, rather than more, likely to tell anyone what she was up to. Yesterday, she'd made a phone call after she'd spoken with Cassie. What Cassie had said about Alfie Jeffreys had troubled Paige. The man was staying with Dom and Paige was as protective of her *grandpère* as he was of her. Paige pulled up in the car park of The Imperial. The pub, situated on New North Road, has an interesting history. It houses an impressive Orangery that was originally a heated palm house designed by Isambard Kingdom Brunel for Streatham Hall. It was moved to its present site at the beginning of the twentieth century. The steel and glass construction is stunning, especially when the setting sun catches on its glass roof. Tonight there were no solar pyrotechnics, just a dull reflected greyness.

Entering the bar, Paige spotted the person she'd arranged to meet. A large, chubby man wearing a black shirt and black trousers sat at a table. He waved a pudgy hand in her direction. She hurried over.

"Bill, thank you so much for agreeing to see me," she said. "What can I get you?" she asked, noticing he hadn't ordered a drink yet.

"A glass of Bordeaux, please Paige," he replied in his soft Welsh accent.

Each time they met Paige was reminded that they

were not friends. They tolerated each other at best. It was no secret that Bill's wife, Penny, had hoped to buy River Books from Dom and had never forgiven Paige for having been chosen by Dom as the new owner instead of her. Bill was fiercely loyal to Penny and had himself been angry that his frenemy, Professor Dominic Giraud, had favoured Paige over his wife. The situation hadn't been improved by the involvement of one of Penny's relatives in a murder investigation at River Books last year. A murder that Paige had helped solve. No, Bill didn't like her and the feeling was mutual but what did unite them was their affection for Dom.

"Bill, as I briefly explained on the phone, I need your help and your extensive knowledge of university politics and, more importantly, scandals that may have been buried concerning Alfie Jeffreys. It's one of your areas of expertise, is it not?"

Professor Williams puffed out his already expansive chest and trained his raisin black eyes on Paige. He took a long sip of his wine, licked his moist lips and gave her a calculating look. "I recognise when someone is massaging my ego, you know?" he said.

"I wouldn't expect anything less of you, Bill. That's why you're my best chance of finding out the information I need. I realise that both you and Dom are masters at picking up on the rumours running through the ivory towers," Paige paused as Bill gave an imperceptible nod. "However, as the information I'm searching for could have a direct impact on Dom, there was no way I could ask him."

"It wouldn't have done you any good, even if you had," Bill said smugly.

"Why?"

"Because Dom was away on a research sabbatical in France when the Alfie Jeffreys' scandal was the top topic in our ivory towers."

Paige let this information sink in while she sipped at her apple juice. "So, if my memory serves me right that would have been before I started at Exeter University? I remember him telling me about how much he enjoyed the time. It resulted in a well-received paper and several conference appearances, didn't it?"

"Correct. He was so engrossed in his discoveries that petty politics in another department at the university passed him by. That was seventeen years ago. By the time he returned to Exeter the dust had settled and the university had swept the whole affair under the carpet."

"What happened seventeen years ago with Alfie Jeffreys?" Paige asked her pulse racing. She'd known that if there was dirt to find on Alfie, Bill would find it.

Bill interlinked his sausage-like fingers and placed his elbows on the table. His eyes glowered with contempt. "In my opinion, a travesty of justice," he pronounced censoriously.

"Go on, Bill. You've got my full attention."

"Alfie Jeffreys was found to be appropriating Roman artefacts from an archaeology dig that he'd been working at."

Paige gasped. "No! So it's no coincidence that he's interested in this most recent Roman dig then."

"Indeed it isn't. The official story is that he had taken some of the Roman finds back to his house for safekeeping because he'd been concerned that the person logging the finds hadn't been doing their job properly. He claimed that that person wasn't making sure the artefacts were stored securely."

"Ouch. He pointed the finger at someone else?"

"It gets better," Bill's pasty face took on a rosy hue as he warmed to his subject. His Welsh accent thickened. "Guess who the person he pointed the finger at was."

"I don't know. A student? Another member of

staff?"

"Close. It was a post-doctoral student. Who could have been a post-doctoral student seventeen years ago?" Bill was grinning now with delight as Paige scrunched up her face in concentration. "Come on, don't be slow, Paige. Aren't you meant to be a super-sleuth?" he taunted.

"How should I know, Bill? Give me a clue." She jutted out her chin in defiance. With Bill you never ceded ground.

"It's someone you met quite recently who met a sticky end," he said, a satisfied smirk on his face.

Paige slapped her hand on her forehead. "Oh my. Not Professor Watkins?" she asked, her voice squeaking with disbelief.

"Congratulations. Not too slow. You got there in the end," Bill said.

"But Alfie told me he'd spoken to Professor Watkins about being allowed access to the Cathedral Cloister Garden site."

Bill chortled. "I very much doubt that, my dear. He would have given the man a wide berth. Watkins testified against him in an internal investigation."

"Alfie asked Dom if he could find a way for him to have access to the site, Bill," Paige said, her voice seething with barely contained anger. "He's using him. Alfie also wanted to talk to Zac when we told him that Zac had been working there. By that time Zac had already disappeared. Bill, do you think he's dangerous?"

"From what I've learnt he's manipulative and cunning but physical violence? Not that I know."

"That's a relief."

"Mind you, he could pay someone to be violent for him," Bill added.

"That's not a reassuring thought, Bill. What are we going to do?"

"I'm not sure I can help you there, Paige. I am most definitely not a man of action - physically." He placed his hands on his copious stomach. "That's your department." Bill stopped when he saw Paige's crestfallen expression. "What I can do is invite Dom for one of our lunches and check up on the old queen. And naturally I'll keep my ear to the ground for any whispers."

"Thank you, Bill. That would be great. You've given me a lot to think about. I'll work something out. Can I get you another glass of wine?"

Bill drained the remains of his glass, stood up and checked his watch. "I've got to get going. Penny is expecting me. Take care, Paige. Don't worry too much about Dom. He's a tough old bird."

"Before you go, Bill, one more question," Paige said, her nose twitching. As Bill had risen to his feet she'd smelt the same fragrance she'd detected on her pursuer at the dig site. "What aftershave are you wearing?"

"What on earth! Why are you interested in my aftershave?" The tone of his voice was sardonic.

"Just humour me, okay?"

He shook his head. His jowls wobbled like pink blancmange. "It's Kouros by Yves Saint Laurent."

"Thanks Bill. Take care and say hi to Penny for me."

He snorted with laughter. "I'll pass on that one. I didn't actually tell her it was you I was meeting. I didn't want to upset her unnecessarily. There's no need to pretend there is any love lost between the two of you."

After Bill left Paige sat at the table lost in thought. What Bill had told her put a whole new light on the murder of Professor Watkins. Could Alfie have been responsible? But there was no way that Alfie Jeffreys was the person she'd disturbed that evening at the cathedral site. More digging was needed. She allowed herself a small smile at her wittiness.

Chapter 33

Tuesday was Paige's day off. She had a lot of investigating to do and she was going do it on her own terms. No more pussyfooting around to please others. It was a strange sensation but she felt so much freer since Alex had told her he couldn't be involved with someone like her. She really liked the Spaniard. There was no doubt about that. However, she'd sworn that she wouldn't be controlled by a man again after what happened with her abusive ex, Xavier, in France. Controlling men and Paige's free-spirited approach to life were like oil and water - they didn't mix well. Even if Alex dressed it up as concern for her welfare, his insistence on following the rules still felt restrictive. Paige admitted that she'd isolated herself from her friends and family. Had she done so unconsciously to give herself freedom to act as she saw fit? Possibly. She'd managed to exasperate Mary, Sunny and Alex in quick succession. The one person she hadn't upset was Dom but the fact that he had Alfie as his house guest made it difficult for her to just pop in and talk things over with him like she was used to doing. Was Dom unknowingly harbouring a murderer? Paige had to move fast. This had become personal. Yes, she cared about Zac. The young man was her employee but Dom was special. He'd been her rock when life in France had become unbearable. He'd offered her an escape by selling River Books to her for a nominal amount. That generous act had enabled her to start afresh in Exeter. He'd even renovated his Lodge House so that he could rent it to her. He was her *grandpère*. There was nothing she wouldn't do to protect him.

Paige's first action of the day was a calculated risk. She planned to visit Mica. There was a high possibility that the woman would kick her out and refuse to speak to her. There was only one way to find out. On her way to Mica's lodgings Paige decided to call in on Miss Fletcher. The elderly lady was still nursing a broken ankle. Paige pulled up in front of Miss Fletcher's neat terraced house. As she made her way to the gate with Sprite, Paige saw the old lady wave to her through the window. Paige signalled that she'd use the key safe to get into the house. Once inside the pair made their way to the front room where Miss Fletcher was comfortably installed in her armchair watching the street.

"Hello, dear. This is a lovely surprise. And how are you my pet?" she said, lowering her hand to ruffle Sprite's neck.

"We were in the neighbourhood and thought we'd pop in to say hi. Faithful at your post I see," Paige said, nodding to the elderly lady's binoculars sitting on the coffee table next to her.

"What else can I do? I read a little. I listen to the radio and I spy on the neighbours," she said with a mischievous smile on her face.

"Seen any murderers lurking in the vicinity?" Paige asked.

"Not that I'm aware of. How is poor Zac? I saw his photo splashed all over the news."

"If only I knew. He's still missing. When the police turned up at the campsite where he'd been hiding out he'd gone. There have been no sightings of him since." Paige sighed.

"We both know he didn't do it. Haven't you solved

the murder yet?"

Paige's shoulders drooped. "Unfortunately, not. I believed I had. I was wrong. I was convinced it was Mica, who's one of Zac's housemates. You must have noticed her. A statuesque Grace Jones lookalike?"

Miss Fletcher nodded. "Oh yes, I've seen her around. Quite a madam, that one. I saw her having a row with a skinny student with lanky, greasy hair. I say a quarrel but it was more like a rant. He just stood there and took it. That was until an elderly gentleman with gingery, grey hair pulled up in a black Mercedes and the young man jumped in the passenger seat."

Shivers ran down Paige's spine. "Are you sure it was a Mercedes, Miss Fletcher?" she asked in a wobbly voice.

"I may be old, dear, but I know my cars," she replied somewhat indignantly. "My grandson, Russell, has one. When he comes to visit, he takes me out in it." Miss Fletcher was staring at Paige's face. "Are you alright? You've gone very pale. You look like you've seen a ghost."

"I'm fine," Paige replied unconvincingly.

"Go and put the kettle on. A sweet tea is what you need," Miss Fletcher ordered.

Paige walked into the kitchen in a daze. A black Mercedes was the make of car that had tried to run her down. Miss Fletcher's description of the driver sounded like it could be Alfie Jeffreys but he'd told her and Dom that he no longer drove a car. As far as Paige knew the man didn't live in Exeter, nor did he know Kevin from Zac's student digs. No, she was letting her imagination run away with her - or was she? Paige went through the motions of filling the kettle, making the tea and carrying the tray into the front room while her mind sorted through the new information Miss Fletcher had provided.

"Miss Fletcher if you see that black Mercedes again could you note down its number plate?"

The old lady's eyes lit up. "Another mission for me. Count me in, dear. Can I ask why the car's important?"

"A black Mercedes tried to run me over the other night," Paige said.

Miss Fletcher looked horrified. "Were you hurt?"

"I managed to dive over a low wall into a garden when the car mounted the pavement. Sprite and I survived."

"It was a targeted attack then?"

Paige nodded. "Definitely."

"Don't you worry, my dear. I'm on the case. Anyone who tries to kill this gorgeous young dog deserves to be locked up," she said, ruffling Sprite's ears.

"Thank you," said Paige, thinking that she obviously ranked below her dog as far as the old lady was concerned. "It may be a coincidence that one of Zac's flatmates got into a black Mercedes but I've got to chase down every lead. Oh, and before I forget," Paige said, reaching into her bag, "here's the next book in that cosy crime series you were reading." She handed over the paperback.

"You're an angel. Take care, Paige, and thank you for dropping in," Miss Fletcher said.

"Bye agent Fletcher."

The old lady giggled as Paige and Sprite let themselves out of the house.

Mistress and terrier walked to the end of the road and turned into Zac's road. Their next meeting most certainly wouldn't be as pleasant as that one had been. Paige repeated the mantra *With courage, nothing is impossible* as she knocked on the door. A few minutes later she heard someone in the hallway. The door cracked open and Mica looked out.

"You've got a cheek coming here," she shouted.

"I'm here to apologise," Paige said.

"Oh, is that so? Really?" Mica raised a sceptical eyebrow.

"Yes. Can I come in?"

The door opened and Mica let her inside. "Follow me. We'll go in the kitchen. I don't want you poking about in my room. The police and your Spanish friend have already done that," the girl said as she marched ahead of Paige and Sprite down the hallway.

Dirty dishes were piled high in the sink. Work surfaces were covered with a greasy film. A typical student house kitchen. Mica picked her way through the chaos until she reached a small Formica table and pulled out a chair. Paige did the same.

"I won't offer you anything to drink," Mica said. "I'm doing you a favour, believe me. This dump is a health hazard." She arced an arm to encompass the mess.

"I see what you mean," Paige said. "I appreciate your concern."

"You taking the piss?" Mica snarled.

Paige held up her hands in surrender. "No. Look Mica we haven't exactly got off to a good start. Can we try to get on - if only for the time this chat takes."

Mica glared at her and then her expression softened. "I can do that. What do you want?"

Getting her thoughts in order, Paige began. "Firstly, I apologise for believing you'd committed the murders. I shouldn't have gone rushing to the police without checking more facts."

"Yeah, you shouldn't have. Okay, apology accepted," she said grudgingly. "Now what do you really want?"

"I need your help to catch the murderer. I'm convinced you have information that can help me do that."

"That's the police's job," Mica said.

"And how has that been working out so far?" Paige said. "They arrested you - they got that wrong. They've issued a country-wide warrant for Zac's arrest but haven't found him."

"You repeating that Zac's innocent doesn't make it true," Mica sneered.

"I'm not stupid," Paige said. Mica allowed herself a smirk. Paige chose to ignore it. "Mica can you tell me about the coin I saw you handing to Professor Watkins?"

"I wasn't handing it to him, I was handing it back. He's was really upset. Ranting about Roman coins being stolen, as if I'd know anything about that. He wasn't usually like that. I told him I found it outside Zac's door. I thought he should have it. He cross-examined me about how it had got there, but I couldn't tell him. I told him to ask the two students in this house who actually know something about Roman coins."

"That makes sense," Paige said. "Maybe that's what got him killed."

"You can't be serious," Mica gasped.

"Honestly, I don't know. He's dead so we can't ask him if he followed through on finding out the origin of the coin."

"He was okay, you know. A bit up himself but a fair man."

"How did you know him?"

"I bumped into him on campus when he was talking to Zac. When Zac saw me he skedaddled. Marcus invited me for a drink and we got chatting. He wasn't a client. Turns out he knew my dad from way back. We sort of got on." Mica dipped her head as if admitting getting on with anyone was a sign of weakness.

"Can I ask you what was your alibi for his death?" She held her breath waiting for the vitriol to spurt from Mica's lips.

"Not that it's any of your business. I was with a client all night. After a little persuasion they agreed to vouch for me. Not every married man would have been so forthcoming." She gave a satisfied smile.

"No, they wouldn't. But did the police take his word for it?"

Mica looked like the cat who'd got the cream. Paige could almost imagine her licking her whiskers. "Let's say that I had *hard* evidence," Mica sniggered.

"The evening was videoed," Paige said, understanding Mica innuendo. "Talking of filming, someone paid the landlord to install the spy cams and to receive copies of the SD cards."

Mica's dark eyes narrowed into a squint of suspicion. "How do you know that?"

"The landlord told me. The way the system worked means someone in this household had to be in on the scam. As you were so worried about the proliferation of the spy cams video footage in cyberspace, I'm assuming it wasn't you."

"But what do the spy cams have to do with the murders?"

"I don't know exactly. It wouldn't be a stretch to imagine that the person saw something that led to both deaths, would it?"

"Perhaps." Mica rubbed goosebumps on her arms. "Are you saying I'm living in a house with a double murderer?"

Paige ran her fingers through her hair. "I'm not saying the person living here is necessarily the murderer but I'm sure that someone living here is helping them."

"That's not funny," Mica replied, a tinge of apprehension in her voice.

"What can you tell me about the under stairs cupboard?"

"What?"

"The SD cards and the cash were left there," Paige explained

"Sorry, I've never seen anyone go in there except for Handy Andy."

A shiver of disappointment ran through Paige. Of course, it would have been too easy if Mica had seen someone. "What trainers do you wear, Mica?"

"Really, Paige? Trainers? I don't wear trainers," she said, wincing at the thought.

"Anyone wear brown trainers with orange writing on them?"

"I couldn't say for sure, maybe Kevin? Not that I ever give that worm as second glance," she said with contempt.

"Thanks, Mica. On the subject of Kevin, I heard you had a row with him in the street and that a black Mercedes picked him up."

"I assumed it was some old pervert wanting Kevin's services."

"What?" Paige asked stunned.

"He's part of the *incel* movement, isn't he? Hates women. I assumed he liked men."

"But you don't know for sure?" Paige asked.

"No," Mica admitted with regret.

Paige turned her attention back to Mica. "Once again, I'm sorry I thought you were guilty of the murders."

"Paige you made the mistake everyone makes," she paused, "You only see my dominatrix persona. No one sees the real me." Sadness flashed across the girl's face. When she lifted her head again the disdainful mask was firmly back in place. "You've taken up enough of my time. Goodbye."

"Hang on. Can I take a peek in the cupboard?"

"Knock yourself out," Mica said disinterested, already negotiating her route out of the hazardous kitchen.

"Thanks."

Paige poked around in the under stairs cupboard and came up empty. No envelopes were hidden inside. The mysterious accomplice would have cleared them out at the first opportunity after the murder of Andrew Hammond in Zac's room. Did the police search the cupboard? Unlikely. And she'd alienated Alex who could have found out if they had. "Come on Sprite, I've still got you," Paige said as her terrier gave her an encouraging bark.

Chapter 34

Back home Paige contemplated her next move. She had to track down Kevin and work out if he was the murderer. There were several black marks against his name. Spreading out a sheet of A4 paper on the table she made a list of what she knew so far.

1. Kevin was on the same archaeology course as Zac yet he'd pretended to hardly know him.

2. Kevin had been jealous of Zac being chosen to work at the dig. Had he since been chosen to replace Zac? If yes, that would have given him the opportunity to scope out the site.

3. Kevin had been annoyed with Professor Watkins for favouring Zac. Was that an important enough reason to kill the man? That would be a stretch.

4. Kevin lived in the Heavitree student house. Could he be the person who had asked the landlord, Dave, to put in the spy cams? It was unlikely. He was a student. According to background checks that Mary had carried out on the student tenants, he and Zac were the only two who didn't have financially comfortable families. He couldn't have paid for the copies.

5. As Kevin was not from a wealthy background, he would be more open to being bribed. Was he paid to carry out the exchanges of SD cards and cash payments?

6. The young man was rumoured to be an *incel* - a term for men who wanted a romantic or sexual

relationship with women but unable to get one. The majority of them had a big chip on their shoulders. In Paige's opinion that summed up Kevin's character. However, if Kevin was an *incel* then Mica had been wrong about him preferring men. Being an unattractive young man in a house full of self-assured female students from privileged backgrounds who, at best ignored him and at worst disparaged him, would be a strong motivator to get his own back by exposing the girls in their most intimate moments to the world on the web. If you added in Mica's part-time job as a black dominatrix, his motivation sky-rocketed. If Kevin wasn't the instigator of the spy cameras, it could have been relatively easy to convince him to act as the courier.

7. Physically, Kevin was tall and skinny. The person who'd chased Paige at the archaeology site had had a similar silhouette to him. Did Kevin possess a pair of those distinctive trainers? Another fact to check.

8. Had Kevin killed Handy Andy accidentally? Paige had trouble imagining Kevin as a killer. He struck her as a weak-willed individual. Yet, Paige knew from past experiences at chasing down murderers that anyone can kill.

9. Had he been blackmailed into placing the Roman coin in Andy's mouth? Had he thought he was being clever leaving a coin by showing his knowledge of Roman customs relating to death? Or had he thought it was a way of implicating Zac because of his access to coins at the archaeology site when he was logging finds?

10. What about Professor Watkins' death? Could Kevin have been involved? The police hadn't uncovered the reason for the professor being at the site in the evening. What if he'd been searching for what Paige witnessed the intruder digging up? Or had Watkins agreed to meet someone there? If yes, would

he really have agreed to meet a student that he didn't particularly like late at night? It was unlikely.

11. Whose black Mercedes had Kevin got into? Was it the same car that had attempted to run Paige down?

12. Who was driving the car? Could it have been Alfie Jeffreys? He'd told her and Dom he didn't drive anymore. Had that been a lie? If yes, why?

13. But how would Kevin and Alfie know each other? It didn't make sense.

Paige laid down her pen and rubbed her brow. Time for a run. Paige's go-to-activity when she was struggling to think clearly was exercise. She went upstairs and changed into her jogging gear. Back downstairs in the kitchen she laced up her trainers. Sprite looked at her mistress' sports clothes and settled back in her basket. The dog's action signalled that she didn't fancy a run and preferred to stay in the warm.

"I won't be too long," Paige said to Sprite as she locked the back door behind her.

Paige set off for the King George V playing fields. The early spring sun was attempting to break through the grey clouds. At the park, crocus, daffodil and narcissus plants were doing their best to brighten the area with patches of purple, yellow and white flowers. Paige's mood felt lighter taking in nature's colourful tapestry. She ran several circuits of the playing fields. The endorphins coursed through her body. Knots of tension released from her shoulders and neck. As she returned home to continue with her investigation her feet pounded the pavements along Topsham Road. Turning into the drive down the side of the Lodge she saw Dom and Alfie getting into a taxi. She whistled to get their attention. Both men waved to her before climbing into the car. Paige stepped inside her gate and watched as the taxi drove past. Dom caught her eye and winked. He seemed happy. Paige sighed with relief.

A hot shower and a quick change of clothing later Paige was on her way to the university campus. If her sources were correct Kevin's lecture should be finishing at 3.15pm. She planned to corner him on his way out of the lecture theatre. Parking was never easy on campus except when Paige had Dom as a passenger and they could use his Blue Badge parking permit. It took her a while to find an empty space. By the time she arrived outside the lecture room all the students had dispersed except for one. A lad lingered behind packing up his bag. Paige hurried over.

"Hi, I'm looking for Kevin Stevens. Have you seen him?"

"No. Didn't come in today," the lad said.

"I don't suppose you know why or where he is, do you?" Paige asked, giving the young man her brightest smile.

"No. We're not mates. He keeps himself to himself. Mind you, he doesn't usually miss lectures. He fancies himself as an expert on all things Roman." The tone of his voice was sarcastic.

"I heard he wasn't best pleased when Zac was given the responsibility of logging finds at the Cathedral dig."

"Right annoyed, he was." The young man peered at Paige more closely. "Hey, you're Zac's employer, aren't you? Run the bookshop?"

Paige preened a little. "Yes. I'm Paige Harper. Are you a friend of Zac's?"

"Sure. He's alright Zac. Helped me a bit. I'm not as smart as him. Can't believe the police would think he'd murder Prof Watkins. Worshipped the ground he walked on, he did."

"I thought they'd had a falling out?" Paige ventured.

"Not exactly. Something was up with the Prof though. I overheard him asking Zac to check the logs from the digs several times."

"Do you know why?" Paige asked hopefully.

"Sorry. Not really. Zac went a bit weird after that - secretive, edgy. Prof was the same." The lad gave her a shy grin. "I've got to dash. Got a tutorial. Nice to have met you, Paige. If you get to see Zac again, tell him Jay says hi." He gathered up his belongings and hurried away.

"Thanks Jay. I will," Paige called after him.

Paige's suspicions of items missing from Cloister Garden's dig seemed to be confirmed by what Jay had said. Why had Zac feared Professor Watkins? Could it be because Zac believed that the Prof held him responsible for the missing objects? What if the reason the professor had been asking questions everywhere was because he was trying to track down who had stolen them? Or maybe Zac thought the professor was the one who'd stolen the items and was going to pin it on him, his research assistant? If neither Zac nor the professor had stolen the artefacts, who had? Kevin? It was urgent that Paige track him down.

Back in her Mini Paige headed for Heavitree and Kevin's lodgings. It was the end of the school day and the traffic was snarled up as school buses ferried pupils home. Paige tapped her fingers on the steering wheel in frustration. Finally, she pulled up close to where Kevin lived and parked. Walking past the rickety gate down the front path, Paige caught it with her knee. It swung back and banged loudly against the fence. A net curtain twitched in the first floor window. That was Zac's room. No one should be in there. She accelerated and rapped loudly on the front door.

An angry Mica pulled open the door. "Not you again. Go away," she snarled.

Paige pushed past the stunned girl and bounded up the stairs two at a time. On the landing she caught a glimpse of Kevin quickly slamming his door behind him. She pounded on the wood. "Let me in, Kevin. I saw you in Zac's room. What were you doing?"

There was no response. Paige rattled the handle. "Open up," she shouted. She pressed her ear against the door and listened. There was a scraping and then a distant thud. "Kevin. I know you're in there," she yelled. The muffled noise of a metal object crashing on concrete reached her. "The blighter. He's gone out the window." She thundered down the stairs and bolted into the kitchen. As she flung open the back door Kevin was disappearing over the garden fence. On his feet were brown Solar Glide Gore-Tex trainers. In her hurry to run after him, Paige crashed into the dustbin he'd overturned after sliding down the drainpipe. She fell. Swearing under her breath, she scrambled to her feet. She winced as she put weight on her knee. Bummer. She'd never catch him now. Paige brushed herself off and limped back into the kitchen where she was met by Mica's amused expression.

"That was entertaining. What do you want with *Cheese straw*?" asked Mica.

"I need to talk to him," Paige said.

"I gathered that much by the screaming and pounding on his door." A sardonic grin accompanied her deadpan delivery.

"Mica, can I ask you a favour?" Paige said, holding her hands together in a begging gesture.

"As you've provided me with a dramatic diversion by chasing that little scrote, I will."

"When I was walking up the path I saw the curtains in Zac room move. Kevin was in there. Can you come with me to the room? I need a witness if I find anything incriminating."

Mica grinned with wicked enjoyment. "Lead the way," she said.

When Paige had last been in Zac's room it was to discover Andrew Hammond's dead body. Since then the police crime scene cleaners had removed the blood but the chaos of the ransacked room had been left untouched. Paige turned to Mica. "I have a photographic memory. I'm going to close my eyes and recall how that room was last time. Okay?"

Mica looked sceptical but nodded all the same. "Fine."

Paige focused on the images in her head. Then she opened her eyes to compare the scene in front of her. Zac's pink shirt was scrunched up differently. Paige dug out her phone and turned to Mica. "Can you record me?" she asked, turning on the video camera.

Mica held out her hand and focused the camera on Paige who spoke to the camera. "It is 4.05pm on Tuesday 12th March. I'm standing in the doorway of Zac Jones' room. I witnessed Kevin Stevens exiting this room fifteen minutes ago. He has fled the scene. I have requested that Mica Murrel record my entry into Zac's room." Mica flipped the camera round and said, "That's me," to the camera before angling it back onto Paige. Walking towards Zac's pink shirt, Paige pointed to it and said, "This shirt has been disturbed. I believe that Kevin planted something in it." She took a pen from her pocket and bent down over the pink fabric. With care, she lifted the material using the end of the pen. A watch fell out of a fold onto the carpet. "If I'm not mistaken, this is Professor Watkins' watch," she said addressing the camera.

Mica stopped the recording. "That's definitely Marcus' watch. Wow. That was impressive. Did that slime ball kill Professor Watkins?" she asked through gritted teeth.

"It looks that way."

Chapter 35

Paige rang the police. She and Mica chatted in the hallway while they waited for them to arrive. A patrol car drew up outside and DS Brown jumped out of the passenger side. She stormed through the front door and pointed an accusatory finger at Paige, "I told you not to interfere with my investigation," she snarled.

"Whoa, lady. That's not a nice way to treat someone who's found some vital evidence, is it?" Mica said, peering down on the sergeant from her six foot frame.

DS Brown turned purple with rage. "Who do you think you are talking to a member of the police force like that?" she roared.

Mica didn't flinch. "I'm a concerned citizen who just witnessed you harassing a member of the public. I shall be making a complaint."

Paige bit the insides of her cheeks to stop the laughter that threatened to bubble through her lips. It was fun to see the sergeant on the receiving end for once.

"I can have you arrested again, Miss Murrel," DS Brown said.

"Adding intimidation, eh? I'm certain the inspector will be thrilled, as well as the illustrious person who is my alibi," Mica drawled. She turned to Paige and said, "Did you capture that? You're still recording aren't you?" She gave Paige a sly wink.

Paige made a show of holding her phone up as if filming. Her mind was racing. Just who had Mica's client been? Obviously someone with clout judging by Brown's reaction. The sergeant had blanched and was now holding up her hands. "I think there's been a misunderstanding. Please, Miss Harper, Miss Murrel, we can sort this out."

"That's better," Mica said. "Still waiting for the apology though." The young woman stared hard at DS Brown.

"Please accept my apologies Miss Murrel and Miss Harper," DS Brown said through teeth clenched so tight she was at risk of dislocating her jaw.

Paige and Mica exchanged a glance and then graciously accepted. "Now perhaps we can show you what we discovered. We recorded finding Professor Watkins' watch and will forward the footage to the police," Paige said, leading the way up the stairs.

Once DS Brown had retrieved the watch, sealed off the room and taken statements from both Paige and Mica about Kevin's actions, she scuttled away. Not quite so many sharp edges were on display now. Mica had shaved off a few of the woman's corners. PC Patel was waiting to drive the sergeant back to the station. As DS Brown dipped her head to climb into the car, Office Patel gave Paige a big grin and a thumbs up.

"Looks like you've got yourself a fan there," Mica said.

"He's kind. It's not the first time he's seen her lay into me. Thanks for sticking up for me and that was an ingenious idea to suggest that I was still recording."

"Don't you go telling anyone I was nice to you. I've got my reputation as a heartless bitch to uphold," Mica replied.

"Your secret's safe with me," Paige said, as she mimed sealing her lips.

Back home, Paige collected Sprite's lead and set off for the park. Once there, she unhooked the dog's collar and let her scamper off. Other dogs were running around with their ears and tails flying in the light breeze. Paige mulled over the events of earlier. Kevin was definitely involved in the murders. It had to have been him who collected the SD cards and picked up the cash. However, Paige was convinced he wasn't the criminal mastermind behind the murders. So who was? Could it be Alfie Jeffreys? He came across as a friendly, affable bloke, although Bill had painted a very different picture of a man obsessed with Roman artefacts who had attempted to steal from a previous dig. Because there was no mistaking from what Bill had said that if Alfie hadn't been caught, he would have kept those objects found at his house. Instead he'd made up a cock and bull story about not trusting the post-doc student. The fact that the person in question had been the now deceased Professor Watkins was even more suspicious. But Alfie lived up North and, as far as Paige knew, had only recently returned to Exeter. Paige remembered what Cassie had said about Alfie hanging around in her shop and leaving to join the tour group. She still hadn't checked whether he had been part of that group. Maybe Mary still had the tour guide's details. Before Paige could continue with that train of thought her phone rang.

"*Hello, Sheila,*" Paige said, recognising Zac's grandmother's number.

"*Paige, I'm sorry to bother you,*" she said in a voice laced with anxiety.

"*What can I do for you, Sheila?*" Paige asked.

"*I weren't too honest with you last time, love, about not knowing where Zac was...*" her voice trailed off.

"*Go on,*" Paige said, feeling herself bristle.

"*Thing is, this time I'm telling the truth. Zac's missing. Til last Tuesday when the police took me in for questioning he rang me regular like at work. Not on my home phone 'cos he was afraid of the police monitoring it. I haven't heard from him for seven days now,*" the old lady sobbed.

"*Sheila, Zac knows that the police are actively looking for him. He also knows that you were taken in for questioning. He's unlikely to contact you knowing all that,*" Paige said.

"*Has he got in touch with you?*" Sheila asked in a hopeful voice.

"*I wish he had, but no. I'm sorry,*" Paige said gently.

As Paige put her phone away in her pocket a large brown furry canine cannonball crashed into her legs. "Rafa," she exclaimed as she landed with a thump on her bottom. The brown Labrador clambered on her lap and began licking her cheeks enthusiastically. Sprite sprinted over to join the melee. "Hey, you two, let me up," Paige said grabbing both of them by the scruff of the neck in an attempt to free herself.

"Need some help?" asked a sexy Spanish voice.

Paige's insides melted. "Alejandro," she stuttered as she finally managed to disentangle herself from the dogs' limbs. She held out her hand and he pulled her to her feet. His touch sent electricity burning up her arms. "How are you?" she asked as the tingling continued along her spine.

"*Bien. Y tú?*"

"Well, apart from being mobbed by an exuberant four-legged friend and landing on my backside, I'm fine," she said, brushing down her jeans.

"*Lo siento*. I'm sorry. Rafa was so happy to see

you that I couldn't stop him."

Paige grinned. "Nothing new there then, is there, Alex?"

"He is more obedient," he declared in a serious tone. "Just not when he sees his favourite girls." His gold-flecked eyes twinkled.

"Are you trying to flatter me, sir?"

His cheeks dimpled as he smiled and said, "Is it working?"

Paige's stomach spun like a Catherine Wheel. "I thought you didn't want to see me again." Her breath caught in her throat.

"It's difficult, no?"

"Yes. But Alex before we go any further you should know that I've just had a call from Zac's grandmother."

His mouth pulled to one side in a grimace. "And?"

"She's worried because she hasn't heard from Zac for seven days. She admitted to me that they'd been in contact until she was taken in for questioning. Since then, nothing. I told her it wasn't surprising that Zac was afraid to ring her. I told her I hadn't heard from him."

His tense shoulders visibly relaxed. "You did the right thing, Paige."

"It was hard to tell her that," Paige said.

"But responsible." Paige shuddered inwardly at his choice of words. He continued, "I will let DI Denton know what you've told me, if I have your permission?"

"Of course. I'm sure he'll follow it up. It was lovely to bump into you and Rafa, Alex. Must rush. Take care," Paige said with forced brightness as she turned to leave.

"*Adios, cariño.*"

Calling to Sprite to follow her, Paige walked away quickly. On the positive side, he'd called her *cariño* and she could feel her resolve weakening. On the negative side, he'd also praised her for being 'responsible'. She didn't want to be 'responsible'. She wanted to be adventurous and daring. An exciting partner, not a damp squid. A sigh escaped her lips. "Kryptonite," she whispered.

Chapter 36

Paige walked back home with Sprite trotting along beside her. The phone call from Zac's grandmother had upset her and yet she knew there was nothing she could do to help the woman. Also, Sheila had lied to her. Paige had a big problem with people lying to her. She prayed that the old lady's lies hadn't put Zac in more danger. Then meeting Alex had been difficult. Their physical attraction was undeniable. You could almost see the electricity arcing across the space between them. Yet, with Alex' past reinforcing his need to control situations by playing by the rules, how could there be a future for them?

It was 6pm when Paige pulled out her keys from her pocket and walked down the side of the house. The drive bordered her garden fence and back gate. It continued on to Dom's house. A sharp stinging sensation hit her throat as her dream catcher burned against her skin. She cried out in pain. "What the…? What's happening?" Danger was lurking.

Her phone pinged with a voice message, *'Bonjour mon chéri, it's Dominic here. I've something urgent to tell you. Come round immediately'*.

Paige listened. A clutch of panic gripped the pit of her stomach. Dom was in danger. There was no mistaking the coded message. An Emeritus Professor in French did not make a language gender mistake that would cause a schoolboy to blush - no way would he use the masculine *'mon'* form to address her. And he never called himself Dominic when leaving her a message. He used either '*grandpère*' or 'Dom'.

Paige scanned her surroundings. Her blood ran cold. A black Mercedes was parked outside the front of Dom's house. Could she reach the house unnoticed? Taking off her bright jacket Paige placed it on the ground. Sneaking around and vibrant clothing didn't mix. She'd learnt that the hard way on a previous investigation in Topsham.

Paige broke into a sprint with Sprite fast on her heels, both keeping to the shadows of the tall yew hedges. Paige went round the back of the house. If the owner of the black Mercedes was expecting her to waltz into their trap through the front door, they'd be sorely disappointed. Very gently she pushed down the kitchen door handle. Damn. It was locked. Probably to force her to use the front entrance. Not going to happen. Whoever had locked it hadn't counted on her knowing where Dom kept the spare key. Feverishly she probed the soil under the empty geranium pots. At last her fingers curled around the cold metal. Dusting it off, she peeked in the kitchen window. The room was empty. Next she surreptitiously checked out the dining room. Alfie and Kevin were standing in front of Dom. Paige bit back a moan of anguish. Her beloved *grandpère* was tied to one of the high-backed dining room chairs. Kevin jabbed Dom's silver-topped walking stick in the old man's face. The silver pommel swished back and forth around the professor's skull. Dom shrank back. Alfie held Dom's phone in his hand. Paige tried to read his lips. She thought he said *Where is she?* Dom shook his head and closed his eyes. Alfie stepped forward and slapped Dom's cheek. Startled, his eyes flew open. A red patch bloomed on Dom's normally pale face. Paige swallowed a cry. Anger blazed hot in her belly.

"You'll find out soon enough where I am you evil bastard," she hissed.

With both Alfie and Kevin standing with their backs to her, Paige popped her head up just long enough for Dom to see her. He gave an almost imperceptible shake of his head. She ignored his signal. How could she not rescue her *grandpère*? She crept to the back door. Sitting on the low step she quickly sent a text to Alex, *At Dom's. He's in trouble. Please call the police.* Immediately afterwards she turned her phone on to mute. The last thing she needed was for her phone to ping and alert Kevin and Alfie to her presence. Paige looked down at Sprite. She couldn't let the dog come in with her. It was too great a risk. Kevin was armed. He could really hurt Sprite. Gathering the terrier in her arms she whispered, *"Grandpère's* in danger. Stay and wait for Alex." The dog's golden eyes radiated understanding. Paige gave her a kiss and put her finger to her lips. Page slid the key in the lock, whispered "Wish me luck," and slipped quietly inside the kitchen. Sprite stood sentry next to the partially open back door.

The layout of Dom's house was as familiar to Paige as her own house. She silently negotiated her way round the kitchen furniture and into the hall. Moving as swiftly as the wind, she was a ninja. At the dining room door she paused. It was ajar. Good. Easier to get inside the room. She peered through the crack.

Kevin's voice reached her ears, "Do you want me to brain him, boss?"

"Not yet. I want the proud Professor Dominic Giraud and his dearest Paige to suffer. The woman has caused me too many problems. You're going to watch her suffer, Dom," he sneered. "I expect her to be ringing the front door bell any moment now. Your little lap dog will come running when you call." His face contorted with disgust. "Do you know what it's like to not have anyone who cares about you? To be discarded for a small error of judgement? To be banished from Exeter, the city you love because of a snitch who frames you? To be excluded from your one passion? I'm an expert on Roman artefacts. Roman artefacts in Exeter," he emphasised. "I want to be recognised as the Roman expert who unearthed rare coins minted by the Emperors Galba and Otho who reigned from 68-69 AD to April 69 AD." Alfie's voice roared.

"Listen, old boy," Dom said in a soothing voice. "Let's be reasonable, shall we."

"Don't you old boy me, you fag," Alfie said, spittle gathering at the corners of his lips. "That Watkins man had me banished. Banished. Me!" he raged. "When I heard about the new dig in the Garden Cloisters I knew I had to come back and claim what was mine. Kevin was all lined up for the job of logging artefacts at the dig, but Watkins preferred that Zac boy. So we had to act fast. I paid for spy cams to be installed so I could monitor the situation with Watkins' favourite student," he spat out. "Unfortunately, Zac turned up just after Kevin had killed the handy man. Andy was getting greedy. Couldn't have that. We were respectful though, we placed a coin in his mouth to pay the ferryman to cross over to the underworld," he bragged.

Paige couldn't believe what she was hearing. A shiver ran like a ghostly touch over her skin. This man was demented. He believed he could kill a man and, as long as he put a coin in his mouth, that was okay. There was no doubt that either him or Kevin had killed Professor Watkins too.

Alfie continued, "Kevin hid while Zac discovered Andy's body. Lily-livered ginger idiot ran away. Kevin had already searched Zac's room for the SD cards from the fake smoke alarms. Zac must have had them on him when he fled. Kevin couldn't find the coins either. We wanted to frame him like I'd been framed, but the coins weren't there. Then that interfering protegee of yours, Paige, turned up so Kevin couldn't follow Zac. Ruined our plan, nosy bitch. Complicates my life that one. Shame I didn't manage to finish her off with the car. A hit and run accident would have tied up that loose end nicely. But I intend to rectify that very soon." He glanced at his watch. "What's taking her so long?"

Paige smothered a gasp. The bastard had tried to kill her. She balled her fists. 'Patience,' she told herself. 'You'll get your revenge.'

"You know why I decided to renew our friendship, Dom? Didn't you wonder? We weren't exactly mates back then, were we?" he asked with a smirk of malicious amusement.

A vein throbbed on the professor's forehead. "Perhaps not, but I was glad to offer you hospitality."

"More fool, you. Anyway, I used you to track Paige's progress and get information on Zac's whereabouts. The fact that you weren't on campus during the months leading up to my dismissal helped," he gloated. "You didn't know the real reason I'd had to leave, did you? Surprised me, that. Weren't you meant to be gossip-in-chief, eh? The one in the know. How's that working out for you now?" he mocked.

Paige had heard enough. Time to attack. She charged into the room. The door bounced off the wall behind her with a loud bang. The men gaped slack-jawed as Paige targeted Kevin. Before he could react she rugby tackled him. The tall, skinny boy landed with a thump. Paige wrestled the stick from his hands. She whacked him on the back of the head. He slumped and passed out. One down, one to go.

Alfie sprang into position behind Dom using him as a human shield.

"Surprise or should I say 'woof'?" Paige gave a throaty little laugh. "Payback time, Alfie. No one messes with my *grandpère*. You're going to wish you had killed me."

Alfie, cast around him with the desperation of a trapped animal. His trembling hands grasped a Chinese vase from the shelf behind him. Shakily he raised it above Dom's crown. "Another inch and I'll smash his skull to smithereens," he warned.

Paige calculated her chances. Every muscle was on alert, ready to spring into action. How fast could she move? She couldn't risk Alfie dropping the heavy vase on Dom's head. How was she going to disarm him?

"*N'aie pas peur*," she mouthed to Dom. (Don't be afraid).

"*Ma chérie, il faut mieux faire ce qu'il dit*. Do what he says," Dom pleaded.

Alfie screamed, "Stop talking that French crap."

Raising her hands aloft still holding the stick, Paige pretended to surrender, "Sorry Alfie."

"That's better," he said. Perspiration pooled under his unsteady arms, staining his pale blue shirt dark blue. Rivers of sweat streamed down his pink face. The effort from holding the vase up was beginning to take its toll. "Now put the stick down," he ordered.

In slow motion Paige began to lower the stick. But she wasn't surrendering, no, she was a ninja manipulating a Japanese Bojutsu fighting staff.

"*Baisse-toi*," she yelled. Dom ducked forward obeying her instruction in French. Paige pivoted on her left leg. Swung the stick with all her force. She hit Alfie square on the shoulder. He toppled like a rotund skittle. The vase flew from his slippery grasp. It crashed to the floor. Splintered into shards. Alfie scrambled to his feet. Paige rotated on her heels. The stick whistled through the air, swiping Alfie's legs from underneath him. His fat body slammed into the floorboards. Winded on the broken pieces of china, he squealed like a pig as the sharp splinters pierced his flesh. She was very tempted to sit on him to make the jagged pieces cut deeper. Instead she trod on his arm and was rewarded by a howl of pain. "Oops, how careless of me," she exclaimed.

Leaning over him, Paige said in a low, fierce voice, "I warned you. No one hurts Dom." She placed the tip of the stick on Alfie's throat. "One move and my hand might just slip."

Alfie began to sob.

"Let me get those ropes off you," she said to Dom while keeping an eye on Alfie. Once Dom was free, she gave him a hug and breathed in deeply his familiar scent of Aramis.

"I'll just deal with this disgusting excuse for a human," she said, roughly hog-tying Alfie. The man squawked and wailed as she pushed and shoved his body around on the ceramic slivers that sliced into his blubber. "Do you want me to shut you up for good?" she asked, hovering the stick's tip over his voice box.

"No," he whimpered.

"Shame. I would have enjoyed it," she said with icy contempt, as she scraped the tip over his larynx.

Satisfied that she'd intimidated Alfie into compliance, she stood the stick against the chair where Dom was rubbing feeling back into his legs and wrists. Next she checked on Kevin. The scrawny young man was lying prone, but still breathing despite the large lump on the back of his head. She shivered with revulsion as her nostrils drew in the scent of Kourus. That odour would be forever linked to this memory. Taking another section of rope, she secured Kevin's hands behind his back.

Assured that neither Kevin nor Alfie were a physical

threat, Paige knelt next to Dom and stroked his cheek. He seemed to have aged ten years. "Dom, I was so frightened," she said, her voice shaking, betraying the tsunami of emotions that were coursing through her.

"*Merci, ma chérie*, you saved me. That's my ninja." He attempted a smile. It fell short.

"One ninja reporting for duty, sir," she joked, giving him a salute.

"I can't believe that Alfie masterminded all this," Dom said hollowly. He rubbed his hands over his eyes. "You realised I was in danger?"

"Yes. Your coded message worked. You'd never call me *mon chéri*. And you don't refer to yourself as Dominic."

In a voice that trembled, he replied, "Glad I taught you well."

She turned to Alfie, "You were outsmarted by a cleverer man than you, although I hesitate to use the term 'man' for you. And it wasn't exactly your best move to leave the black Mercedes out the front in plain sight. Or was that your idiot sidekick's mistake?" She stopped and said, "Ah, if my ears are not mistaken, I think the cavalry has arrived."

The wail of sirens grew louder. DI Denton, PC Patel and Alex burst into the room. Sprite followed and immediately jumped on Dom's lap, covering his face with warm licks from her tiny pink tongue.

Dom gathered Sprite to him and held her close. "Was I glad to see your mistress," he whispered to the furry ginger ball.

A loud barking came from the garden. Outside the dining room window Rafa bounced up and down, desperate to join them. He placed his big, brown paws on the window sill and pressed his muzzle against the pane.

Alex stood just inside the doorway, his eyes taking

in the carnage. "Two men and a vase, *cariño*?" he said in a husky voice that turned her insides to liquid fire.

Paige waited for the lecture on being responsible. Instead he strode across the room and crushed her in his arms. "One more than usual," he said, his warm breath fanning her skin. He took a step back, searching her face while a hint of laughter edged his mouth.

She tossed her head back. "Only the best for my *grandpère*."

"That's my girl," Dom said, finally relinquishing Sprite. Leaning heavily on his stick he joined the group hug. Outside Rafa's barking ratcheted up several decibels. "Let's leave the police to deal with these two while we have a cuppa and let one very impatient dog inside to join us."

Alex roared with laughter. "The English - always the cup of tea."

Chapter 37

Paige sat in the kitchen with Dom, keeping a close eye on him. DI Denton had insisted on calling an ambulance to the scene. For one thing, he was worried about Kevin's concussion and Alfie's deep gashes which continued to ooze blood all over the floor. The medics patched up Alfie's cuts and checked Kevin out after the boy regained consciousness. Once DI Denton was satisfied that they were fit to be transported, officers came and hauled Alfie and Kevin off to the police station for questioning. Secondly, the inspector was worried about Dom who'd had a nasty experience. His skin was pallid and clammy. Despite Dom waving away his concerns, the paramedics took his vitals and prescribed a sedative. Only when Paige insisted that she was going to be staying with him overnight did they abandon their attempt to persuade him to go to hospital.

"Professor Giraud, I'd like to ask you a few questions, if I may?" DI Denton said.

"Of course," Dom replied in his refined voice, that held no hint of a tremble.

"How do you know Mr Jeffreys?"

"I knew him vaguely about twenty years ago. He worked in a different department to me but occasionally there were inter-departmental gatherings. His wife was a very sociable woman."

"How did he come to be staying here if you didn't know him that well?"

"We met by accident at River Books. Although now I'm sure it was anything but accidental. He said he'd travelled down with a coach trip and was interested in the archaeology digs. We had lunch together and I offered to put him up if ever he passed through Exeter. Last Thursday evening, the 7th, he turned up in a taxi and asked if he could stay a few days. He told me he'd heard of the death of Professor Watkins and wondered if his extensive knowledge of Roman history in Exeter could be of help to the new person in charge of the digs at the Cathedral's Cloister Gardens."

"And you didn't suspect that he was staying with you for ulterior motives?"

Dom shook his head. "Unfortunately not, Inspector. I felt sorry for him. He told me he'd been widowed and was lonely. I swallowed his lies whole." He dropped his gaze.

Denton spoke gently. "You were being a kind former colleague. You mustn't beat yourself up about this."

Dom's lips twisted in a wry smile. "Don't worry, Inspector, Mrs Violet Tucker will make sure that I never live this one down," he said, his voice heavy with sarcasm.

The inspector passed a hand across his forehead. "I imagine she will," he acknowledged. "Perhaps you can explain how you came to be tied up?"

The old man blinked as if reliving the moment. "Alfie and I were in the dining room. He received a text. Told me he needed to pop outside to make a call. I heard a car pull up on the drive. Then two male voices talking - one Alfie's and another I didn't recognise. The animated tone of their voices suggested an emergency. Then Alfie walked into the room with a tall, thin young man in tow. He introduced him as Kevin, a promising archaeologist. Kevin was holding a backpack. Alfie told

Kevin to place the bag against the wall behind my chair. The next thing I knew was that Kevin had looped a rope over my torso. I cried out to Alfie to help me. He began laughing. "Not likely, old chap," he'd said mimicking my accent. Then he and Kevin attached my ankles to the chair legs and tied my wrists together. They wanted to know what Paige had found out about the murders. I told them I couldn't tell them. I hadn't seen or heard from Paige for a few days. They forced me to send a voice message to Paige asking her to come here immediately. A short while later, Paige arrived and rescued me." His eyes sought out his granddaughter's. She smiled at him through a sheen of tears.

"Thank you, Professor, you've been very helpful. We will keep you informed if we need anything else from you, sir," DI Denton said.

Denton turned to Paige and said, "Miss Harper, I'd like to ask you a few questions, please. Perhaps we can go next door and leave the professor in Dr Ramos' capable hands?"

"Alex, Dom. What would you prefer?" Paige asked with a wicked twinkle in her eye. No way was Dom going to pass up the opportunity to hear how she'd turned up at the house. He may have had a shock but he was still an inveterate gossip and gatherer of information.

"Here will be fine, Inspector," Dom said solemnly.

"Very well. Miss Harper what can you tell me?"

"Inspector as you are probably aware, earlier this afternoon, just after 4pm, I reported seeing Kevin Stevens planting Professor Watkins' watch in Zac's room. DS Brown arrived at the scene and myself and Miss Mica Murrel showed her a recording we made on my mobile of us discovering the watch. I tried to detain

Kevin, but he locked himself in his room and then clambered down a drainpipe into the back garden. He knocked over a dustbin on his way down, which I fell over when I gave chase. While I was getting to my feet, he escaped over the fence. I noticed that he was wearing the same trainers as the man who chased after me several nights ago near the Cathedral dig site." Paige paused.

"Trainers?" Denton asked.

"Yes, I told you I'm an aficionado of trainers. Kevin was wearing Brown Solar Glide trainers with Gore-Tex written in orange on them."

"Very well. Now explain how you came to visit Professor Giraud this evening."

"I'd been to the park with Sprite. Just as we reached home, I received a voice message from Dom, but it was full of obvious mistakes that a professor of French would not make. I was on high alert. When I saw a black Mercedes parked outside, I knew Dom was in trouble. It was a black Mercedes that had tried to run me down. Oh, and by the way, Mr Jeffreys has just admitted that it was him who attempted to kill me."

Denton raised his eyebrows in surprise. "Has he indeed? That's good to know. And the professor witnessed this admission?" he asked Dom.

"Yes, I did," Dom confirmed.

"Also one of my elderly customers told me she'd seen Kevin climb into the passenger seat of a black Mercedes. I thought Kevin had come to kill Dom." Her breath caught in her throat. "I'd begun to suspect Jeffreys of being involved in the murders. There were several elements of his story that didn't add up. For one, he told Dom and myself that he was part of a coach tour visiting Exeter. That's not true. My friend, Cassie Carmichael, who runs Cellar 7 on Riverside, told me he was hanging around in her shop before the coach group arrived at River Books. He left her place to mingle with the group when they entered the bookshop. Also Mary had the contact details of the tour leader and checked with her if Alfie Jeffreys was part of her tour. She confirmed he wasn't."

Paige paused and looked at Dom. "Dom, do you remember when Alfie went to inform the group leader that he was going out to lunch we didn't actually see him talking to her?" Paige asked.

"Yes. He went outside and then came back into the shop saying he'd sorted it out," Dom said scowling. "He did nothing but lie to me."

DI Denton said, "Don't distress yourself, sir." He focused his dark eyes on Paige again. "Please continue, Miss Harper."

"When I saw the car I knew in my heart that something was wrong. I made my way to Dom's house, hugging the shadows of the yew hedge just in case they were in the front room. Then I sneaked round the back with Sprite. The door was locked. I searched for the spare key. I checked whether anyone was in the kitchen and the dining room. The kitchen was clear but then I saw Dom tied up in the dining room." Her voice caught in her throat. "Kevin was threatening Dom with his stick, swinging it near his head. I couldn't stay outside and wait for the police. I sent a text to Alex to report it and then entered the house. As you saw, I managed to overcome the two men and free Dom." She leant back and pushed her fingers through her hair.

Paige was surprised to see a grin spread across Denton's face. "Very impressive, Miss Harper. And of course, you didn't use undue force, did you?"

"Certainly not, Inspector. However, I will let no one harm my *grandpère*," she said fiercely.

Alex, who'd been listening and observing the questioning broke his silence and said to Dom, "You have one fiery tiger cub protecting you, Dom. Anyone who dares to hurt you is lucky to survive."

Dom plumped out his thin chest. "Paige is my ninja girl. You should have seen her wielding my stick. Magical."

DI Denton rose to his feet. "Thank you. I must get back to the station. I'm afraid the forensics team will be here for a while longer, Professor. Once they've processed the dining room, they'll be combing through Mr Jeffreys' belongings in his room. We will arrange for a crime scene cleaning team to come in tomorrow to deal with the dining room." He lifted his gaze to Paige and said, "They are excellent at removing blood stains."

Paige sent him her most innocent smile. He laughed as he strode out the back door.

"Dom, you'll come and stay with me tonight. Alex can you inform the officers here that Dom will be staying at mine?"

"*Claro, cariño*. I will take care of this and then I will join you at yours, no?"

"Definitely. It'll have to be takeaway. For some strange reason I haven't had time to cook," she said, the release in tension causing giggles to bubble to the surface.

Chapter 38

After Alex had dealt with the police he joined Dom and Paige at her house.

"Come in, Alex," Paige said, opening the back door to the handsome Spaniard and one very excited Chocolate Labrador. "Rafa, sit," she commanded. The dog sat on his back haunches waiting for his treat. Paige gave him a dog biscuit. Sprite bustled up and gave an indignant bark. "Here you are little Miss." Paige handed the terrier another biscuit. "Now both of you in your baskets," she said pointing at Sprite's basket and the spare basket she kept for Rafa. With a jaunty step towards their respective beds the dogs settled down with their treats and ignored the humans.

"Right, now that the youngsters are occupied, let's order some food. I'm starving," Dom said, rubbing his thin hands together.

Paige took this as a good sign. "What do you fancy?"

"Pizza," declared Dom. "It's something I rarely eat but this evening I've a hankering for a crispy thin crust pizza."

"Alex, is pizza okay with you?" Paige asked.

"*Perfecto, cariño*. I'll have a pepperoni. And you Dom?"

"A meat feast. I'm starving after being held hostage. I need to build my strength up." He grinned but Paige caught the flicker of concern behind the bravado.

"I'm going to be exotic and have a Hawaiian," said Paige. "I fancy a bit sweetness." Her lips pinched together briefly as she remembered what had happened.

Alex pulled out his mobile. "I'll order for us all. My treat, okay?"

"Wonderful, my man." Dom beamed at Alex.

"Gracias, Alejandro." Paige let the sound of his name roll around her tongue. It felt more intimate to her when she spoke his name in Spanish. He glanced up at her, his almond eyes flashing gold sparks. Her blue-grey eyes twinkled holding his gaze.

Dom's words cut through the invisible cord that seemed to attach them. "An old man is dying of thirst here."

"Sorry, Dom. What would you like to drink? More tea or something a bit stronger?"

"A glass of Bordeaux would be welcome," he said.

"And impossible," Paige replied deadpan. "Unless you send Alex to raid your cellar."

"What an excellent idea. Alex, could you?" Dom lifted an eyebrow questioningly.

"Of course. Write down which bottle you want me to fetch and I'll go over now."

Paige pushed the Post-it pad over to Dom who scribbled the name of the wine he wanted. "You'll find it down in the cellar in the rack on your right," Dom said. "A Chateaux Frontenac 2019. I deserve a good wine after defying death."

"An expensive wine with a meat feast pizza, Dom? Are you sure that Kevin didn't make contact with that skull of yours?" Paige joked.

"I'll have you know that I can be unpredictable too, young lady!"

Alex was watching the exchange as if at a tennis

match. He shook his head in amusement. "I will go now," he said, walking out the back door.

While Alex was on his mission to bring back Dom's Bordeaux, Paige took the opportunity to speak to Dom frankly. "Dom, you had a very nasty shock and if at any time during the night you feel unwell you must come and wake me. Is that understood?"

"Aren't you being rather dramatic, *ma chérie*?" he asked.

"No," Paige replied. "Let me ask you this. If it had been me who'd been tied up and had a deranged youth ready to brain me, would you not be just as concerned about me as I am about you right now?"

Dom's facade crumpled. "I admit I was petrified. When you came storming in I was even more afraid." He gulped down some air. "By then I'd understood how much Alfie hated you. You'd spoilt his plans. I was sure he'd kill you." He placed his shaking hands on his knees to steady them.

"Alfie was no match for me," Paige said flexing her biceps and eliciting the faintest of smiles from Dom.

Dom stood up and cupped her face with both hands. He studied her face for a long moment. "My ninja," he whispered, planting a kiss on her forehead.

Alex returned with the bottle of wine to find Dom and Paige hugging each other in the middle of the kitchen.

Dom broke away first. "Ah, Alex," he said, "did you find the Frontenac?"

Alex waved the dark green bottle in front of the professor.

"Perfect." Dom straightened his tall thin frame and said to Paige, "Can you fetch the corkscrew, *ma chérie*?"

Paige pulled open a drawer and passed it to him. Next she took two wine glasses from a cupboard and placed them on the table.

"Aren't you joining us?" Dom asked.

"No. I'll toast to the capture of Alfie and Kevin with a glass of sparkling apple juice," Paige replied.

Dom expertly opened the wine and poured himself and Alex a generous glass. Paige filled a tumbler with her soft drink. "To the capture of those murderers," she toasted, raising her glass.

"And to my saviour," Dom added.

"To the feisty, strong warrior queen and the stoic academic," Alex said. He winked at Paige as he stressed the word 'feisty'. She glowed.

They clinked their glasses together. The dogs barked their approval. The barking turned into a frenzy as the front door bell rang.

"I do believe the pizzas have arrived," Alex said as he hurried down the hallway.

The three adults sat round the kitchen table with their pizzas and drinks. Rafa and Sprite had elected Dom as the most likely candidate to drop a tidbit their way and were lying on the floor either side of him. Their faith was rewarded with a sliver or two of ham.

The evening passed pleasantly in general chat and banter. All talk of murderers was purposefully avoided. At 10pm Alex and Rafa left for home. Paige let Sprite out in the garden for a final tour of the perimeter and then locked the doors securely. Dom headed upstairs and she left him to go through the bathroom before she mounted the stairs to her bedroom. She poked her head round the door to wish him goodnight. He was already asleep. Paige whispered, "Sweet dreams, *grandpère.*"

Early next morning the local media stations reported

the arrests of Alfie and Kevin as suspects in the murders of Andrew Hammond and Professor Watkins. When Dom came downstairs Paige was relieved to see that he'd regained a little colour, although to her eyes the traumatic experience had aged him. Somehow he seemed even more skeletal. His skin stretched like thin rice paper over his prominent cheek bones and patriarchal nose while pale blue veins ran just below its surface like a miniature waterways map. She prayed that he would make a full recovery. Of course, she mentioned none of this to him. He had his pride and she didn't want to dent it anymore than it already had been by Alfie's deception.

Once Dom had finished his breakfast he prepared to go home. The police SOCO team had rung him to let him know that they'd completed their work. The crime scene cleaning team was due at 9am. Paige was glad that there would be people in the house with him.

"*A toute à l'heure, ma chérie.*" He headed out the door.

"Do you want me to accompany you?" she asked.

"Stop fussing. I'm a grown man. I can find my way across the lawn to my house," he said tetchily.

She didn't rise to the bait. "Fine. Take care. I'll see you later."

Paige collected her bag, phone and keys. Sprite waited by the back door as her mistress put on her coat and gloves. Outside Paige clicked the remote to unlock the Mini. She attached Sprite in her harness and set off for work. Today was going to be yet another interesting day as soon as the news of her involvement in the arrests became common knowledge.

Chapter 39

River Books beckoned as Paige and Sprite walked from the car park. She wanted to have a chat with Mary and Sunny before the media turned up. Unlocking the entrance door, Paige disabled the alarm and sprinted up the stairs to her office. Sprite trotted after her. Paige hung up her coat on the hook inside the door and locked her bag in her desk.

"Are you staying here or coming downstairs?" she asked her terrier.

Sprite's ginger eyebrows rose in surprise as if to say, 'Are you kidding me? I don't want to miss out on all the fun.'

"Come on then. Let's go and get ready for our day."

Mary arrived looking flustered. "Paige have you heard the news?"

Paige grinned at her big sister. Mary narrowed her eyes and said, "No. Don't tell me you were involved?"

Feigning nonchalance, Paige replied, "Actually, I was the one who caught them."

"Them?" Mary screeched. "You took on two grown men? Were you completely off your head?"

"Whoa," Paige said holding up her hands. "They were holding Dom hostage. I had to save him."

Mary's face softened. "Sorry, little sis. That must have been tough. I know what he means to you."

"It was horrible, Mary. He looked so vulnerable

tied to the chair with that horrid Kevin swinging a stick at his head."

The door bell jangled and Sunny trudged in with her arms full of fresh produce. The sisters rushed over to help.

"Sunny, let me take something. It's too much for you," Paige said.

Sunny smiled her luminous smile and said, "I'm stronger than I look. But thank you." Between the three of them they arranged the food in the café kitchen in record time.

As soon as Mary turned the sign from *Closed* to *Open* Riverside's gossip-in-chief powered into River Books. Today Violet was wearing a lavender twin set that was just a little too tight for her plump form. Knitted fabrics can be so unforgiving, Paige thought waspishly.

"Violet, how lovely to see you," Paige and Mary chorused.

Violet waved away their greetings and plonked herself on the first available chair. "Sunny dearest, could you bring me a cappuccino, please?" she pleaded.

Sunny brought over the coffee and Violet took a delicate sip. Her scarlet lipstick left a crooked smile on the cup's rim.

"Ah, that's better." She turned her beady eyes on Paige. "Now, tell me about the arrest. Is it true that you saved dear Dominic from certain death?" she said, her breathing quickening.

Paige heard Sunny gasp. "Paige are you and Dom alright?" the young Nepalese woman asked, her chocolate drop eyes wide with fear.

"We're both fine." She fixed her gaze on Sunny and Mary. "I had hoped to have time to explain what happened before anyone…" At this point she stared pointedly at Violet. "Before anyone else did."

Violet leaned back in the chair. It creaked ominously under the assault. Interlocking her pudgy fingers and placing her hands on her stomach she gave a grin of complete and utter satisfaction. "Why don't you tell us now?" she said.

Paige knew that she wouldn't get rid of Violet until she'd at least given her some information. For the next quarter of an hour Paige gave an edited version of events; a bit like one of those reports that are heavily redacted. Violet oohed and aahed as Paige described how she'd tackled Kevin and whacked Alfie. At the mention of Alex arriving with the police Violet's eyes lit up with interest.

"So did Alex have to rescue you?" she asked Paige.

"No, sorry to disappoint you Violet, but I'd already disabled both men before Alex and the police arrived."

"I heard that there was a lot of blood." Violet's voice shimmered with excitement.

"Alfie may have been cut in the struggle," Paige said. No way was she going to tell the nosy woman about the 'accidental' way she'd stepped on his arm.

"From what I heard there was blood streaming down his arms, his torso. A real bloodbath."

"I'd be intrigued to know who your source is Violet," Paige said. Her remark hit home.

The woman winced and changed the subject. "How's dear Dominic?" she simpered.

Paige laughed. Dom was Violet's arch enemy when it came to gathering gossip on Riverside. He'd be amused to hear her refer to him as 'dear Dominic'. "He went through a traumatic ordeal," she said, in a low fierce voice. "To think that he offered hospitality to that two-faced liar makes me so angry. I could have torn Alfie limb from limb. What a nasty piece of work. A real psycho. Believes himself to be the all-knowing oracle on everything Roman. He's just a washed-up has been.

I learnt that he left the university in disgrace after trying to steal Roman artefacts from a archaeology dig twenty years ago."

"How did Professor Giraud, who has always been party to all the campus scandals, not know that?" Violet asked, goggle-eyed.

Paige was not fooled by the woman's shock surprise. The gloat in her voice had given her away. "Dom was away in France on a research sabbatical," Paige replied. "The incident was hushed up by the university and, to be fair, Alfie worked in a different department from Dom."

Violet nodded sagely like a wise Buddha. Her jowls wobbled like powder-covered blancmange. "Thank you, Paige. I must dash. Do give Dominic my best wishes, won't you?" She rose from her seat and moved across the floor like a ship in full sail. She'd got enough information to dish out to her acolytes in the retail premises on Riverside.

The day dragged on. Paige was bored. Part of her was still hyped from last night's showdown. She rang Dom to check all was well and passed on Violet's message. He roared with laughter when he heard it. They both speculated on who could be the Riverside President's mole inside of the police force but didn't come to any conclusion.

By closing time Paige was desperate to escape. She and Sprite jumped in the car and drove straight home. As they climbed out of the car, the little ginger fur ball gave a low growl. Her hackles rose. The dog was on full alert. Paige surveyed the surroundings. Although her dream catcher remained cool against her skin, something or someone was here.

"Come out now," she yelled. Her back gate opened. Sprite rushed forward and then skidded to a halt when she recognised the person.

"Zac? Zac, what are you doing here?" Paige asked, taking in his flushed face.

"It's safe now, isn't it?" he voice trembled. "They can't hurt me, can they?"

Paige stepped towards him and gave him a hug. "No, they can't. Oh, Zac, I'm so relieved to see you're safe. Where have you been? We've all been worried sick. Your grandmother is beside herself."

"I knew they were watching her. I caught a glimpse of Kevin when grandma came to see me at the caravan site where I'd been hiding. I had to leave. I couldn't risk putting her in more danger by maintaining contact. If she didn't know where I was, it was better for her."

"Let's go inside and you can tell me all about it. Then we need to inform the police, okay?"

Paige, Zac and Sprite went into the kitchen. "Cup of tea?" she asked.

"Yes, please."

"How do you take it?"

"Milk, two sugars."

"Sit yourself down," Paige said as she busied herself filling up the kettle, getting mugs out from the cupboard and hunting down the sugar that she rarely used.

Once they both had their hands wrapped around their mugs, Paige began. "Where have you been staying these last few days since you cut off contact with your grandmother?"

"I'm not going to reveal the person's name to the police but she gave me permission to let you know. In fact she told me I had to come and see you first. She told me to say *Murder She Wrote*." Zac looked perplexed.

Paige chortled. "Miss Fletcher. Still playing at being

a super sleuth. But she's housebound at the moment with her broken ankle, so how did you make contact?"

"When I dropped off the envelope for you at her house she gave me her phone number to ring in case of an emergency."

"There's more to that woman than meets the eye. She told me she saw you dropping off the envelope through the window but said nothing about speaking to you."

"Yeah. She told me to apologise for that little white lie. She'll make it up to you next time you visit with a freshly baked Victoria Sponge."

"I'm going to hold her to that," Paige said, her mouth watering at the thought of the cake. "But where were you hiding? She's got carers coming in and out. How did they not see you?"

"Miss Fletcher's smart. She knew when they were due and I'd go into the garden shed while they were there."

"I still don't understand why she'd help you," Paige said, rubbing a hand across her brow.

"Because of you," Zac said.

"Because of me?"

"Yes. You were certain I was innocent."

Paige looked astonished. "That's a big leap of faith she took. I could have been wrong."

"But you weren't. I'm sorry I ran away. Maybe if I'd come to you straight away…" he trailed off.

"What's done's done, Zac," Paige said firmly. "Finish your tea and I'll take you to the police station to make your statement."

Paige accompanied Zac into the police station. Before they left home she rang Dom so he could organise a solicitor for Zac. The local Bideford police were going to bring Zac's grandmother to Exeter.

Reassured that Zac would not be questioned until his legal representation had arrived, Paige left.

Chapter 40

It was Easter. The archaeology murders had grabbed the headlines immediately after the arrests. River Books had done a roaring trade from those people curious to see the woman who had captured two murderers single-handed. Paige told Mary that she'd tolerated her five minutes of fame for the sake of the business, but there was a part of her that actually enjoyed the limelight. She scolded herself for being so shallow. However, when a group of the shop's young video gamers had wanted her to dress up as a ninja for them, she'd drawn the line and flatly refused. Finally the public's interest in the murders had peaked and life slowly returned to normal.

On Easter Monday Paige hosted an afternoon tea. Dom, Mary and her husband, Peter, Sunny and Cassie gathered in the garden. It was a warm spring day. Pink and purple tulips stood to attention in the borders. Bright yellow forsythia lit up the hedges. The grass, a vibrant green carpet, welcomed a new season. Paige gazed at her friends sitting in deckchairs with fleece blankets over their knees enjoying each other's company. She gave thanks for having these special people in her life. A year and a half after leaving the horrors of an abusive relationship behind in France, she'd found her tribe. Part of her still didn't entirely trust that it would last. Hopefully, she'd be proved wrong.

For a moment her smile faded. One person was

missing. Alex. He'd gone home to Valencia to be with his family for Easter's Holy Week or *La Semana Santa*. In Spain, Easter is a time of processions, religious and cultural activities. The celebrations in Valencia focus particularly on the city's seafaring heritage and deep connection to the sea, which is why it's called *La Semana Santa Marinera* in that particular city.

"Hey, why so sad?" Mary asked.

Paige put on her happy face. "Nothing," she said. "Has everyone got a slice of cake and a drink?"

Dom turned to Sunny and said, "Thanks to Sunita we have a wonderful selection of cakes."

The young woman blushed, a faint pink colouring her amber features. "Thank you, Dom." She grinned at Paige. "Of course, you would have baked cakes for everyone, wouldn't you have Paige?"

The friends roared with laughter.

"I would have but they wouldn't have been as delicious as these," she replied.

Mary snorted. "Not delicious at all you mean. Little sis, you are many things, but a baker you are not."

"No, I'm a ninja who fights off murderous villains when they threaten my *grandpère*. Just don't put me near an oven. I did offer you all hot cross buns on Good Friday," she countered.

"Shop bought," Mary said in a loud stage whisper, which was met with much hilarity.

Cassie asked, "So are you going to give me a quick recap of the main points of the murders? I don't trust the press."

"Sure," Paige said. "Basically, Alfie Jeffreys held a grudge against Professor Watkins, who he blamed for his sacking from the university twenty years previously.

When he heard that a new dig for Roman artefacts was taking place at Exeter Cathedral he made friends with Kevin Stevens. Kevin was on Watkins' course and planned to be involved with cataloguing the finds at the archaeology dig. The plan was to steal coins from the dig and blame Professor Watkins. Unfortunately, the professor chose Zac for the job. Kevin has a real problem with women in authority and the lead archaeologist being female, Professor Watkins didn't think it appropriate for Kevin to work with her."

"So they needed a plan B?" Cassie said.

"Yes. They paid for spy cams and tried blackmail Zac into stealing artefacts. They knew about his thefts. Zac refused, partly because of his love of archaeology and also because of what Dom said to him about being a custodian of Exeter's history." She glanced at Dom who looked like the cat who'd got the cream.

"Someone appreciates my pearls of wisdom," he purred.

"Moving swiftly on," Paige said with a soft laugh. "We don't want someone to get too big-headed."

Dom placed a hand on his heart and said dramatically, "*Moi, surement pas.*"

"Yes, most certainly you," Paige said, grinning widely at Dom's antics. He was gradually bouncing back from his ordeal. "On with my story. One day Zac saw Kevin hanging around the Cloister Garden dig site. Worried that Kevin would attempt to steal the Roman coins uncovered that day, Zac decided, foolishly as it happens, to take the coins with him for safe-keeping. Kevin saw him slip them in his backpack."

"That's why he was searching Zac's room," Mary exclaimed.

"Yes." Paige lowered her voice. "I'm telling you all this next part in strictest confidence. Zac realised the coins he'd unearthed were the first examples of extremely rare Roman coins to be found in Exeter. Between 68-69 AD three Emperors - Galba, Otho and Aulus Vitellius - ruled for the briefest of periods. As you can imagine their coins are invaluable."

Dom whistled. "Priceless. He wouldn't want those falling into Kevin or Alfie Jeffreys' hands."

"Exactly. Zac took them and hid them in a neighbour's garden shed," Paige continued.

"That was risky wasn't it?" Mary asked.

"Perhaps. He returned from hiding them and found Andrew Hammond dead in his room. He panicked and fled. Kevin was going to follow Zac but I turned up and scuppered his plans."

"Tsk, tsk," Dom said, waving a finger at Paige. "Always in the thick of it, *ma chérie*."

"I don't go looking for trouble, Dom. It finds me," Paige protested. She pouted at him.

"Indeed, it does," Mary said, shaking her head.

Cassie, sensing that the conversation was about to be side-tracked, brought it back on topic, "What about Professor Watkins? Why was he so interested in tracking down Zac?"

Paige explained that he'd thought that Zac had stolen some artefacts and fled. It had brought back horrible memories of the Alfie Jefferys' scandal, except this time it was Professor Watkins' reputation on the line.

"Poor man," Cassie said.

"It awful for him and for Zac. With Kevin feeding them false information and planting incriminating evidence, both were desperate. That was what Alfie Jeffreys had hoped for."

"So who was following you?" Cassie asked.

"That was Kevin." Paige grinned. "No way was he going to catch me."

"Modest as always," Mary chirped.

"Of course, big sis."

Sunny popped to her feet. "More tea anyone? More cake?"

"Yes, please. All this talking has made me quite thirsty." Paige cleared her throat. "And hungry. Bring on the cake." Her hands rubbed her stomach.

"Has there ever been a moment when you're not hungry for cake?" Mary laughed.

Paige pretended to think about the question before replying with an emphatic, "No."

After a cup of Assam and slice of lemon and blueberry sponge, Paige turned to her guests. "Anything else you want to know?" she asked.

"What about Alfie? I can't figure him out. Why did he come back to Exeter?" Sunny asked.

"To seek revenge on the man he considered had ruined his life. After he was sacked his life collapsed like a house of cards. His wife divorced him." Paige paused and turned to Dom, "She's alive, not dead like he told you."

"Lies, lies," Dom muttered.

"Yes. He became obsessed with proving everyone wrong and finding the ultimate Roman artefact. Couldn't hold down a job because of chasing his Roman Holy Grail. Did a bit of chauffeuring."

Dom interjected, "But he said he didn't drive anymore."

"Another lie, I'm afraid," Paige sighed. "That black Mercedes Kevin arrived in, is the car that tried to run me over. The police have matched the paint left on the wall at the scene of the hit and run to it. Alfie will be charged with my attempted murder and," Paige paused, "for the murder of Professor Watkins, who he lured to the archaeology site to kill. The police found a bloody Roman brick with traces of Professor Watkins' skin and hair on it." Paige shuddered as she thought about what could have happened to Dom. "It was carefully preserved in a plastic bag, as if he wanted to gloat over it."

"He's going to be locked up for a long time," Dom said. "You know I began to suspect that he hadn't been telling me the truth, but…" He trailed off. "Why was my 'poppycock' radar so dysfunctional?" His shoulders drooped. Dom prided himself on his perspicacity.

"I don't know, Dom. Luckily our friends were on the ball. Cassie, you flagged up inconsistencies with his story. Mary, you confirmed them with the tour manager. Then Bill filled me in on the university scandal."

"Good of old Bill to meet with you," Dom said.

"Bill and I have our differences, Dom. However, there is one person who unites us - you. We both care for you. For the space of an evening in The Imperial we laid down our arms and called a truce."

"Do we know what's going to happen to Zac?" Mary asked.

"He's agreed to give evidence at the trials of Kevin and Alfie, whenever that may be. The university and the archaeological team are extremely happy with how things turned out. Without Zac's intervention, those valuable coins could have ended up in the hands of private dealers and been lost to history. As it is, the university now have them locked away safely and they get international recognition for the amazing discovery. They're creating a Professor Watkins Scholarship and the first recipient next year will be Zac."

"Jolly good. That's marvellous news," Dom said.

"Yes." Paige grabbed Dom's hand and said, "I almost lost you though."

"But you didn't my brave ninja," he said passing

Paige his walking stick. "You protected me."

She sprang to her feet and reenacted some of the ninja moves that had disabled Kevin and Alfie.

Mary groaned and covered her eyes with her hands, "Lord, give me strength. Do not encourage her Dom."

Professor Giraud's smile lit up the garden.

Chapter 41

Several days later Paige was ruminating about the past month. River Books had been busy over the Easter period. The takings had been good. Financial pressures were easing as the shop's popularity grew. The supplementary translation work wasn't as essential as it had been during the first months in keeping the shop afloat. Paige regretted that she'd been so occupied with solving the murders that she hadn't been able to decorate the shop with Easter bunnies and chicks. Mary, on the other hand, had celebrated. She claimed that vivid memories of how the bookshop's Christmas decorations were so bright that they must have been visible from space still haunted her. Leading up to Easter, Paige had worn a headband with fluffy bunny ears. Mary most definitely had not. Sunny had baked cupcakes and decorated them with eggs, chicks and bunnies. They'd sold extremely well to regular customers and holidaymakers. Paige could personally vouch for the deliciousness of the cakes.

She hadn't even organised an egg hunt. "That's something to add to the list for next year," she said to herself. Paige stopped herself and looked down at Sprite who was lolling in her basket.

"Did you hear, girl? I can't believe I'm already thinking about what I'll do with the shop next Easter! I'm planning ahead. Isn't that astounding? I'm actually thinking of my future here in Exeter."

Sprite sprang to her feet. "Are you as excited as I

am?" Paige asked. But Sprite was charging towards the kitchen door barking loudly. Paige's heart skipped a beat as she heard the sound of another bark. "They're back."

She ran into the kitchen and flung the back door wide open. A large brown ball of fur bounced in. Rafa put his paws on her shoulders and gave her a big slobbery kiss. "Hello boy," she said, hugging his neck, "I'm pleased to see you too."

"*Hola cariño.*" Alex's gold-flecked almond eyes sparked with amusement. "You are pleased to see me also, no?"

Paige opened her mouth to reply but, as Alex stepped forward and gathered her in his arms, her throat constricted.

"Lost for words, Paige?" he teased, his voice laden with emotion. His lips brushed across her forehead. Heat zigzagged through her at his touch. Her breath caught in her throat as she raised her lips to his.

"Never," she whispered before kissing him. She would always have the last word.

About The Author

Christine Tipper lives in the West of England. Over the years she's also lived in France, Spain and Nepal. Filled with a natural curiosity (some would say nosiness) she is fluent in several languages. A translator and interpreter she loves being able to join in conversations around the globe. A great lover of sport, she is a vocal and enthusiastic supporter (rowdy and embarrassing if you believe her family) of Exeter Chiefs Rugby Club. Her hobbies include travelling, reading - especially crime fiction - painting, creating mosaics and keeping fit.

Her favourite phrase is, 'Let me tell you a story…'

Want to keep up to date with Christine's latest releases? Sign up to her mailing list here to receive an exclusive short story, absolutely free!

https://christinetipper.com/join

Thank you.

Printed in Great Britain
by Amazon